JUNE IN WINTER

JUNE IN WINTER

Patricia Anne Phillips

DAFINA BOOKS
Kensington Publishing Corp.
http://www.kensingtonbooks.com

DAFINA BOOKS are published by

Kensington Publishing Corp.
850 Third Avenue
New York, NY 10022

All Kensington Titles, Imprints and Distributed Lines are available at special quantity discounts for bulk purchases for sales promotions, premiums, fund-raising, and educational or institutional use. Special book excerpts or customized printings can also be created to fit specific needs. For details, write or phone the office of the Kensington special sales manager: Kensington Publishing Corp., 850 Third Avenue, New York, NY 10022, attn: Special Sales Department. Phone: 1-800-221-2647.

Kensington and the K logo Reg. U.S. Pat. & TM Off. Dafina and the Dafina logo are trademarks of Kensington Publishing Corp.

First Dafina Mass Market Printing: June 2003

10 9 8 7 6 5 4 3 2 1

Printed in the United States of America

In loving memory of Ophelia Washington,
William and Carol Thompson.

ACKNOWLEDGMENTS

I would like to thank my family for their support and believing in me. Karen Thomas, my editor at Kensington Publishing, for your patience. I hope you will always be my editor. Dr. Rosie Milligan for publishing my first novel, *Something In Common*. Maxine Thompson of Black Butterfly Press for editing my book well enough for me to get an agent to represent *June In Winter*. And to all the authors I've met, thank you all for your encouragement.

One

June 1999

"Hi, Baby. My plane will be in at five. I'll see you tonight around six-thirty. I'm taking a cab home, so don't bother to pick me up."

Tracey Woods smiled as the recorded message confirmed that her husband's flight would arrive on time. Listening to his voice purr over the machine, she tingled inside. Goose bumps rose on her arms and her face flushed with excitement. Donald's baritone had the timbre of a sassy, silky saxophone.

She couldn't believe today was their third wedding anniversary. Soon her husband would be home after a four-day business trip. Boy, how she'd missed him.

Tracey had decided to celebrate this anniversary differently. They would stay home. There would be dinner with the family, which consisted of his mother, Mildred, his twenty-six-year-old daughter Janet, from his first marriage, Tracey's Aunt Flora, her sister and brother-in-law, and her niece, Lisa. Dinner would be served at seven. Everyone knew to leave by ten o'clock so that Tracey and Donald could be alone. After three years, one would think that she would have grown used to his traveling, but she had not. Donald was a prominent real estate developer and, since Tracey was a real estate broker, she had been impressed by his reputation long before they had ever met.

She frowned. "Forgot to chill the wine," she whispered to

herself. Tracey ran down the hallway and went to the kitchen. She grabbed two bottles of Bordeaux from the wine rack and put them in the refrigerator.

She stood before the full-length mirror in their bedroom to see if she had completely zipped the back of her black dress. Her high neckline skimmed across her throat, while the back worked into a draped-cowl effect. The dress was made of crepe and was cut with superb skill. It was a demure style, but nevertheless caught the eye. She ran her fingers through her jet-black hair, which framed her velvet brown face like shining gilt. She was only five-foot-six, but her slender figure made her look taller. *Donald loves this dress,* she thought. It fit close and revealed the long, shapely legs he constantly complimented. She slipped into a pair of black, open-toed pumps and hurried down the long stairway.

Tracey went to the kitchen to check on dinner. She threw a bibbed-apron over her dress. The prime rib was medium rare, just as Donald loved it; the vegetables were not too soft, and she baked his favorite dinner rolls.

Her impeccable dress gave her the look of someone who had never been in a kitchen. To everyone's surprise, Tracey was a good homemaker. She liked having a meal ready for Donald when he came home. With their salaries, she could have easily hired someone to cook and clean their house. As large as their house was, Tracey still preferred to do her housework. She felt no one else could.

Donald had built the house two years before he and Tracey had met. The moment she saw it she knew it was her home. The English Tudor house had four bedrooms, three baths, and a game room with the most beautiful pool table that she had ever seen. A large foyer opened onto a central living and dining room, flanked on one side by a kitchen and family room. The house sat on a hill in View Park. From their family room, the couple had a panoramic view of Los Angeles.

After Tracey and Donald were married, he let her redecorate as she chose. She had a flair for decorating and enjoyed making changes to make her husband more comfortable. In spite of the age difference, the two were compatible in every area. Tracey was thirty-six years old and Donald was fifty-two. He had the body of a thirty-five year old and worked out in their home gym to maintain it. He also had the prowess of a much younger man.

She sighed, and looked at her watch. It was six o'clock. Hearing the doorbell ring, she rushed to the foyer to admit her first guests. Tracey smiled, knowing that it was her family because her brother-in-law was early for everything. She opened the door wide and laughed out loud. She had guessed correctly.

"I knew it had to be you guys," she said, as she stood back so they could come in.

"John's been rushing me since four, girl. Why he has to be an hour early for everything, I don't know," Robin said, and gave Tracey her jacket. Tracey kissed Aunt Flora and grabbed Lisa's hand.

"You're almost taller than I am, and you're only eleven years old."

"I know. I'm already taller than my mom. Am I going to be the only kid here?"

"Yes, honey, but you can go into the den and watch television. I've told you before when you come over here, you should bring a friend."

Tracey went to the kitchen to check the dinner again and walked back into the living room with a tray of hors d'oeuvres in her hand.

"Well, it won't be long now. The others should be coming along, and Donald should be arriving in about thirty minutes," she said and her eyes lit up, as they always did when she spoke of her husband. All she could think of was lying in his arms later that evening. He had been working so hard, and she had been so involved in the sale of a twenty-five-unit apartment complex, that they hadn't made love in more than a week. *Everyone better remember to leave early tonight,* she thought, with a smile playing across her lips.

The doorbell rang again. Tracey opened the door and hugged her mother-in-law. When Tracey held her arms out to hug Janet, Donald's daughter, she pushed past her.

Tracey pretended that she hadn't noticed the icy treatment. Three years, and one would think Janet had accepted her father's marriage, and realize that he would never go back to her mother. She never hid the way she felt about her parents' divorce. But she had to invite Janet for Donald's sake. After all, it was their anniversary, and nothing or no one would spoil her night, Tracey decided, as she welcomed her guest.

Mildred looked at Tracey with a warm smile. "Is there anything I can do to help?"

"No, Mildred. I have everything under control." Tracey smiled back, feeling her spirits lift. She remembered how, at first, she had sensed that Mildred wanted her son to marry a woman who was close to his age. But now, Tracey knew Mildred liked her. Over the past three years, Mildred had accepted Tracey as part of their family. Tracey was Donald's wife, he loved her, she loved him, and that's the way it would stay.

The adults gathered in the family room and watched the big screen TV. They chatted, waiting for Donald to arrive.

Tracey looked at her watch again. It was close to seven. Donald should have been home half an hour ago. Through their laughter, Tracey heard the shrill of the phone.

"That's probably Donald, with some explanation about why he's so late," Tracey chuckled, as she moved quickly into the foyer. "I'll be right back."

She was still smiling when she picked up the phone.

"May I speak with Mrs. Woods, please?"

Tracey frowned slightly at the unfamiliar, formal voice. She hesitated. Who could this be at this time of night? "This is she."

"Mrs. Tracey Woods?"

It took a moment for Tracey to answer through the sudden lump in her throat.

"Yes." Her fingers instinctively gripped the receiver tighter.

"Mrs. Woods, this is Teri Myers from San Francisco General Hospital. I am sorry to inform you, but there's been an accident . . ."

A scream welled deep inside, but Tracey's throat clamped shut. All that came out was a rasping breath, as if she were being strangled. And when she heard the nurse's voice again she screamed, dropped the phone and slid against the wall.

"Tracey, what is it?" John yelled from the living room.

A thick glaze covered her eyes, but Tracey could still see her brother-in-law rushing toward her, followed by the rest of those gathered for the party. The laughter that filled the house only moments before was replaced with questioning screams.

"Tracey, what's wrong?" Robin asked, moving toward her sister.

"Has something happened to my father?" Janet asked.

"What is going on?" her brother-in-law asked.

John picked up the cordless phone and spoke into it, while Robin and Aunt Flora helped Tracey stand. The quiet was broken only by John's staccato utterances.

After several eternal minutes, John slowly dropped the phone into the cradle and turned toward the others.

"Donald is still in San Francisco. He was in a car accident and he's unconscious. It sounds serious," he choked out the words, looking at Mildred as she began to scream. Janet grabbed her, and they both cried, holding on to each other.

"I've got to get to San Francisco right away," Tracey cried. "Robin, call the airport and make reservations for the first flight out, please." She started to take a step but her legs were weak.

"John, help her up the stairs," Robin said, holding the phone in her hand. Mildred, Janet, and Flora went back to the living room and waited. No one thought of dinner.

While Tracey was upstairs changing, Robin was making

reservations for three, including Janet. They decided that Mildred would stay in Los Angeles. As upset as they were, no one wanted Mildred's high blood pressure to flare up again.

"I'm going with you, Tracey. I made reservations for Janet, too," Robin said.

"Thanks," Tracey turned to face Robin. "The nurse said that a Miss Howard was with him. Maybe she was taking him to the airport."

While slipping into a pair of slacks and matching sweater she felt a chill come up her back and frowned. "Damn, it's cold for the month of June." She trembled, and was colder than she could ever remember.

When Tracey and Robin came downstairs everyone was sitting in the living room with their coats on. The room was silent, and everyone looked at her as she walked in.

"Tracey, did the doctor say how bad Donald's condition was? Is he dying?" Mildred cried. "He's my only son. Oh Lord, don't let him die"

Flora sat on the couch next to Mildred. "Honey, don't say things like that. As soon as he knows that Tracey and Janet are there, he'll be all right." Flora looked at Tracey. "We should all leave. But you call us as soon as you see him, Tracey."

"I will, Aunt Flo," Tracey said, with a sudden electric tingle of fear running down her spine. "Mildred, try not to worry too much. We'll call you." She wondered what condition she would find her husband in.

Everyone rushed out of the door at the same time and Tracey, Robin and Janet left in a taxi headed for the Los Angeles Airport. Tracey cried the entire ride. Now feeling a terrible pain in her right temple she laid her head back on the car seat and closed eyes. Robin was trying to console her and held her hand. Janet was quiet when they arrived at the airport and during the flight. Tracey could imagine how painful it must be for her, too, and took her hand.

"Tracey, I wonder if he's dead," Janet cried.

"Of course not. Your father will never leave us. I just wish that I was with him. We have to believe that he'll be all right," she said and wiped her eyes. She knew that she had to stop crying and be strong for Janet. But she was just as afraid as Janet was, and it seemed like they had been in the air for hours as Tracey looked at her watch.

On the plane, a man sitting in front of them overheard their conversation. He turned and looked at them, but he didn't say anything.

When the plane landed, they got off and rushed through the airport. All three, looking straight ahead, ran down the escalators into the streets to flag a taxi.

Robin and Janet each held one of Tracey's hands as they rode to the hospital. No one spoke.

When they walked into the emergency room they went straight to the nurses' station to ask where they could find Donald Woods. Tracey was so upset, she didn't even read the nurse's badge.

"Is my husband conscious?"

"Just wait here, I'll get the doctor." But as she started to walk away, Tracey grabbed the nurse's arm.

"Please, tell me if he's conscious. I have to know." She looked to see if she saw any doctors around who could tell her. She needed an answer, now. Janet and Robin stood next to her, each holding her arm to support her.

"I'm sorry, you'll have to talk to Dr. Stone. Wait right here and I'll get him." The nurse walked off leaving them pacing in front of the counter.

"Where is the doctor?" Janet asked impatiently.

They looked at each other as the doctor walked toward them. He looked grimy and tired.

"Mrs. Woods?"

"Yes, I'm Mrs. Woods. Will you take me to my husband?" Tracey asked apprehensively, afraid of what she might hear. "He needs me with him."

The doctor looked at Robin and Janet. "Are they family, too?" he asked.

"Yes, this is my husband's daughter and my sister."

The doctor nodded. "I think all of you should come along." Tracey's heart felt as if it was closing. She held Janet's hand tightly and said a prayer to herself as they walked down the busy hall.

They followed the doctor into the room. There were three nurses and another doctor standing around the bed. The room was warm, too warm, and too much light and the smell of medicine made Tracey nauseous. She opened her hands, and closed them again. They were moist and shaky, and she felt beads of sweat on her forehead. One nurse had a pen and pad in her hand, taking notes. Tracey wrinkled her nose as she noticed another smell. What was that smell? It smelled like—like blood. Suddenly Tracey's eyes fell upon Donald's body.

"The time of death is nine-thirty P.M.," the doctor said.

She was so grief-stricken, bereft of words, suffering the death of her husband, that she was hardly aware of what was going on around her. She closed her eyes against the dull ache that she still felt in her head, feeling a knot in her stomach. This wasn't really happening. How could her life change so in one day? One minute she was looking forward to celebrating her anniversary and the next she was staring at her husband's corpse. This was a nightmare. She looked from one doctor to the other, searching for an answer, but there wasn't one. Her breathing was shallow, as her chest constricted.

"I want to stay with my husband, touch him, and be near him." But when she started toward his bed where he lay covered with blood, she stopped as if she couldn't move.

A nurse walked toward Tracey and held her hand, leading her away from the bed. She felt sorry for her. Tracey was so distraught, so frightened. She felt numb. She couldn't believe she had lost her husband. This couldn't be happening to her.

Janet looked as though she was in shock, never saying a word, not crying, just looking straight ahead as Robin led both of them out of the room. All three stopped as Tracey cried out.

"Why, why? Oh God, why my husband?" she cried, and leaned against the wall.

Robin put her arms around Tracey and Janet. "Let's get out of here."

As they walked down the halls of the hospital, there were two men and two women looking in their direction. A younger woman who was tall and composed was leading the older woman in the opposite direction. One of the men stepped closer to Tracey and stopped in front of her. Robin looked up at him, wondering what he had to say to them. He was handsome, brown-skinned with close-cropped black hair, with eyes that were far too serious and sad.

"I'm Travis Howard. I take it that you are Donald's daughter?" he asked looking directly at Tracey. "Susan Howard was my sister," he said, before Tracey could speak. "She and your father were deeply in love and were planning to get married." He stopped for a moment, as if he couldn't continue.

Everyone looked at him as though he was out of his mind. Tracey knew this man was mistaking Donald for someone else. He couldn't be speaking of her husband. She opened her mouth to speak, but before she could, he was composed and continued to talk.

"He was a good guy. I'm speaking on my family's behalf. We're very sorry," he said and held his hand out to Tracey.

Tracey looked up into the man's face with wide eyes, confused at what he was saying. Who was this stranger?

"It's just so horrible the way death happens. Susan was just saying at lunch today that they were going to get married as soon as possible. Now, it's too late. She was dead when they arrived at the hospital. At least they were together," he sighed.

She clenched her slender hands together and struggled valiantly to comprehend what he was saying to her. Robin held her close.

"What in hell are you talking about, you fool? Are you—crazy? Do you even know who you're talking about?" Tracey heard her voice getting louder and louder. "I'm Donald's wife, not his daughter. And do you expect me to believe what you're saying about my husband? You are mistaking him for someone else. If your sister knew my husband at all, then she was probably no more than a business associate, or maybe she was dating someone that my husband knew."

As her anger rose, Tracey balled up her fists and clenched her teeth. She wanted to strike out and hurt someone. Whoever this man was, he had set himself up as a good target. She ignored the stunned look in his eyes as he stepped back. She raised her fist in the air.

"My husband is dead and I don't wish to discuss this any longer," she yelled. Her voice began to crack, her fists stopped in the air and fell to her sides. "I've got to get out of here. This is just too much for one night." And before she could say another word, the tears began to flow uncontrollably.

Even Janet seemed to feel sorry for Tracey. For the first time in three years, she placed her arm around Tracey's shoulder.

"Tracey, don't pay this man any mind. He's mistaken my dad for someone else."

Robin hugged her. "Come on, Tracey. Let's go to the hotel."

"I'm sorry, miss," the strange man stammered. "I didn't mean to upset you." He had been stupid to say such things, but he didn't know that Donald was already married. For the last year, Donald had been dating his sister, and she'd told them he was divorced with a grown daughter. He looked at Tracey again and even with the embarrassment, hurt and pain she wore, she looked so young. *There's no way,* he thought to himself. *This woman has to be in her twenties.*

He reached out for Tracey's hand, but she pushed his hand away and faced Robin.

"Get me to the hotel, Robin. I can't take anymore tonight," she cried, and looked at the man one last time as though she wanted to say something to him. But she didn't. She couldn't. He had made an awful mistake. Let him deal with it.

They were quiet in the taxi. Tracey just wanted to get to the hotel. She laid her head back and closed her eyes as she thought of her husband. Today was their wedding anniversary, and she was supposed to be happy and in love. Donald was supposed to be surprised and happy when he walked into their home. He would have kissed her and said that he had missed her, that he couldn't wait until everyone left so he could make love to her.

"Happy anniversary, Love," she whispered to herself.

They went inside the hotel and stayed in one room. Janet sat on the edge of the bed and began sobbing for her father, beginning to feel the loss inside of her. Tracey sat next to her and held her in her arms.

"My father is dead, Tracey. Dead. No warning. No words. The last words I had said to him were out of anger. I didn't even get a chance to say I'm sorry, or that I loved him. Now, I will never get the chance," she cried and Tracey cried with her. Robin lay across the bed next to them.

Donald Woods was dead.

Two

Tracey stood at the window looking out as she watched three long black limousines line up in front of her house. Her mood blended in ominously with the gloom of an overcast and cool June morning, with gray clouds that threatened to open and overflow with rain. She heard footsteps and turned around. It was Mildred standing in back of her.

"I don't think that I can take it, Tracey. I'm not as young as you are. Donald was my only child," she cried and held Tracey's hand.

"I know, Mildred. It's hard for me, too."

Tracey's family and Janet were sitting in the family room. Tracey's best friend, Wendy, was there for moral support. She had even closed her business. Everyone was so quiet it seemed as if no one was in the house.

Tracey heard the doorbell ring. "It's time, Mildred."

Mildred trembled so hard that Tracey was afraid for her health. She had had a stroke three years earlier, but now that Donald was gone, Tracey thought the funeral might be too overwhelming for her. The doorbell rang again and Robin answered. Tracey's legs got weaker with every step she took. And the first person she saw standing on her porch was Norma, Janet's mother, waiting impatiently for them to come out. Tracey could see that she had been crying.

* * *

Tracey had decided on a graveside ceremony because it would be fast and easier for everyone who was close to Donald.

As everyone stood around the coffin, the pastor talked about Donald's childhood. Tracey held her head down, her arm linked through John's for support. Wendy walked up beside her and placed her arm around Tracey's neck.

Janet stood on one side of Mildred and Norma was on the other. The funeral was small and private. The pastor finished and Tracey placed a spray of orchids and roses on top of her husband's coffin. And when everyone turned away to move, Tracey couldn't move her feet or will them to walk. How could she leave her husband to be put in the cold ground? Her legs were beginning to buckle. She broke down and sobbed. "How could this have happened, and why Donald?" she asked.

John caught her weight. He held her tight and led her away. She took two steps and heard a loud, animal-like cry. Tracey's head snapped up, and she glared at Norma. Everyone stopped and turned around. Norma was screaming, falling to the ground, repeating over and over again, "I can't believe he's gone. Lord, he was my husband for twenty-two years."

Janet tried to hold her up but she was just too heavy. Her purse had fallen on the coffin and the pastor picked it up. The black wide brim hat she was wearing had slid down her face.

"I can't believe he's gone," Norma cried again.

Tracey stood, her mouth open, and couldn't move. Two men had to literally drag Norma to the car.

Mildred stood behind Tracey. She said, "Oh, God. Can you believe that woman?"

But Tracey couldn't answer. She was looking at the tall man standing at a distance away from everyone. He was dressed in a gray suit, but she didn't recognize him. Then, she wondered if he was the man that had mistaken Donald with his sister's lover. "Yes, that's him," she said to herself.

Tracey looked at Norma and the two men who were finally

pushing her into the car. "So inappropriate," Tracey thought. Donald would not approve of this kind of behavior at all.

Everyone met at Tracey's house after the funeral and stayed most of the day. She was quiet, and stayed to herself. Occasionally, someone would come to her and say they were sorry, but she had just lost her husband so no one started a lengthy conversation. Still, she was able to force a smile now and then. Robin and Aunt Flora stayed with her most of the time. Janet was with her mother in the living room. Wendy made her laugh when she talked about the trouble they had gotten into as children, but most of the time she just wished that everyone would leave.

"I'm sorry, but I have to leave, Tracey. I would stay longer but my mom isn't feeling well." Janet felt bad about Tracey being so unhappy. Even though she had wanted her mother and father together, she didn't want to see Tracey hurt. She was smart enough to know that once her father had married Tracey, there was no going back to her mother. Tracey was pretty, smart, and she was younger.

"Take her home. She should be in bed," Tracey said, and hoped that she would never have to look in that woman's face again. How dare she make a complete ass of herself at her husband's funeral? She squeezed Janet's hand. "You need some rest yourself. Maybe you should stay at your mother's tonight so you won't be alone."

"Will you be all right?" Janet felt ashamed. It took her father's death for her to show any consideration toward Tracey.

"Yes. My family is here with me. Go home and get yourself some sleep."

Tracey sat in the family room. She thought of the man at the funeral. Why would he even come? His last name sounded familiar to her but she couldn't remember where she had heard it. She tried to remember if she had ever had a client with the name Howard. She would never forget Travis Howard's face or his words. "Howard," she said to herself. Where had she heard the name? She knew that she wouldn't rest until she remembered.

After everyone left, Aunt Flora and Robin stayed until late that day. John went home to be with Lisa.

It was getting dark and Tracey closed the drapes and all the blinds. She went back into the family room with Flora and Robin, and they all had a cup of coffee and cake that someone had brought over.

"Tracey, there's potato salad, fried chicken, and green beans left in the kitchen. Why don't I fix you a plate?" Robin asked.

"No, thanks," she said and lay her head back on the couch. Flora sat at the other end and Robin sat in the chair in front of them. The house was neat with everything in place as always.

"So, what did his ex-wife have to say today after she finished getting everyone's attention at the funeral?" Flora asked. "That woman just rubs me the wrong way."

Tracey held up her head. "She didn't have much to say. Just that she can't believe he's gone. She repeated it over and over, just as she did at the funeral. I think she's still in love with him. She'll probably never remarry. But, I doubt I will either."

"You're too young to make a decision like that, baby. Everyone thinks like that when they lose their spouse."

"Listen to you two," Robin said. "You have to decide what you are going to do, Tracey. Not tonight, but you will have a lot of thinking to do. We'll be here if you need us, honey."

"I know. I just don't know where to start. I have to go and see the lawyer tomorrow. Then I have his things to pack at home and at his office. I have some things to settle with Janet and Mildred, too." She shook her head. "So much to do." She laid her head back and cried.

After Flora and Robin put Tracey to bed, they cleaned the kitchen, put all the food away for her, turned out the lights, and said good night.

As Robin was driving Aunt Flo home, she felt as if she wanted to cry for her sister. They were so close, and the only other person they had was Flora, who had been like a mother to them.

"I don't know what we can do for her, Aunt Flo. She seems so withdrawn from everyone. Did you see how she just sat alone today, or she would go outside so no one could get close to her?"

"Yes, I saw her, but it's natural for her to feel this way. She just lost her husband. You know how much they were in love. They were so good together."

"When we were at the hospital, a man told Tracey that Donald was in love with his sister. She was conducting some business with Donald and was in the accident. She died before they got to the hospital. He must have gotten Donald mixed up with the man his sister was involved with," Robin said, and parked her car in front of Flora's house.

"His timing sure was bad," Flora said. "Tracey didn't mention that."

"Aunt Flo, she's had so much to deal with. I bet she has forgotten all about it."

"Well, all we can do is be there for her. I don't know if she'll keep the house or sell it. Tomorrow, I'll tell her that, if she decides to move, she can stay with me. That may be good for her," Flora said.

"I think it will be good for her, too." Robin kissed Flora good night and watched her go inside.

That night Tracey tried to sleep but too much had happened and too quickly. She had said good-bye to her husband a week ago, and now he was dead. Her life had completely changed with just one phone call. She went downstairs and got a glass of water. She crawled back in bed and tried to sleep, but she kept seeing the man at the funeral.

Why was he there? she wondered. Maybe he'd wanted to apologize for the mistake he'd made. She pushed the memory from her mind, but she kept hearing the name "Howard." Finally, she fell asleep.

In the middle of the night, Tracey jumped up as if someone had thrown cold water in her face. "Howard, Susan

Howard." She gasped and put her hand over her mouth. She remembered the name. It was also mentioned in the phone call from the hospital, but she was so upset that she had forgotten. Tracey stood up and ran her fingers through her hair. Two weeks ago she was in her husband's office in their home. His phone rang and she answered. It was a few seconds before the caller spoke.

"May I speak to Mr. Woods?" she asked. Tracey told her that Donald would be home soon.

"Will you please tell him that Susan Howard called?"

Tracey told Donald but he seemed distracted at the time. Later that night she walked into his office and he was on the phone. He was yelling and hung up the moment she walked in. Donald said that it was only business. Tracey closed her eyes, remembering that night. He had put his arms around her, kissed her, and they had gone to bed.

Unable to sleep she went back downstairs and slid into her comfortable chair. She had to get a hold of herself. "Donald was a good man. Hadn't the man said that?" She felt as if she was betraying her husband's trust. But she couldn't stop. Tracey got up and marched into Donald's office. Maybe if she looked around and found nothing, she could forget this man, once and for all.

Methodically, she looked through his desk, pulling out one drawer after another, dumping everything onto the floor, on top of his desk, in his chair, reading every piece of paper she saw, but came up with nothing. Her heart beat fast and hard against her chest as she dashed through the room like a tornado in a winter storm.

Suddenly, she remembered bringing his briefcase from the hospital and pulled it out of the study's closet, but it was locked. "Where's the key?" she whispered to herself. She found it in the pocket of the jacket that he was wearing during the accident. She felt a knot in her stomach as she laid the jacket over the chair. It had been cleaned because there was blood on it from the accident. She felt as though she was obsessed, but she couldn't stop herself. Tracey needed

to remember her husband loving her and know that he was
true to her.

Unlocking the briefcase, her hand trembled as she pulled
out more papers. Nothing. She lifted up the secret com-
partment and pulled out a white envelope full of receipts.
This was too bizarre. This couldn't be happening to her.
Tracey felt as though she was dying inside as she read one
by one, for flowers that were sent to San Francisco, a $900
necklace, a bracelet, and designer gowns. When she found
hotel receipts she flew into a fury. Without giving it thought,
she tore the receipts into small pieces. She threw the pieces
up in the air, and they fluttered down around her like a bliz-
zard. Some of the pieces landed in her hair. She was too
livid to brush them out.

She turned on Donald's private answering machine.
"Donald, it's Susan. Sweetheart, I can't wait until you get
here. I love you. . . ."

Tracey couldn't take anymore. She threw the answering
machine against the wall, the briefcase in the trash. She
cried, screamed, and pushed his blotter, his ink weight, and
all the neatly stacked papers on his desk to the floor.

"Liar! You lied to me!" she screamed. She sounded
breathless, felt as though she couldn't get enough air. Panting, she kicked at the papers and ripped them apart. She
wanted to burn the whole room down, but as she and Donald were nonsmokers, she couldn't remember where they
kept their matches. For a moment, her eyes roamed around
the room. What could she do? Frustrated, she walked over
to the window and tore down the vertical blinds. The noise
of the clanging metal surrounded her and added to her sense
of impotence.

Looking up at the ceiling, with her fists raised, she let out
a loud bellow. "God, how could you do this to me?" She
crumpled to the floor, with her head in her arms. She
sobbed and sobbed, as tears sluiced down her face.

Finally, spent, she leaned against the wall, panting.

How long had she been stupid and incredibly foolish? A

year . . . two? How could she have been so blind? Her worst nightmare had come true. She had thought their life together was good, then to find out about this—under these circumstances. This was too much! Had her whole marriage been based on a lie?

"Damn you, Donald!" she yelled into the empty room. She was overwhelmed with rage. Tracey stood in the door of Donald's office and was shocked at what she had done. Everything was on the floor, the trash knocked over, and the phone hanging off the hook. Donald's briefcase was thrown against the wall. The office was upside down. On her way out, she grabbed the bottle of brandy and ran upstairs. She sipped from the bottle and cried herself to sleep.

The next day Tracey was talking to her lawyer on the phone when she heard the doorbell ring and hung up. It was past one P.M. and she was still in her nightgown and robe. Her head was killing her and her stomach was upset. She opened the door and was surprised to see Norma, Donald's ex-wife, standing on her porch.

"Come in, Norma. What can I do for you?"

Norma followed her into the family room, looking around the beautiful house. *This should have been my house,* she thought.

"Would you like a cup of coffee, Coke, or some brandy?"

"No, thanks, Tracey." They were sitting opposite each other, wondering what the other would say next.

"Tracey, this isn't a friendly visit. We have never liked each other and there's no use acting like we do now," Norma said sitting straight and looking uncomfortable.

"I agree," Tracey answered.

"I came to see what Janet will be getting now that Donald is dead. As a mother, I don't want my daughter to be cheated out of anything that belongs to her." Norma moved around in her seat awaiting Tracey's answer.

Tracey just stared at her, speechless. For the first time,

she realized why Donald never wanted her back. She had large round eyes. Her hair was gray around the temples and thinning on top. She was two years younger than Donald but looked older and, for the first time, she looked ugly to Tracey. It was quite obvious that Norma was looking out more for herself than she was for Janet.

"Janet will get exactly what her father left for her. I'm moving out of this house and going to buy one of my own, so she can have this one." She watched Norma's eyes light up and Tracey frowned. "I haven't seen the lawyer yet. After all, Donald was just buried yesterday. Janet will get what belongs to her, but you will have to ask Janet for some of what she gets. I'm sure that Donald didn't leave you anything, Norma. Now, if you will leave my house, I have some business to take care of," Tracey said and stood up.

Norma didn't like the way Tracey was looking down her nose at her. Who did she think she was? She stood up and started walking toward the dining room when she heard Tracey call her name and turned to face her.

"You're going the wrong way. The door is to the right." Tracey opened the door and watched her as she quickly walked toward her car. She stopped again and turned around to face Tracey.

"You know, he only married you because I wouldn't take him back."

For the first time since Donald's death, Tracey laughed. "You're insane. Go back home, Norma, and dream some more." She laughed again and closed the door.

Tracey sat back on the couch and closed her eyes. "The nerve of that woman," she said out loud to the empty room. She went upstairs and was changing into a pair of jeans when the doorbell rang again. She was sure that she heard Norma's car drive off but maybe she was mistaken. She slung the door wide open.

"What now?" she blurted, expecting to see Norma.

Her eyes blinked wide when she saw Travis Howard

standing face to face with her again. She never wanted to
see this man again. "How can I help you?"

"I just wanted to say that I am sorry and to see if you
were all right," he answered.

"And you came all the way to Los Angeles to ask me
that?" She touched her hair, hoping that it was in place.

"No, I live here. I was on vacation in San Francisco when
we met in the hospital. Maybe I did make a mistake about
your husband and my sister."

"You didn't make a mistake and you know it. I'm the
one who made the mistake. I found out about Donald and
your sister," she said vaguely, wondering why she was
even talking to this man.

"I'm so sorry about everything. Are you going to ask me
in?"

She didn't say anything for a few seconds, and she con-
sidered slamming the door. "Come on in," Tracey said. She
led him to the family room and wondered what unwelcome
person would ring her doorbell next.

"You have a beautiful home, Mrs. Woods," Travis said.
You are also a beautiful woman, he thought, admiring her
plentiful black hair.

"Did you say that you live here?"

"Yes. I've been living here for ten years now. I think that
Susan may have met Donald on one of her visits here. Anyway, I just wanted to say that I'm sorry for everything." She
looked into his eyes and he looked just as sorry as she did.
Her heart went out to him. After all, Susan was his sister
and he had lost her, too.

"Did you ever see Donald here?"

"Yes, a couple of times. But, my sister could have come
out here a few times without me knowing it. She was a
grown woman and had her own life."

Tracey nodded her head in agreement. She was sitting on
the couch, and he sat in the chair opposite her.

"What was she like?" Tracey asked him.

"Believe it or not, she was a good, decent woman. She

was smart, worked hard as a nurse, and loved helping others. I'm sorry to say, but she loved Donald. She always talked about him when I saw her. She's not at all what you think of her, Mrs. Woods."

"I had to ask," she paused, fighting back the tears. She wanted to ask if she was beautiful, did Donald act as if he really loved her. But how much more could she bear hearing?

"What are you going to do now, Mrs. Woods?"

"Go on with my life. That's all I can do. I'm a real estate broker. First, I'm moving in with my aunt until I buy myself another house. And after that, all I can do is go on and make the best of it." They were talking as if they were old friends.

He looked around. "But this is such a beautiful house. Why would you want to sell it?"

"I'm not selling it. Donald built this house before we knew each other and I think his daughter should have it. I told him to leave it to her in his will two years ago. I have money of my own and can buy a house of my own, Mr. Howard."

"Please, call me Travis."

"Do you have other family here, Travis?"

"Yes. My mother. She has been hurt so deeply by this. She had only one daughter. My father died four years ago," he said sadly.

"I'm sorry, Travis, for all of us."

He stood up. "I don't want to take up any more of your time. I just wanted to say that I am very sorry for the way I went on at the hospital. I really put my foot in my mouth," he said, and wondered if she would have found out if he hadn't opened his mouth. It was such a bad time, and he thought that he was doing the right thing. He should have known better. She looked so hurt, so broken that night, and he felt just like the jerk that she said he was.

Tracey walked him to the door and they said good-bye. She thanked him for coming by. When she heard his car drive off, she ran upstairs and cried. She stayed inside and walked from room to room, still feeling her husband's presence in the house. She would miss this house, miss her husband. But, right now she didn't know whether she loved him or hated him for what he'd done to her. She opened the door of his office and looked at the picture on the floor that they had taken two years ago. "Lord, we were so happy. Why? Why?" she kept asking herself. She saw no signs, and he hadn't changed toward her. "Was he really in love with that woman?" She went back to her room where she remained the rest of the day.

Robin left work at eleven-thirty to have lunch at Flora's house at noon. She could smell something cooking when she walked in.

"Aunt Flo, I'm here and I'm starved," she yelled from the living room.

"Come on in. I'm setting the table." Flora set two plates on the table and filled their glasses with iced tea. Robin took the strap of her purse and slung it on the door.

"It's been a busy morning. I wanted to call Tracey, but I couldn't get any privacy with people walking in and out of my office. Have you talked to her today?" Robin asked, as she took a bite out of her turkey burger.

"Yes, she's packing, poor child. She must have been packing something of Donald's because she was all choked up when we spoke. I feel so sad for Tracey. She never hurt a fly, you know."

"Yes, I know, Aunt Flo. Life can be so rotten, and so was Donald. I know that you were never crazy about him."

Flora got up to get some more napkins. "You're right. He was too old for her, too demanding, and he thought that he was better than anyone else, if you ask me. I just thank the good Lord that he couldn't change Tracey. One thing that I can say about her, she's her own woman. But, I never thought that he was cheating on her."

"She'll be all right, Aunt Flo. She has her work and she has us. She'll get through it. I just don't know how long it will take her, but she will."

Flora sighed. "I'm going to call her and go over and spend the night. Tomorrow is Friday, and we can get a lot accomplished. There's so much in that big house to pack and move. I need more ice. Do you?"

"No, mine is cold enough. Saturday Lisa and I can come over and help you guys. At least it may take her mind off the worst part of it. We can laugh and talk and have something delivered for dinner. John has a lot of work to do anyway. He'll be glad to get me and Lisa out of his hair for a day."

Robin took the last bite out of her burger and wiped her mouth with the napkin. "It was so horrible at the hospital, Aunt Flora. I wanted to hit that woman's brother over the head with my purse. He just went on and on about how much his sister and Donald loved each other. He's one person that I never want to see again, and I'm sure that Tracey feels the same way. But I had no idea that he was telling the truth. We all thought he had mistaken Donald for someone else. I even thought the man was crazy."

"What was he like?" Flora asked with interest.

"Tall, good-looking, talked as if his sister was the luckiest person in the world," Robin frowned, displeasure reflected on her face. "I'll never forget it. Poor Tracey was shocked but she didn't believe it either. She was so distraught over Donald's death. Now, she's devastated knowing that it is really true."

Flora got up and touched Robin on her shoulder as she went to put the dishes in the dishwasher.

Robin went to the bathroom to wash the smell of pickles off her hands, put on fresh lipstick, and comb her hair. She walked into the living room where Flora was hanging up the phone. "I have to get back now, Aunt Flo. It's really busy at work today. I have a large project to complete this month."

Flora stood beside her. "How long have you been managing at that bank?"

"It's been eight or nine years now. It doesn't seem that long. I put in a transfer to go to the main office. It's more work, but also more pay and more of a challenge." She kissed Flora on the cheek as Flora walked her to the door.

"I'll call Tracey later. Call me and let me know if you go over there tonight, Aunt Flo."

"I'm telling you now, I'm going over as soon as I can get a few things together and throw them in an overnight bag."

An hour later, Flora was at Tracey's front door. Tracey was seated at the far end of a long, dimly lit room when Flora rang the doorbell. She answered wearing a pair of blue jeans and an oversized faded blue sweatshirt. Flora walked right past her and set her overnight bag in the chair, sighed, looked around the room, and opened the blinds.

"I'm staying overnight so that I can help you pack and get things ready to move back home. Now, where should I put my bag and purse?"

"Aunt Flo, you didn't have to do this. I could have handled it myself."

Tracey looked as if she hadn't slept for days. Her hair was in a ponytail and she looked as if she had lost about ten pounds.

"I know that you could do it all yourself. But, I'm here to help you, honey. The two of us can do it much faster, don't you think?"

Tracey knew from the look on Flora's face that she was going to stand her ground, and there wasn't anything that she could say to change her mind. But, what the hell? She could use the company. With Aunt Flo here, she wouldn't cry every time she packed something that belonged to Donald. "Okay, Aunt Flo. Let me put your things away. Would you like something to eat?"

"No, I had Robin over for lunch today. I called you earlier but you didn't answer. Were you out?"

"Maybe I was in the shower or in the backyard."

Flora stood back and took a good look at Tracey. "Well, we should get started. The sooner we finish the sooner you can move out. You'll feel better once it's all over."

"Yeah, I'm sure I will."

They started in the pool room where Donald used to play with his friends. Tracey picked up a picture that they had taken together in England, and Flora saw tears fall from her eyes. When she saw her aunt watching, she turned her head and wiped her eyes.

"Come here, Tracey."

"What is it, Aunt Flo?"

"Just follow me." She led Tracey to the family room and patted the couch so she could sit next to her. "Do you need to talk it out?"

"No, Aunt Flo. Talking can't take away the pain. I just can't understand how I couldn't see what Donald was doing. I wonder how many more women he had while we were married?"

"Probably none. He was in love with you, Tracey. Weren't you two still living as man and wife?"

"Yes, I thought so, but . . ."

"You were. You went places together. That doesn't seem like a man ready to leave his wife. Maybe he wasn't as in love with that woman as her brother thinks he was. Maybe he was just playing around with her or just passing time. Who knows why men do those things? Donald wasn't a completely stupid man. He knew that he couldn't just walk out and find another woman like you. He was lucky to have a woman as young and as beautiful as you are," she said laughing and adjusting the hairpin in her hair.

"I don't know, Aunt Flo. Her brother swears that they were in love."

Flora turned to face Tracey. "You were so upset that night, Tracey. Maybe you're making more out of it than you heard."

"He came here, Aunt Flo, and said the same things."

"What do you mean he came here? Why would he be coming over here? What did he want, Tracey?" she asked, her tone rising in anger.

Tracey recognized the same tone that Flora used when they were children and had gotten caught doing something that her aunt had asked them not to do.

"Now, don't get upset, Aunt Flo. He only came to say that he was sorry."

"But, why would you let him in? You should have closed the door in his face. He's got his nerve. The only thing that he's sorry for is the death of his sister, who was sneaking around with your husband."

Tracey wondered why she had even mentioned it to Aunt Flo.

"Don't let that man in here again, Tracey. You don't know anything about him and he has no business coming around here."

"He has no reason to come back again, Aunt Flo. Now, can we talk about something else?" And then she thought of him again and closed her eyes tight to make the vision of him disappear. She didn't want to see him again either.

"Did you eat anything today, Tracey?"

"Yes, I had a peanut butter and jelly sandwich a few minutes ago."

"Well, I guess that's better than nothing," Flo said, as she looked around the room. She stood up, trying to decide where to start. "You want me to start in here and you can get started in one of the other rooms?"

"No, this room is as good as any. This madness won't last forever. I already packed some of the things that were in one of the bedrooms." Tracey started to stand up but hesitated.

"Aunt Flo?"

"What, honey?"

"Why is it you never remarried? Was it because of Robin and me?"

Flora sat back on the couch beside Tracey again. "No, it wasn't because of you and Robin. After Sam died, there were no men good enough. He did everything for me, treated me like a queen, and gave me everything I needed. When he died he left me enough to live comfortably. I knew that I would never find a man like him so I didn't look for one," she said with a dreamy look in her eyes. Her face lit up and she looked younger.

"Were you in love until the day he died?"

"Yes. We were married for twenty years and in love for twenty years. Just like your mother and father were." Tracey noticed the full, soft smile as Flora spoke of her husband.

"Why on earth would you ask me if I didn't remarry because of you and your sister?"

"I just wondered. You are still a pretty woman, and you could have been married again if you wanted to."

Flora touched Tracey's hand. "The day your mother and father died in that terrible car accident, I was so thankful that the Lord left me you and Robin. You two filled my life. I just didn't want another husband. I lost Sam, and then my dear sister. You girls were all I needed, or wanted. In a way, you and Robin saved my life because I had no one after your mother and father died." She kissed Tracey on the cheek.

"And you saved mine and Robin's life, Aunt Flo. You've been a mother to us and we love you dearly for that." Tracey was feeling sad and wiped a tear from her eye.

Flora began crying, too. "Now, let's stop this kind of talk and get something done around here." She stood up and straightened her dress. Tracey smiled as she looked at her aunt's slender figure. She was still stunning at sixty-two.

Tracey and Flora packed boxes until seven that evening. They made sandwiches and sat down to watch television. Both of them were hungry and tired. They sat in the den and looked at the boxes stacked in the corner.

"We've accomplished quite a bit, Aunt Flo. I sure wouldn't have done so much if you weren't here to help me and keep me company. This big house is so quiet and lonely. I thought I didn't want any company, but, to tell you the truth, I was glad when I opened the door and saw you standing there." Tracey smiled and touched Flora's hand.

"You should have known that I wouldn't stay away too long, honey. I knew you needed someone to talk to." Flora picked up an empty glass from the table. "I just wish that things would have turned out better for you. Lord knows you deserve it."

"They will one day." Tracey looked at her watch; it was almost eight. She was dog-tired and knew that Flora was, too. "Aunt Flo, I'll put the dishes in the dishwasher and we can go to bed. You can turn the television on in your room if you are not sleepy right now. But, I haven't slept all week. I feel as though I'm going to fall on my face," she said, blinking her eyes, which were red with fatigue.

At ten o'clock P.M., Tracey was asleep, but at one A.M. she was wide-awake again, thinking of Donald. She still had no answers about why he'd been having an affair. The next day she had to go to his office, clean out his desk, and collect other items that he may have left behind. His partner would be taking over the company. Tracey would sell him Donald's half. She wanted no part of the business. She had her own life and that was all she could handle. But she knew that going to his office would be just as painful as walking around seeing everything that reminded her of him in this house.

She got out of bed and walked to the window. Although it was the month of June, it was still chilly. Los Angeles was never hot in June, but it was unusual to be so chilly, she thought.

She put her robe on and got back in bed. It was past three when she got back to sleep. And when she woke up again, she decided that she would wait until Monday morning to go to Donald's office. She just couldn't do it this morning, not this soon. But deep inside she knew that it would be no better by Monday. She closed her eyes and fell asleep again.

It was morning and the smell of coffee led Tracey to the kitchen.

"How long have you been up, Aunt Flo?"

"Only about an hour. I fell asleep as soon as my head hit the pillow last night and slept all night. Did you sleep straight through the night, Tracey?"

"I wish. I was up at one, then three, and now it's seven." She could see the top of someone's head out the window and heard the doorbell ring. "I wonder who that is and why they are at the back door?" Tracey opened the door, and Robin and Lisa walked in.

"I knew with Aunt Flo being here, you guys would be up drinking coffee," Robin said. Tracey looked at Lisa, whose hands were full.

"What did you buy, Robin?"

"McDonald's big breakfast for everyone. Sausage, eggs, hash browns, and muffins. Then we stopped and got a dozen donuts."

"You think we have enough?" Lisa teased.

"Yes, we have enough," Flora answered and took the food from Lisa. They all sat at the table and ate. Tracey was surprised that she didn't feel sick when she smelled food, as she had yesterday. Maybe she was simply hungry enough to eat this morning. The phone rang, and Tracey took it in the den. It was her employee, twenty-one-year-old Michelle.

"Michelle, you are doing a good job. I'll be in on Monday. Don't forget to call Mr. Smith and have him bring in the counteroffer. I will be in about nine. Oh, and Michelle, why don't you leave at noon today?"

"So how is she, Aunt Flo?" Robin asked with concern.

"She's about what you would expect. Still searching for answers that she may never find. She packs and wipe her eyes, talks about her marriage and can't understand why she didn't see Donald for what he really was."

"She may not ever see that, Aunt Flo. I just wish it wouldn't hurt her so much and hope she doesn't blame herself for his infidelity. Some men will play around, and it doesn't matter how nice or pretty their wives are. They just play around. The dead woman's brother said that they were in love. Maybe it was just his sister that was in love. I believe that Donald was still in love with Tracey," Robin was saying, but stopped when Lisa walked in from the bathroom with Tracey right behind her.

"That was Michelle on the phone. She didn't go in on Thursday and was going to work all day today. But I told her to go home at noon. I'm going back to work on Monday anyway," Tracey said, and poured her second cup of coffee.

"With all the moving and business that you have to attend to, don't you think Monday is a little soon, Tracey?" Flora asked.

"Yes, it's a little soon, but I have a lot to do, Aunt Flo. I have a thirty-unit deal going on and a backlog of paperwork waiting for me at my office. I have a buyer to counteroffer on Monday. I'll get everything done somehow," she said and sighed.

"Don't worry. We are all here to help," Robin assured her, and Lisa agreed.

They finished their breakfast, and Tracey dressed in a pair of faded jeans and sweatshirt. She went to the store to get more boxes. Since she had help, she planned to take advantage and get as much packed as possible.

"I'll start in my bedroom, and Robin, you can start in the guest bedroom. Just pack everything. Aunt Flo, I guess you can finish the den, and Lisa, you can start in the second bathroom," Tracey said and looked around at all the work that she had ahead of her. "I don't know how long it's going to take me to move all of this stuff. Most of it is what I bought. I'll leave Donald's daughter some of the furniture that he bought."

By noon, they had packed the rooms they had started in. Tracey ordered in pizza and Coke for lunch. They stopped, ate, and went back to work. Robin went out to get more boxes.

At six, Tracey sent all three home. Flora wanted to spend another night, but Tracey assured her that she would be all right. She wanted to be alone in the house that she loved so much for the few nights she had left. At eight, she took a long shower, curled up in the black leather chair in the den, and turned on the television. She looked around the room. It seemed strange that there were no paintings on the walls, no pictures over the fireplace, and no waiting for Donald to come home. It was almost as if all life had disappeared from the house. It was once so warm and cozy with so much love in the air. All she felt now was a chill and the quietness around her. Tracey was so depressed. She went to her bedroom, and got in bed wishing for a deep sleep until morning. The days were a little easier than the nights. The nights were so quiet, cold and lonely.

Morning came, but Tracey had gotten very little sleep. She got up at seven and packed until Flora called to see if she was all right. After Flora hung up, the phone rang again and it was Robin.

"Have you had breakfast, yet?"

"No, just coffee. I wasn't hungry and wanted to get an early start."

"But, Tracey, it's noon. You should eat something before you make yourself sick. That won't do you any good, you know."

"I'll make myself a sandwich in a few minutes. I just have a lot to do and the sooner I finish, the sooner I can move out and start a life for myself. I feel so depressed walking around seeing everything packed." She sat on the arm of the couch and looked at the work that she still had to do.

"I know, honey. If you change your mind and want company, just call me. Okay?"

"I will. Don't worry about me. You always worry about me, Robin."

"Sure, that's what the oldest sister does."

On Wednesday, Tracey called Janet and asked her to come over. She had moved everything that she wanted out of the house. "Of course, you will need your own furniture. I left some that your Dad had bought before we were married. But you will still have to buy some of your own. I take it that your mom will move in with you?"

"Yes, and I'm sorry that she came over to see you, Tracey. That wasn't my idea. If I had known, I would have asked her not to."

"I know, and it's all right. The key will be in the same place."

"Tracey, do you think you'll miss the house a lot?"

"Yes, but not enough to want to live in it. I feel better since I've finished moving out. This house has too many memories for me. Anyway, you take care of yourself." She wanted to say "keep in touch," but she knew better.

"You too, Tracey." Janet liked Tracey even though she tried not to, and she hated the way things had turned out for her. She really never understood her father. And they were never very close. Before Tracey, he went from one woman to another. After his marriage, Janet had been sure that he had stopped. And maybe he had, for a while.

Three

Tracey spent the weekend unpacking her clothes at Flora's house. She looked around the room that she and Robin had shared. Aunt Flo had kept everything as it was from their teens. The same pink bedspreads, stuffed animals, and pictures on the walls. She smiled as she looked at her high school boyfriend's picture. At six, she and Flora sat down to eat dinner. When Tracey finished, she went back to her room and continued to unpack until she was too tired and went to bed.

On Sunday morning, Flora went to church, but Tracey stayed home and put away everything she had left out the night before. When she finished, she went to her office for a couple of hours and did some work that was left on her desk. She went over a new listing, made a couple of phone calls, lay her head back and leaned into the leather chair's headrest, closed her eyes, and felt her tired body relax. Feeling exhausted from packing and unpacking, she'd finally gotten some sleep. But it felt like a drugged sleep, she was so bone tired.

The next morning was the first day that Tracey felt thoroughly rested from sleeping through the night. After she showered and dressed for work, she could smell coffee and food cooking in the kitchen. She knew that it was Aunt Flo cooking breakfast for her after she had told her the day before that she never had time to eat, and always stopped on her way to the office to pick something up. When would Aunt Flo realize that she could take care of herself?

Tracey walked into the kitchen where Flora was waiting for her with a plate of food in her hands. Flora sat the plate on the table in front of Tracey as though it burned her hands.

"Are you all right, Aunt Flo?"

"Yes. It's just that my right hand is a little stiff this morning. Must be the cool weather."

Tracey sighed. "Aunt Flo, I told you not to go through any trouble for me. Sometimes I can't eat this early," she said, setting her purse on the table.

"But it's good to start your day with a full stomach. Haven't I told you girls that? Even as children I used to tell you girls that breakfast was the most important meal of the day," she said, determined that Tracey would put something in her stomach before she left the house. Flora was still in her long blue bathrobe and her hair was pinned up in back. Her eyes were round and wide-awake and she seemed to be full of energy.

Tracey just couldn't hurt her feelings and the coffee smelled awfully good this morning. Aunt Flo could still make the best pot of coffee that she had ever drunk before.

"Okay, but I can't eat all of this. I have to get to the office early this morning." But, she hadn't eaten dinner the night before and didn't realize how hungry she really was. She ate the grits, eggs, and bacon and drank half a cup of coffee.

Aunt Flo stood in back of her. "I thought we weren't hungry this morning? You sure seem hungry enough to me," she said with both hands on her hips as she laughed.

"Guess I was hungry. I was too tired to eat anything last night. Now, I've got to get out of here." She picked up her purse, jacket, and briefcase. Flora walked her to the door and said good-bye. She noticed that Tracey looked like she had rested last night, but she had gotten thinner in the weeks since Donald's death.

* * *

When Tracey walked into her office at eight-thirty, Michelle was already there. "What are you doing here so early this morning?" Tracey asked.

"I knew you'd be here early, too, so I came in case you needed me for anything."

Tracey noticed that Michelle was wearing a short black dress and black flats. Her French braids were hanging down her back and she was wearing too much makeup. She would have to remind her again that this was a place of business. Her short dresses were all right as long as she didn't wear them any shorter, but some of the makeup had to go. She just had to figure out how to tell her tactfully.

As Tracey walked into the small room that was used for a kitchen and supply room, she saw Michelle's schoolbooks on the table where she studied on her lunch break, remembering that she used to do the same thing in the office where she worked. The phone rang and she ran back to her desk to answer. It was her client saying that he would be thirty minutes late. Tracey pulled out a file from her cabinet and gazed out the large window behind her desk.

"How's your mother, Michelle?" she asked, as they were sitting at their desks. Tracey's desk sat back in the corner near her file cabinets and a large window with a nice view.

"She's all right, but my sister dropped out of school last week." She turned to face Tracey. "Can you imagine? She has one more year to get her BA, and she drops out?"

"You just keep going. Sometimes it's hard, but it pays off in the end."

Michelle nodded in agreement. "I'm going to finish school," she said resolutely. "One day I'd like to own my own business like you."

Tracey took a long look at Michelle, who was smiling at her. The younger woman's eyes were filled with admiration. She hadn't realized that she was a role model to Michelle.

Tracey lifted her eyebrow, but didn't speak.

"Tracey, why did you become a realtor?" Michelle put her chin on her elbow, her face a study in rapt attention.

Tracey hesitated. She measured her words. "Like I told you before, I worked in an office with four realtors. I was the file clerk and did all kinds of duties, just like you do. This one realtor, Linda, was in her fifties. She used to let me drive her car to make her bank deposits for her." The phone rang again. "Here, I'll get it," Tracey said. She talked for a few seconds.

"That was Wendy. Now, like I was saying, Linda only sold units or commercial buildings and made big commissions. I knew then what I wanted, and I told her. She took me under her wing and taught me everything I know. When she thought that I knew enough, I studied for the realtor's exam and passed it, also with her help."

The phone rang again. "I'll get it this time," Michelle said. She only answered a question and hung up. "That was my mom."

Tracey smiled. " Like I was saying again, Linda got very ill and had to stay home. I even helped her work from her home until she got too ill." Tracey's eyes started to water as a sense of gloom fell over her. Lately it had been so easy for her to cry.

"She died of breast cancer," she said, and took a deep breath, but continued on. "I went into a small office with three other realtors in Inglewood and did well. My husband also taught me a lot," she had to admit.

Michelle listened to every word Tracey said to her. She knew what she wanted.

"Would you teach me, Tracey? I've been working with you for a year and I want to learn."

"There are so many other fields a woman can go into. But, if you really want to learn, I'll give you more to do and teach you. There is one more thing, Michelle. Your appearance means everything."

"What do you mean?" Michelle sounded a little miffed; she folded her arms in front of her and stared Tracey up and down.

"You have a pretty face, but you wear a bit too much

makeup. Let people see the beautiful Michelle under there."
There, she'd said it as tactfully as she could, without hurting
her feelings.

Michelle looked in her purse and pulled out her mirror.
"Maybe it is a little too much. My mom says she thinks I
overdo it, but she wears a lot sometimes, too," she said and
held her head down.

"I'm sure she means well when she tells you. Now, I'd
better get ready before Mr. Smith gets here. It takes all the
strength I have to work with him. He doesn't understand the
business so I have to explain the terms of his loan over and
over. But, dumb me, whenever he calls, I never refuse him.
I end up being his realtor again."

"Yes, but look at the good deals he gives you," Michelle
said with a smile. "I hope that I can find a Mr. Smith when
I start selling real estate."

"You will. Just learn everything and you will do well,
Michelle. Some people settle for one deal a month because
you can make lots of money. Me, I take all the deals that I
can handle so I can retire early and do a lot of traveling."

Mr. Smith wasn't so bad this time. He had used Tracey
as the broker on four other deals and by the fifth one he
understood. After his third cup of coffee, he was gone
and Tracey could submit his counteroffer to the selling
agent.

It was Friday morning, and Tracey was depressed. She
had told Donald's business partner that she would be in his
office the next morning to pack his things. She had put it
off before. What would she do with his things after they
were packed? She didn't really want them after finding out
about that woman he had been cheating on her with. She
still loved him, but she hated him, too. She wondered how
you could love someone one day and hate him the next day.
The phone rang and it was Robin.

"You don't sound too good today, Tracey."

"I know. I have to clear out Donald's office tomorrow, Robin. I just don't have the energy to go through all his things. Right now I don't feel that I will ever be free of the hurt he caused me. It's all I think about."

"You'll feel differently later when the hurt isn't so bad."

"Will I? I wonder."

"Hey, how about if I go with you?"

"I can't have you always holding my hand through this. You have your own family to do for. I'll go alone."

"Okay. How is work?"

"Work is the only thing that keeps me going these days. Aunt Flo is running me crazy. I know she means well, but she is always there. 'Eat breakfast. You shouldn't go without eating.' 'Did you have lunch?' And on and on. She goes on all the time."

Robin laughed. "Better you than me, honey. But if you change your mind about tomorrow, just give me a call."

The next morning, Tracey got out of bed and sighed at the thought of what she had to do. She hadn't changed her mind and left early, still determined to get it over with.

When she walked in, Chuck was in his office and offered Tracey a cup of coffee, which she declined. She sat at his desk in the chair opposite him. He was a portly, dark-skinned man who weighed more than two hundred pounds. He wheezed with every breath, and she could smell cigar smoke in the office.

"I'm sorry about everything, Tracey. I'm going to miss Donald. We've been in business together for fifteen years. I still remember your wedding day. I told Donald that you were the prettiest bride I had ever seen," he said and smiled again. "I remembered Donald saying that you were all the woman that he needed. I believe that, Tracey. He wouldn't have left you for anyone."

"How long had you known about his affair, Chuck?"

"From the beginning, but he was my friend," he said

ruefully. He hung his head, casting his eyes onto the papers on his desk.

"I thought I was your friend, too, Chuck."

"You were—and still are." Chuck began to shift restlessly in his seat. "I—I tried to talk to Donald," he stammered.

Tracey glared at Chuck. She folded her arms across her chest.

"He's a man who did what he wanted, got what he wanted," Chuck said in a rush of words. "You know that, Tracey."

"Yes, I guess I do," she said, showing no emotion, but trying to hold back the tears. She cried all the time now. But there was plenty to cry about, she thought.

Tracey was silent for what felt like an interminable time. In the absence of small talk, Chuck looked like he wished he could sink into the ground under her icy gaze.

Finally, she stood up. "I'd better get it over with, Chuck."

He stood up and walked her to the door of Donald's office. "If you ever need me for anything, Tracey, you know that you can call me." He kissed her on top of her head.

She nodded stiffly, walked inside, and sat in the chair behind Donald's desk. Chuck had three boxes stacked in the corner for her. She grabbed one and started to pack. While rummaging through a drawer she pulled out an envelope and opened it. She sucked in her breath as she stared at the couple. It was a picture of Donald with his arm around a woman's shoulder. "This must be her," Tracey whispered. She was wearing a pair of white shorts and a tight blouse. Her legs were short but nicely shaped. Her face was pretty and she wore a short, pixie haircut. How many times had he told Tracey to never cut her hair?

"How could you, Donald?" she hissed.

She threw everything into the box, but with trembling hands, she tore the picture into pieces and threw it into the trash. Tracey sat behind his desk and looked around his office. This would be the last time she would see it.

"Why did it have to end this way, this soon, and with another woman involved?" she asked out loud, feeling his presence in every corner of the room.

She walked out with one box that she was going to take home. She stopped to give the office one last look. Forget him, she thought, still standing in the doorway. I will never be anyone else's fool. I keep my hair long for him and he falls in love with a woman with hair as short as his. She kicked the door closed to his office and went to her car. But, instead of putting the box in her car she changed her mind, walked behind the building, and flung the box into the trash Dumpster.

No more crying, no more sitting around and wondering why he did it. I was a good and loving wife. He lied and cheated on me. But that's that and it can't be changed. It's time to go on with my life, she thought. But, she knew that it would be much easier said than done.

When Tracey walked inside of her office the next morning, she listened to her messages. The first one was from Michelle. She said that she had a cold and wouldn't be in. The second was from Wendy. She said it was important that Tracey call her back. But before she could return the call, Wendy was walking in.

"Hi. Are you all right, Wendy? Your call sounded urgent. I was just about to call you back."

Wendy sat in the leather chair in front of Tracey's desk. She looked tired—as if she had a lot on her mind. "I could use a hot cup of coffee."

"I could use one myself. You sit, and I'll pour you one, too."

Tracey came back to her desk with two cups of coffee in her hands. "So, what is that worried look on your face about, girl?"

Wendy threw both hands up in the air and stood up. "Honey, the building where I work is for sale. I've got to find myself another space. I only have a few weeks to find one."

"Is that why you are so out of breath? A few weeks with

all your connections? Girl, you looked as though you had only one week left."

Wendy eased back in her chair. "Tracey, my business is doing well. I hate moving into another building. Moving from one office to another is so much trouble."

"You should have rented a space from me. You see, I won't be selling anytime soon. All this time, you could have been on the second floor."

"Lot of good that does me now," Wendy said. "So how have you been these days?"

"I could be better, and I will be soon, I hope."

"How's Miss Flora and Robin and her family?"

"They're all right. I'm the only one that has been under the weather."

"You have a right to be. You just lost your husband."

"Twice. I lost him to another woman, and to his death. I get so angry, my blood just boils. Now, enough of that. The space upstairs just happens to be empty. The tenants moved out two weeks ago. Now, will you listen to me and lease it? You know I'll give you a good deal, girl. It would be good seeing you everyday. But, on the other hand, it may not be too good," she laughed.

Wendy looked at Tracey as she smiled. Tracey was starting to sound like her old self again. "I'll take it. It's not that far from my old office, anyway," she said.

Tracey got up and took the keys from Michelle's desk. "Come on, I'll take you up there. It's been awhile since you've seen it."

"I still kind of remember what it looks like. You know that I was with you when you first moved in, but I had no idea that you would buy the building," Wendy said as they climbed the stairs.

"That was Donald's idea. He did have a good head for business." They stepped inside and Wendy stood in front of the two large windows.

"It's about the same size as your office," Tracey said.

"Almost. It's just a little smaller. But, it's still lots of room. I love the windows." She followed Tracey around the office.

"When can I move in?" Wendy asked anxiously.

"Anytime you want. I'll draw up a lease agreement and you can start moving whenever you're ready. What about the girl who works with you?"

"She'll love it. It's not that far from her house. She lives in Inglewood. It's only a few minutes to West LA."

Tracey locked the door and they walked back downstairs to her office.

"I'll give you a call tomorrow. I have an appointment in thirty minutes," Wendy said as she rushed out the door.

"Good," Tracey answered. The phone rang and she picked it up. It was a man who had been referred by one of her clients. He wanted to sell his home in Ladera Heights and needed a realtor. Tracey usually refused to sell single-family homes because the commission was smaller, but in this case she made an exception. Mr. Green was a friend of a good client, with whom she still did business, and he wanted to sell fast. His wife had died a year earlier and he needed the change. He had decided to relocate to Detroit. Tracey asked if she could meet him at two o'clock so that she could get a better idea of what she had to work with.

She left the office at one-thirty so she could be at Mr. Green's house early enough. She parked the car and got out. What a lovely house, she thought. She could smell the roses that were blooming in the front yard and she admired the brown-wooden trimming around the windows. She started to take a look in back of the house but the owner opened the door and stepped outside.

Mr. Green was in his seventies, an attractive man with sad eyes. He showed Tracey around the house. There were two bedrooms, one with a fireplace, two baths, a kitchen, den, an office, and a living room with a fireplace. She walked out back, and in the center of the backyard was a beautiful, gurgling, two-tier fountain. Potted plants along with leafy green ferns and palms accentuated a tropical setting. Tracey smiled, and breathed in the warm summer air she felt against her face. Suddenly a thought hit her. This was where she would be during the summer evenings when she wanted to read or relax. This house had her name written on it. She knew it in her gut. This was her house! Talk about serendipity. Today was her day.

"How much do you have in mind to sell it for, Mr. Green?"

"What do you think I could get for it, Mrs. Woods? I'm not sure what the houses are going for around here. I've been so wrapped up in other things that I've had to take care of after my wife's death." But after a few seconds he gave her a price hoping that he wasn't asking for too much.

Tracey was ecstatic. This was the first time she'd felt enthusiastic about anything since Donald's death. Could she dare hope to be happy again?

"I'll take it. I'll draw up a purchase agreement and bring it back signed tomorrow," she said smiling. " I knew today would be a better day for me."

Mr. Green's mouth dropped open. "You mean you want it for yourself?"

"Yes, absolutely. It's a beautiful house. I used to live just ten minutes away from here." As she walked into the kitchen again, he followed her.

Tracey caught him staring at her.

"What's the matter, Mr. Green?"

"I was just thinking of my wife. Your hair reminds me of hers when she was young. Your hair is so black it is almost blue. You're a lovely woman, and I'm not saying that to flirt with you. I'm old enough to be your grandfather."

"Why thank you!" Tracey needed to feel attractive again, and she knew Mr. Green spoke to her in a fatherly tone. She beamed at the compliment.

"I think I'll have the wall between the dining room and kitchen knocked out, and have a bar to divide it. I love a bar in my kitchen," she said, already visualizing it.

Mr. Green appeared to be speechless. He stammered, "Why—why, I had no idea selling would be this easy. I'm so happy that you love this house. My wife and I had lots of happy years here together. You know, I think a bar would look real good here, Mrs. Woods. You have great taste," he said, talking fast, amazed at their mutual good fortune.

When Tracey got home and told Flora that she had found a house, Flora looked disappointed. "Are you sure that you are up to moving so soon, Tracey?"

"Aunt Flo, I won't be that far away from you. I'll see you as much as I always have. It's just that I want to get on with my life. I'm tired of crying every time I think of Donald."

Tracey sat on the couch and gestured that Flora should sit next to her. "You're going to love my new house, Aunt Flo. It's right off Corning Street and Slauson Avenue. Only fifteen minutes from my office. We can drive by Saturday. I'll still be here for a while anyway," she said excitedly.

Flora smiled as Tracey talked about her new house. It was good to see her so enthusiastic again and looking forward to her future. "Okay, but don't you forget. I'll be glad to go with you Saturday."

Tracey inhaled deeply. "What smells so good?"

"I cooked dinner for us. I was hoping that you would come home early enough for dinner."

"Well, I'm famished. I had a light lunch today. I was so excited about the house that I wasn't hungry. I'll go and slip into a pair of jeans and be right back."

At dinner they laughed and talked. Tracey told her that Wendy was going to lease an office from her.

"Is she all right?" Flora asked. "The last time I saw her she had put on a few pounds, she had aged, and she didn't look happy. She always seems to have problems."

"She's all right, Aunt Flo. Probably that young husband

of hers is getting her down. You know how he flirts with every woman that passes him by. He never has a job. Can you imagine? He's twenty-five and she's almost forty. He's going to divorce her and take every cent she has." Tracey shook her head in disgust. "She'll never learn."

As Tracey got up to put the dishes in the dishwasher, the doorbell rang. Flora looked at her quizzically.

"Are you expecting anyone?"

"No. Maybe it's Robin." Flora went into the living room and Tracey followed. Flora opened the door and was surprised to see that it was Wendy. She looked as if she had been crying.

"Girl, I was just telling Aunt Flo that you were at my office today. Come in and have a seat."

"Have some dinner, Wendy?" Flora asked.

"No, thank you, Miss Flora. I had a large lunch today."

"Well, I'm going to leave you girls so I can watch *Hollywood Squares*," Flora said and left the room.

"So, what brings you this way?" Tracey asked with concern. She could see that Wendy had been crying, but before Wendy could answer she put her face in her hands and began sobbing.

Tracey rushed to her side and led her to the couch and sat next to her.

"Honey, what is it?"

"William hasn't come home since he left yesterday. I know he's out with some woman. The last time this happened, it was another woman. I can't take this any longer, Tracey. It's just taking too much out of me," she said, wiping her eyes. "And please don't say, 'I told you so.' I'm just so tired and fed up with him."

"I wasn't going to. I'm just sorry that you have to go through this shit with him. Haven't you had enough, Wendy? When will you stop punishing yourself?"

"I guess not. I still think that if he finds the kind of job he wants, he'll be happier. Maybe then, he'll settle down and be a husband. He's just so unhappy now."

"It's been four years, Wendy. He still doesn't have the kind of job he wants?"

"Look, everyone doesn't have money and a business like Donald had, you know."

"No, everyone doesn't. But, William could do better and you know it."

"Yes. I know you're right. I'm just not ready to let him go." Wendy sniffed, then threw back her shoulders. "Anyway, the owner of the building has a buyer already. I just dropped by to tell you that I would be moving in soon. No use waiting any longer."

"Whenever you're ready."

Wendy held her head down. "Maybe I'll wait a couple of months and see what happens with William. I have too much going on to make any rash decisions now. Who knows, he may decide to do right, for a while anyway. I just have to wait and see."

"You need him to do right for more than a while, Wendy. Don't you think that you deserve more?" Tracey asked warmly, touching her hand. "I promised myself as I cleaned out Donald's office that I'd never let another man hurt me. Can you imagine how it feels to hear that your husband is dead, and was with another woman? The woman's brother told me that, but I didn't believe him," she said, remembering every word. "I just knew he wasn't talking about Donald."

"No, what I can imagine is how much of a fool he must have felt when he found out that you were Donald's wife and not his daughter. The man must have been in some sort of shock to say anything about Donald's relationship, even to his daughter. How would he know if his daughter knew about it or not? What a fool."

"Did I tell you that he came to see me the day after the funeral?"

"No. What did he want, girl?"

"To say he was sorry. He was really very nice."

"He should have been. He let the cat out of the bag. If

he hadn't, at least you could have remembered your husband in a better way. I was so sorry, Tracey. I couldn't believe it when you told me." And she couldn't. Donald always seemed to be the perfect husband. "Well, I guess I'd better be going to my lonely house." Wendy got up and Tracey walked her to the door.

"Call me tomorrow if you need to talk."

"I will. If I'm not too busy with clients tomorrow, maybe we can meet for lunch."

Wendy left and Flora came back into the living room. Tracey was going through her mail. Flora always left it on the table where she could see it.

"So she left, huh?"

"Yes, and as usual she's having trouble with William. He hasn't been home since he left yesterday. I don't know why Wendy tolerates him. I know that I couldn't," Tracey said and sat in the chair opposite the couch where Flora took her seat. She absently studied her aunt and decided that she didn't look any older than fifty, not the sixty-two years old that she was. Aunt Flo's skin was still Hershey brown and unlined. She had maintained a slender figure with a small waist.

"Anyway, I'm going to bed early tonight," Flora said, standing up.

"Are you feeling well, Aunt Flo? It's only eight o'clock," she asked with concern.

"I'm all right. I went to see Marilyn today. She's a member of my church. I cooked and cleaned for her. It wasn't much, but helping her in and out of bed is what got me so tired. The lady who helps her wasn't feeling well today. She didn't ask me, but I went over anyway."

But Tracey noticed that Flora had rubbed her right hand and flexed her fingers more than once.

The next day Wendy came to Tracey's office at noon with Chinese food for the three of them. They all went into the small kitchen for lunch. Wendy told Tracey and Michelle her plans for her new office. She would start to move in on the weekend.

After they finished eating, Michelle went to the post office to buy some stamps and left Tracey and Wendy alone.

"He came home last night like he hadn't done anything wrong. Kissed me on the cheek and went into the bedroom. When I asked where he had been, he said at his brother's house. I asked, 'William, why didn't you call me?' And he said that he had, but I didn't answer the phone." Wendy frowned and shook her head in disbelief.

"That lie was an insult to my intelligence. I know that he was with another woman. Sometimes he's like a kid, Tracey. Something has got to change."

"Well, don't ask me because you know exactly what I will say. Put him out, get a divorce, and forget him, girl."

"I know it will happen sooner or later."

"It's just a waste of time, Wendy. I'm not going to say any more about it. And, by the way, thanks for the lunch. I didn't feel like going out."

"Have you talked to Janet or anyone in Donald's family lately?"

"His mother called me yesterday. She's still taking his death very hard. Too bad she only had one son. I couldn't talk to her too long." Tracey sighed and ran her fingers through her hair. "It only made it harder for me, and I'm so tired of being depressed and not getting a decent night's sleep. I don't really expect to hear from Janet. When Donald was alive, she kept her distance from me. We talked more after he died than we did the entire three years that Donald and I were married."

"Spoiled brat," Wendy said, looked at her watch and stood up. "I have an escrow to open for a new client, so I better leave."

"It's going to be convenient for me to have an escrow office upstairs. I'll be glad when you move in, girl."

Tracey walked Wendy outside to her car and looked up at the sun. It felt good and warm for a change. She heard the birds singing in the trees, and the leaves were greener. Finally, summer was here and the chilly, gloomy days were gone. If only my life would change as well, she thought as she walked back inside of her office.

Four

September 1999

It was a hot day. Tracey put all the paper plates and cups in the trash. She was glad that Robin, Aunt Flo, Lisa and Wendy had helped her line the cabinets in the kitchen and helped put everything away in her new home. The movers had put all the furniture in place the day before. She had decided to have Thanksgiving dinner at her house this year.

As Tracey put sheets and a blanket on her bed, she sat down and sighed. How many times had Donald left her alone to go on his business trips, and to be with his woman? Or was it women? She often wondered. But, she wouldn't let thinking of her marriage ruin her first night in her home. She would just plan her decor and get a good night sleep. Tonight was the first night of her new life, alone. But, that was all right with her, too. Who said that a woman couldn't have a good life without a husband anyway? She took a long, hot bath and went to bed.

At eight the next morning Tracey heard the doorbell ring. She looked at the clock next to her bed and wondered who it was. When she opened the door she saw Wendy carrying a bag.

"Come in. Good, you've got coffee," she beamed as she moved aside to let her pass. Wendy followed her to the kitchen and put the coffee and doughnuts on the table.

"Be right back. I gotta wash my face and brush my teeth," Tracey said.

When Tracey walked back into the kitchen, Wendy was already eating a doughnut.

"I couldn't sleep so I got up and decided to get you up, too. But at least I bought you coffee. How was your first night?"

"Just great. Girl, I slept like a baby last night. Maybe I needed the change because I hadn't slept so well in months. And we got a lot accomplished yesterday. I do appreciate your help, Wendy," Tracey said, biting into her doughnut. She got up, adjusted a painting on the wall, and sat back down.

"I left that fool man of mine in the bed asleep. I just needed to get out and clear my head. After I leave here, I'll go to the office and do some work. I have two escrows to open for to-morrow anyway."

Tracey could see that her friend wasn't happy at all. Her business was doing well, but her personal life was sad. It was too bad, because the only thing she had to do to correct it was get rid of William, Tracey thought, but she wasn't going to tell Wendy that anymore.

"William came in right after I did last night. I wasn't as happy to see him as I used to be when he walked through the door. Maybe I'm beginning to feel differently about him and now, maybe it won't be so hard to throw him out." She finished her doughnut. "Anyway, I won't bore you with this. It's something that I have to figure out on my own."

"I'm sure you'll make the right decision, Wendy. But re-member I'm here whenever you need me. You've always been here for me. We've known each other for a long time." Tracey smiled, remembering all the years they had been friends.

"Since grammar school," Wendy laughed.

"Yes, that's a long time." Tracey put her cup down and led Wendy to the dining room. "What would you think if I have that wall knocked out and have a counter built here?" She stood where she wanted it built.

Wendy studied the area. "I think that's a good idea. It will make the dining room look larger, you know, more open and spacious." She smiled, then said, "You're getting on with your life, aren't you?"

"Yes, I have no choice. I can sit here and feel sorry for myself, or I can make things better." Tracey put one hand on her hip. "You know me. I have to keep going forward. Now, come on, I want your opinion on the second bedroom. I already know how I will decorate my room. This is exciting for me." Leading Wendy from room to room, Tracey felt that at last, she had some direction in her life again.

Five

When Flora woke up she placed her hands on each side of her to balance herself, but the right hand was too sore to hold her weight. The night before they were sore and she took two Celebrex, which was a pain pill for rheumatoid arthritis, but this morning the right hand was worse, and swollen.

Finally, Flora slowly climbed out of bed and held her hands in front of her face. A sharp pain from her fingers penetrated up her right arm.

Two years ago Flora was diagnosed with rheumatoid arthritis, an inflammatory condition that caused the joints to ache and throb. But luckily, Flora only had it in her hands.

She went into the bathroom and washed her face and brushed her teeth, but pressing anything against her hands made her flinch and hiss through her teeth. Today she had more use of her left hand, but felt helpless because she was right handed.

By habit Flora made her bed every morning as soon as she got up. But this morning it had to wait until she put something in her stomach and took a pain pill. She limped into the kitchen and managed to make a cup of tea and eat a croissant. As soon as she finished she took two pain pills and went back to bed. Before she dozed off, she could feel the pain subsiding. As she was just falling into a deep sleep, she heard her phone ring, but she couldn't move fast enough to get it. By noon Flora was up again, she still wasn't able to make her bed. The pain in her hand wasn't throbbing, but her left hand was stiff and the right one was still swollen.

Flora managed to dial Tracey's phone number to her office. "You don't have to leave now, Tracey. It's really no reason for you to rush over here."

"Aunt Flo, I know how painful it is when your arthritis flares up in your hands. The last time it lasted for three weeks before you had full use of them. You just go back to bed and I'll be there in an hour."

Flora could always depend on Tracey and Robin when she needed them. They were her life.

She got back in bed and closed her eyes, thinking of the dream that she had earlier. She had dreamed of her sister, Tracey and Robin's mother, and the day she and her husband had that fatal accident.

The day had been cold and windy with no sun in sight. Flora seldom had headaches but she had a splitting one that day. She had just lost her husband a year and a half earlier. As she started to go into the kitchen to get an aspirin for her head, she heard the doorbell. When she opened the door and saw two police officers, she knew immediately that something was very wrong. Flora suddenly slumped, becoming too weak to stand. One of the officers helped her to the couch.

When they had told her what had happened, she thought that she would faint, the pain in her head throbbing. It would have been so easy to just faint, wake up, and not remember. But she thought of Tracey and Robin. Tracey was ten and Robin was twelve. Flora knew that she had to think of the children. It took all the strength that she could muster to identify the bodies, go to her sister's house, and wait for the girls to return from school.

Flora had paced the floor, wondering how she would tell them. Where would she begin?

How would they react? She felt as though she was inside someone else's body and couldn't remember what had happened that same morning. At three, the girls had walked in. They were laughing and talking about their day at school.

"Mommy, we're home," Robin had yelled.

Flora was walking in from the kitchen and saw Tracey skipping across the living room.

"Mommy said not to run or skip in the house, Tracey," Robin said.

"Girls," Flora said in a soft voice. The girls' eyes lit up. They were always happy to see Aunt Flo because she would bring presents. Sometimes she would come over and baby-sit when their parents went away.

"Hi, Aunt Flo. Are you baby-sitting us today?" Tracey asked, raising herself on her toes to hug Flora. Robin ran up beside her and gave her a hug, too.

"Come here and sit on the couch with me, girls. I have something to tell you both." The girls eyes widened as they followed her and took a seat on each side of Flora.

Flora knew there was no easy way to do this, but it was the hardest thing she had ever had to do in her life.

"I got a call from the hospital today with some very, very bad news."

Robin's young, innocent face scrunched into a worried expression, but Tracey's demeanor hadn't changed.

"Your mom and dad were in a car accident today. They're both dead," Flora said it and held her breath, waiting for their reactions.

The girls looked at each other, not knowing what they were supposed to say or do. Tracey looked at her aunt as if she was waiting for her to say more. After seconds had passed, Robin eyes started to water.

"Are you here to take us to a foster home?" she asked, and started to sob. When Tracey heard her, she started to cry, too.

"I don't want to go to a foster home. I'll run away so no one can find me," Tracey cried. Flora felt tears running down her cheeks and she grabbed both girls. "Of course you don't have to go to a foster home. Both of you are going to live with me. Aunt Flo will take care of you." She sat back on the couch rocking the girls back and forth, and all three cried together. Under the circumstances, she knew that it would take time for the girls to heal. She would need time, too.

The next day Flora had kept them home from school. They talked and she reassured them that she would always be there for them and would always take care of them. She had their twin beds moved into the guest bedroom and did everything to make them feel at home. She had lost her only sister, but she had her daughters. Flora got down on her knees and prayed, "Thank you, good Lord, for the girls."

The first month the girls had constantly cried for their parents. Even so, Tracey tried hard to be a "good girl" so that Flora wouldn't put them in a foster home. She had heard so many sad stories about children who had no parents, and now their parents were dead. And she tried to be the perfect little girl, make perfect grades, and do everything that she was told to do. But after she realized that Flora really did want them she began to relax into a normal child. The girls loved Flora and wanted to stay with her. After a year, the girls had become the center of her life.

Even as grown women, they remained her greatest joy.

Barely an hour had passed when Tracey was rushing into Flora's house. She called out her aunt's name.

"I'm in the bedroom, Tracey."

Flora was sitting up in bed watching her favorite soap opera on television. She took her hands from under the blanket and placed them flat on the bed. She held them up so Tracey could see. "Both of them hurt, but I can't use the right one."

Tracey sat on the bed, too, and gently touched Flora's hands. "Aunt Flo, why didn't you tell me or Robin about it? I know they didn't just start to hurt you today."

"They weren't so bad and they just got worse last night."

"Do you need to go and see your doctor?" Tracey asked with concern.

"No, dear. I took my medication." Flora placed both hands under the blanket to keep them warm. It hurt more if they got too cold.

"Well, I'm going home and get a change of clothes. I'm sleeping over here tonight."

"Tracey . . ."

"No, Aunt Flo. We're not going to argue about this. I'll be back in twenty minutes. Can I get you anything before I leave?"

"No," Flora said as if she were defeated.

The next day when Tracey got to work Michelle called and said that she wouldn't be in.

She chatted with Wendy for a while and returned downstairs to her office. Tracey was surprised that she actually got some work done and was glad to be alone on a day like this.

The office was quiet and her phone wasn't ringing off the hook. But it seemed that every time the phone did ring she thought of Donald. He used to call and have her meet him for lunch or dinner. She had to admit that she missed the good times they had together. It seemed as though every time she took one step forward, she took two steps backward. How depressing she felt. And why was she remembering so many things they had done together, and so many times he said that he loved her when all those times, he had lied. But she knew why she felt so depressed. Today was Donald's birthday. He would have been fifty-three years old. If he was alive, she would have been planning a nice dinner for the two of them, or she would have taken him out, or even planned to go away for the weekend.

Tracey had worked earnestly to flee from her own private torments, but today it wasn't working. Frustrated and angry, she lay her head on her desk and cried.

She looked at the clock on her desk and it was five-thirty. Tracey decided that she was finished in the office today. As she opened the drawer to her desk to place a file in it, she saw a small white envelope and felt as though she had stopped breathing. She held the envelope in her hand. Should she open it, or not? "No. No," she whispered to herself. She ripped it in half and tossed it into the trash can next to her desk. It was the last birthday card that Donald had bought for her. She was so deeply in love with him and had read the card at least a dozen times. How foolish she felt now.

Tracey grabbed her purse from her desk and her jacket off the hanger and walked out the door.

Six

"Why are you so late?" Those were the first words that greeted her when she stepped inside the foyer.

Robin lifted her eyebrow. "John, I left you a voice mail. Didn't you listen to it?"

"No, after the staff meeting was over, I came straight home. I was hoping that I would have a home-cooked meal when I got here."

Robin watched the familiar creases furl in John's forehead. She could always tell when he was annoyed. Still, he tried to hide it in his voice.

This time, she was the one getting irritated and losing her patience with him. She spoke through clenched teeth. "I work just as hard as you do, John." Robin slammed her briefcase on the hallway table. "You're going to miss a few home-cooked meals. After all, you missed a few when you were working late or when your clients took you to dinner," she snapped. Spinning on her heels, she went into Lisa's room to say hello to her.

When she went back into their country-style kitchen, John was spreading mayonnaise on a ham sandwich. Robin glared at him. "Now that's just perfect. You complained about me not cooking and now you're making a sandwich."

"I'm tired and hungry, Robin."

Robin didn't say anything. John's air of martyrdom pissed her off even more. She walked out again and told Lisa to make herself a sandwich for dinner. "I'm not cooking tonight. It's past seven and I'm tired."

"That's all right, Mom. I can eat a sandwich. Would you like me to make you one, too?"

"No, Love. I'm not hungry."

Robin found John sitting at the kitchen table eating his ham sandwich and drinking a bottle of beer. He had his head down, reading a report that he had brought home. Robin studied him. A fine specimen of carved mahogany, he was still a handsome man. Overall, he was a good man, but sometimes he was selfish and only wanted things to go his way. This was something she should have put a stop to a long time ago. But when they first got married, she was so in love that everything she did was to make him happy. As the years passed, she had changed. She wanted him to consider her as an equal, not just a wife to be there for him. She needed the same things as he. She was still in love with her husband, but there were times that she wanted to walk out on their marriage, like tonight.

By nine, Lisa was in bed and Robin had just stepped into the shower. The water was running hot, and she didn't hear John when he walked in. He undressed, stepped into the shower with her, and put his hands around her waist.

"I'm sorry, baby. I had a long day today."

She nodded and smiled as he moved his hands over her body. She still loved the touch of his hands.

The next day when Robin got to her office, one of the loan agents, Paul—her favorite—was waiting for her with a cup of coffee in his hand. Robin smiled as he met her at the door.

"I saw you parking your car and since I need you to go over this file with me, I thought that the least I could do is make you a cup of coffee." He took her keys from her hand and unlocked the door to her office.

"I feel like a big executive today, Paul," she said as she stepped gracefully into her office.

"You always are to me, Robin." Paul took a seat in front

of Robin's desk while she hung up her jacket. She picked up her cup from her desk and sipped her coffee. "Is there anything you can't do? You make a mean cup of coffee, too, Paul. Just what I needed."

He gave her a long, lazy smile and looked in her eyes. "I wish that I could do more to help you around here, Robin. You're so good at what you do."

Robin couldn't say anything. She just looked at him, and for a split second she wanted to reach out and kiss him. He was so big and so sweet to her. Paul was always there when she needed help. And as their eyes met and locked, her heart accelerated at high speed, faster than she had ever felt it before. But she had never wanted to kiss any man except her husband and the warm feeling that she was beginning to feel for Paul was frightening, and more than a little discomforting. Robin cleared her throat. "What is it you need me to look at in this file, Paul?" Robin opened the file and started to look through the assets.

"Do you think it's enough to use for capital?"

"Yes, Paul, it is." Her phone rang and it was her assistant reminding her of her ten o'clock meeting. "I better get upstairs. Can we finish with this around one?"

"One it is, but don't forget about me, Robin. I have to have an answer for those people tomorrow morning."

Paul helped Robin back into her jacket. Passing him, she felt her shoulder brush against him. Her heart jerked again.

As the weeks passed, Robin and Paul began to work closer together and he began to stay in the office more than he had before. Robin knew that there was only a work relationship between them, and that was all it could ever be. After all, she was a married woman and even if she wasn't, she was older than Paul.

Robin walked into the office one morning and was surprised when her boss, Mr. Holly, called her into his office and gave her a promotion to CEO. She had worked hard for this day. Someone else had been promoted six months before to a job that she should have gotten. But this one was better, and she was happy with it.

Her new office was surrounded with glass windows and an oak desk with high-back office chairs. She stood in the middle of her new office and looked around. Robin picked up the phone to call her husband. But as she dialed the number, she decided to tell him in person. She wanted to see the happiness on his face.

Before she left work, Paul walked into her office. "Congratulations, Robin," he said with a kiss on her cheek. "I'm taking you to lunch tomorrow. So don't make any plans."

"Thanks. I'd love that." She smiled and walked out.

That evening when John walked into the house, Robin yelled for him to come into the kitchen.

"Smells good, baby," he said, reaching over and grabbing a lemon herb chicken leg, taking a big bite out of it. "I didn't even get a chance to go to lunch today." He was still holding his jacket and briefcase in his other hand. Robin had changed into a pair of jeans and sleeveless blouse.

"I got good news today," she said.

"What is it?"

"I made CEO today and I still can't believe it." She beamed at him, waiting for him to join her in her happiness.

"Shouldn't you've thought about it before you accepted a position with so much responsibility, Robin? You have a family, too, you know. I have to work late hours. Did you consider any of this before you accepted the position?"

Her face crumpled with disappointment. She threw the spoon in the sink and stormed out of the kitchen. She wasn't going to let him get away with ruining this moment for her.

Robin walked back to the kitchen where he was still standing and eating his chicken leg.

"Can't you think of anyone besides yourself for a change? If you had the chance to become CEO, you would take it in a heartbeat. But when it's me, the table turns. I stood by for years and accepted your shit, but no more. I accepted this job and I'm keeping it." She began walking out of the kitchen, but stopped to face him again. She put her fists on her waist, arms akimbo. "And if I work late and can't cook dinner, cook it yourself, or better yet, starve!"

John didn't say anything. He just stood there with his mouth open. The silence that fell between them seemed to last forever. Finally, he threw the chicken leg in the trash can and stormed out the house, slamming the door behind him. Robin could hear his car wheels screeching as he sped off.

It was past ten when he got back home. Robin lay in bed, still fuming. When he got in bed, she turned her back to him. So much for surprising her husband with good news.

The next day, Robin and Paul did go to lunch together at a small restaurant around the corner from her job. The weather was warm; summer arrival was late, but welcome.

The restaurant was in the marina, and they were seated at a small table for two with a breathtaking view of the pier. Pelicans and seagulls flew low, and the Los Angeles smog had cleared.

"You've been very quiet today, Robin. I thought you would be buzzing all over the place. Everyone doesn't become the CEO of a bank this size. Some of us don't even become CEO of a small bank." He laughed, and rubbed his hands together.

Robin blushed and glanced down at her long slender fingers. Suddenly she was seeing her hands through Paul's eyes. She was glad she'd gotten her manicure the other day.

"It's my husband . . ." Her voice faltered.

Paul was quiet and looked directly into her eyes.

Robin continued. "He wasn't impressed at all. He doesn't want me to do anything that might change his routine at home."

Paul didn't comment.

"I've been good to that man," Robin added, shaking her head in disbelief at how uncaring her husband had acted toward her promotion.

Paul finally spoke. "I'm sure you have. But some men would see your success as a challenge instead of a compliment. I would be proud to have a wife like you."

She looked at Paul as he was talking, really noticing him for the first time. He was so good-looking, so smart. He was a big man, 6'2", and two hundred pounds. Paul was solidly built with wide shoulders, an unusually thin waist, and brown eyes that seemed to look straight through you. Most of all he was sensitive and listened to her.

They ordered steak, baked potatoes, and salad.

"Paul, you didn't have to go through all this just to take me to lunch. We could have gone anyplace."

"No, this is to congratulate you. It's my treat," he said sincerely. "You deserve it, Robin."

While Robin was driving to her aunt's house, she thought of Paul and wished that her husband were more like him. He was so easy to talk to and so willing to hear what she had to say. Most of all, Paul seemed to know and care when she was happy or sad. She sighed and parked her car. What had happened to her marriage, she thought.

When Robin arrived at Aunt Flo's house, Tracey's car was already parked in the driveway. Good, she would talk to her. They always had been able to talk about anything together.

When Robin walked in, Tracey was sitting on the couch watching the six o'clock news. She looked tired, but Robin knew it was because of the long hours she'd been working lately.

"Where's Aunt Flo?" Robin asked, looking around the room.

"She's next door helping Mary with her sewing machine. The woman bought it almost a year ago and still doesn't know what she's doing. It shouldn't take Aunt Flo too long."

"What were you thinking about? You look like you have a lot on your mind," Robin asked, and sat next to her. "You need to take it easy, Tracey. Does that girl who works for you do any of the work?"

"Her name is Michelle, Robin. And yes, she's good. Maybe when escrow closes on some of the deals I've got open, I can go away for a weekend. I might be able to talk Wendy into going away with me, too."

Robin felt a hint of jealousy when Tracey said that she would ask Wendy and not ask her. "Just don't make yourself sick, Tracey. Work will always be here." Robin tried to sound convincing, although she was shaken inside, too. Ever since their parents' death she'd always assumed the big sister role with Tracey.

Robin decided to change the subject to something brighter. "I was promoted to CEO yesterday," she said proudly. "And Paul took me to lunch to celebrate."

"You worked hard enough for it. I'm so happy for you, girl. I bet John is smiling from ear to ear."

"No, John is acting like a jealous fool." Robin grunted in disgust. "All he thinks about is himself. You know what he said when I told him? He wanted to know if I had thought it through before I accepted the position. He reminded me that I have a family—as if I haven't been a good wife and mother. I'm so disgusted with him right now." Robin wiped tears from her eyes.

"He just has to get used to the idea," Tracey said, holding Robin's hand. "Men can be very selfish you know."

"No, I don't know. Donald was always encouraging you, and he was proud when you made a big sale. That's something that John and I don't have. My friend Paul is very encouraging and he supports me." Robin took a deep breath. Suddenly her face lit up. "Now, take Paul for instance. When they announced my promotion on the job, he hugged me and took me out to lunch today. He's so different from John."

"Everyone is different, Robin. And this is the second time you've mentioned Paul. Do you have the hots for him?" Tracey teased.

"No, but since you mentioned it, he is very handsome." And today she wondered what it would be like to make love with him. John was the only man that she had ever slept with.

"Yes, he's handsome and you're married," Tracey reminded Robin.

"But not happily married. I'm almost at the end of my wits with John."

"Are you still in love with him?"

"Yes, I'm still in love with my husband, but sometimes I wonder if he's still in love with me," Robin said pensively.

Tracey sighed. "He is, Robin. I can tell by the way he looks at you. Just give him more time to get used to the idea."

Robin picked up the magazine that was on the coffee table. "I've been wondering what it would be like if I was divorced and on my own. I make enough money to take care of myself and Lisa."

Tracey gasped. She was startled. "Are you really thinking of that? You've been married for at least fifteen years, Robin."

"Some people divorce after over twenty years of marriage. They do it all the time," Robin said matter-of-factly.

"Think hard before you make a rash decision out of anger. I know that he can get crazy sometimes, but I don't even think that he realizes it." Tracey looked at her sister and wondered if Robin really meant it.

"Do you miss it, Tracey?" Robin's question surprised Tracey.

Tracey grabbed one of the mints on the table and threw it into her mouth. "You mean do I miss being married?" Tracey took a minute and ponderd over the question. She had gone into a second phase of grief since Donald's death and hadn't even realized it. To her surprise, speaking of him today, she didn't feel anger at all.

"I'm not really sure. I guess I miss it sometimes, but lately I've been so busy that when I get home, I sit in that large black chair for a while and then I start to go over papers I bring home from work. But I still need answers that I'm not getting, Robin. I was married to someone that I didn't even know and now he's gone and I will never know him. . . . Maybe I'm better off not knowing him. At least you know who John is."

"Yes, I know who he is, and right now I don't like him very much. Now, let's stop talking about those two fools."

Flora walked in and they changed the conversation. Robin didn't want her aunt to worry about her marriage. She had more than enough to worry about with Tracey dealing with Donald's death and infidelity. They all did.

Seven

Tracey parked her car and went inside her house, still thinking of her sister. She listened to her answering machine, kicked her shoes in the corner, and went to her bedroom to change into a light green bathrobe. When she finished she went into the kitchen, made a tuna fish sandwich, and opened a Coke. She took the simple meal and went into her office to go over some comparables for the purchase of a property that she was working on for one of her clients. She sat back in her chair and moaned when she heard the phone ringing. First it was Wendy calling to see if she wanted to go to a movie.

"Sorry, girl. But I have some conditions to work on for a commercial building. I'm inside for good tonight."

"What kind of conditions?"

"I have to go over thirty-one rental agreements and leases to make sure the tenants are paying what is stated on the application. And tomorrow morning I have to go by the seller's house and pick up his tax bill. The bank wants to see both of them."

"Okay, Tracey. Maybe next week." Wendy sounded disappointed.

As soon as Tracey sat down and took a bite out of her sandwich, the phone rang again. "Who is it this time?" she snapped.

"Hi Tracey, what are you doing?"

"Working, Robin, as always. My life is so exciting, you know. Wendy just phoned to see if I wanted to see a movie and I had to turn her down. How's the new position going?" Tracey asked.

"Busy, but I love it. I've waited so long and worked so hard for it. You've been really working hard lately yourself. You need some real excitement in your life, Tracey, and you know it."

"It's a buying market, Robin. I'm a realtor. Right now I'm too busy to be thinking about going out and having fun."

"How many sales did you make last month anyway?"

"Three big ones. But, I had to work so hard because all three loans closed around the same time. I had to run my butt off." Tracey looked at the stack of papers in front of her and rolled her eyes up at the ceiling.

"See what I mean? You need to go out sometimes and have some fun. You are too young to just work."

Robin's voice took a playful tone. "I know a man I think you may like. Would you like to meet him?"

"No, not interested. I'm at peace with myself and I don't need any problems in this stage of my life. Who is he anyway?"

"A banker. John says he's sure that you two would get along well together. Both of you are ambitious and hard workers. I met him once and I liked him. You won't have to worry about him being too flirtatious. And John says he's a man that was born a gentleman. And if nothing develops between you two, you can always be friends."

"Believe me, nothing will develop between us. If he wants to be friends, fine," Tracey said as though the conversation was over. "Besides, he sounds exactly like Donald did and look where that got me."

"Don't compare every man to Donald, Tracey. You may miss out on a good thing."

"Yeah, and I may miss out on a pain in the ass, which I don't need." Recently, Robin and John were always trying to get her to meet one of their friends or single business acquaintances. Couldn't they understand she didn't want to be bothered? Hadn't she gone through enough?

"I just thought it would be nice if there were another woman going to dinner besides me," Robin coaxed, sounding hurt.

Tracey relented. "Okay, okay. When?"

"Tomorrow evening at seven. It'll be fun, Tracey."

"All right, but only dinner. Now, tell me something about this gentleman, as you called him."

"He works for the same bank that John works for, but he's at the head office in San Diego. John mentioned that he's been divorced for a year. I think you'll like him, honey."

"This is a one-time dinner date, Robin. Where is dinner?"

"At Monty's in Westwood, off Wilshire Boulevard."

"What are you wearing, Robin?"

"A dress. Now you show off those beautiful legs of yours and wear one, too," Robin teased.

"Yeah, sure. See you at Monty's at seven." Tracey hung up and went back to her comfortable chair.

"I thought you would never get here," Paul said, as he took Robin by the elbow to guide her through the restaurant's teeming lobby.

"I know," Robin said, panting. She'd rushed out for lunch. "I had so much to do this morning." She sighed. "It's so nice and cool out here on the patio." Robin looked around Charlie's Restaurant and saw that it had its usual lunch hour rush.

"I thought you would like it here," Paul said as he looked around at the crowd. He had asked to be seated outside since it was such a warm and lovely day. And Robin wanted to eat out. They had a view of the ocean. Today, the surf was calm and the water looked like blue glass.

Paul stood up and held out a chair for Robin.

"I do like it here." Robin slid into her seat, taking note of how chivalrous Paul was. Paul had been on vacation the week before, and she was ashamed to admit that she missed him more than she should have. What was coming over her? she wondered as they waited for the waitress.

Was she going through a midlife crisis? She thought only men went through this syndrome.

Paul was so sincere and caring about everything. Why couldn't John be that way?

Paul stared into her eyes, his gaze lingering. Robin felt exposed, as though his stare bore straight through her. Could he sense her sadness? She dropped her eyes.

"Was it very busy at work last week?"

Robin heard Paul's voice. She looked up and tried to sound more cheery. "Yes, it was. And since I have some new duties, I was extremely busy. I'm glad that you're back." She smiled. "You are so incredible with your work. The other loan officers can't seem to find such good commercial loans like you do."

"Thanks. You didn't take any other guys out for lunch while I was away, did you?" he teased.

"Oh no, never. Would I do a thing like that to you? I'm a true woman."

He laughed and shook his head. "You're something else."

And then for the first time in a week, she laughed out loud, too. God, she had missed him. Maybe she should stop going to lunch and being around him so much, she thought. Lately she had become so unpredictable.

"So, is John taking your new position a little better now?"

"I don't know. We don't really discuss it. As a matter of fact, we haven't discussed too much of anything lately. I come and go, and so does he."

Robin caught herself. She didn't want to whine or disclose too much of her marital business. She changed the subject.

Paul reached across the table and took her hand. His hand felt so big and strong, and warm. He looked into her eyes and her eyes watered. She wiped them with her napkin. She almost started sobbing until she remembered where they were and that she was married. Paul was so young, but so mature and understanding.

The waitress returned with two tall glasses of water, and Robin was grateful for the interruption. Things were beginning to get a little too intense and she wasn't sure if she could stop it, or if she wanted to. Paul was doing everything that John wasn't doing. He made her feel alive.

Tracey arrived at the restaurant at precisely seven o'clock as promised. She wore a black Donna Karan dress with a low V-neck in front, a pair of black pumps and her hair was swept up in back.

She stood in the doorway and saw John waving to get her attention. Monty's was busy during dinnertime and a small band was playing soft jazz.

As Tracey approached the table she could see the face of the man that was her dinner date. He was handsome, just as Robin had said.

"Tracey, this is Carl. Carl, Tracey Woods, my lovely sister-in-law," John said as he and Carl stood up. Tracey nodded in acknowledgment. Carl pulled a chair out so she could sit near him.

Tracey looked at Robin and thought her sister looked beautiful in her close-fitting red knit dress.

Carl ordered another bottle of wine and the waiter refilled their glasses and poured wine for Tracey. Tracey's eyebrow shot up, but she didn't protest when Carl moved his chair closer to hers. The conversation at dinner went well, and when Tracey looked at her watch again it was eight-thirty. She was surprised that she was actually enjoying this man's company.

Carl wasn't very tall but he was built like an athlete. His smooth ebony skin contrasted with his sable eyes that made him appear sleepy, and he had a full sexy mouth. He placed his hands on the table and Tracey noticed that they were large and manicured.

The band played a slow song and John pulled Robin to the dance floor, leaving Tracey and Carl alone at the table.

After they left, Carl began to make light conversation. "Robin tells me that you sell real estate, Tracey. The rates are stable so I would guess that business must be booming."

"It is. But I only deal with commercial buildings and large apartment complexes. And, yes, business is good and I have been pretty busy," she said and looked away. He made her uncomfortable by the way he seemed to look so deep into her eyes. She hadn't realized that his arm was across her chair until she felt it rest against her shoulder. Tracey excused herself, saying that she had to go to the rest room. Once inside, she freshened her lipstick and combed her hair. But the real reason for leaving the table was because Carl was getting too close to her.

When Tracey got back to her seat she was glad to see that John and Robin were seated at the table again. The conversation was better with a party of four. Tracey had no intentions of getting personal with Carl or seeing him again after tonight. But John loved to dance and ten minutes after Tracey took her seat he was pulling Robin back on the dance floor.

Carl moved closer to Tracey, and again she felt his arm resting against her chair. "You have sexy lips, Tracey," he said in a slow, seductive tone of voice.

"Thanks, Carl. The band is very good; don't you think so?" Tracey hoped to change the conversation.

"I wasn't thinking of the band."

Tracey looked at Carl as she felt his free hand slowly moving across her knee. She shifted positions and pushed his hand away. "Please don't do that again," Tracey said calmly between clenched teeth. She looked toward the dance floor to see if John and Robin were coming back to the table. Another song was playing and they were still dancing.

Tracey felt Carl's hand open the split in front of her dress, his large, warm hand against her thigh and she grabbed his hand and held it firmly in hers. "I said not to do that again." She pushed his hand away hard, never taking her eyes from his face.

"If you didn't want a man, then why did you come to dinner as my date? You say no but in actuality you mean yes," he whispered close to her ear.

Tracey couldn't believe this man who was supposed to be such a gentleman. Was this the same man that Robin had told her about? Obviously, John didn't know him very well at all.

Again, Tracey felt his hand raising her dress.

John and Robin were walking back to the table when they saw Tracey suddenly stand up and glare at Carl. And about the time they got to the table, which only took seconds, they saw Tracey pour a tall glass of cold water in Carl's lap.

"What's going on here?" John asked, as he and Robin stood at the table looking at each other, and then at Carl and Tracey.

Tracey smiled calmly. "Nothing's going on, John. I was just helping your friend, Mr. Gentleman Dick here, cool off. I think it got a little too warm in here for the gentleman."

Tracey grabbed her purse and stomped out toward the front door of the restaurant. John and Robin looked at Carl, but he hadn't moved, or said a word. His mouth was opened and he was staring down at his lap as though he didn't know what had happened.

Robin ran behind Tracey and caught up with her as she was rushing through the door.

"Tracey, I'm so sorry, but what did he do?"

Tracey stopped walking abruptly, spun around and faced Robin. "He's no gentleman, Robin. He kept moving his hand under my dress. And you said that he was a gentleman. He's an ass is what he really is. An absolute ass, I tell you. I would have had a better time if I would have stayed home or gone to visit Aunt Flo."

Robin touched her arm. "I'm so sorry, Tracey. I had no idea that he would do something like that. And to think he would just take for granted you would go for it. I'll never speak to that bastard again and he's not welcome in my house anymore. I know that John will agree."

Tracey turned to walk away, but Robin grabbed her arm. "Here, let me walk you to your car."

"It's all right, Robin. I can go to my car alone. It's right out front."

Robin and Tracey looked at each other and hooted with laughter. "Did you see his face?' Robin asked. "I think he was afraid to move."

Tracey laughed out loud. "I wonder what he's doing now." She kissed Robin and went to her car.

As Tracey drove home, she realized that she wasn't ready to start dating again. It was still too soon, even for a dinner date.

When Tracey got home and changed into her nightgown, she sat back on the couch, closed her eyes, sighed, and thought of her life. Where was she going, or was she just existing from day to day? Working and making a lot of money just wasn't enough to complete her life, but work and her family were all she had.

With that thought she was angry with Donald again for what he had done to her. He took back every ounce of happiness that he had given her. In just one phone call, she found out that he had been cheating on her, and perhaps planned to divorce her. She hated Travis. Perhaps this was a case of transference, Tracey thought. What was that old saying about shooting the messenger who brought bad news? How did it go? Whatever, it would have been best if she had never found any of it out at all. Men! Would she ever trust one again?

Eight

"Now Aunt Flo, we've been through all of this. Stella will come and house clean and do your shopping for you twice a week. When the arthritis flares up in your right hand you know that you need help."

"But, it doesn't last that long, Tracey," Flora protested, throwing up her hands. In a couple of weeks I'll be back on my feet." Flora frowned. The pain in her right hand shot up her arm again and she closed her eyes and took a deep breath.

Tracey was watching her and placed her hands on her hips. She knew that she had to stand a firm ground with Flora. "Well, in a couple of weeks, we won't need her. And Aunt Flo, a couple of week's pay will help Stella. Right now poor Michelle is helping her mother pay the bills at home. Hiring Stella will also take some of the financial load off Michelle, and at the same time, put my mind at ease by knowing you're not here alone. Now why don't you go and lay down. She called and said she's on her way over."

Stella was ringing Flora's doorbell at nine o'clock. Tracey answered and showed her in. Stella was dressed cheaply in a gaudy, all-purple outfit, her hair combed high on top of her head. She looked as though she was going out to a nightclub, rather than to work.

"I'm glad that you could make it this morning, Stella. We agreed on noon but I don't think my aunt should stay alone for very long. You can leave her at four and I will check on her on my way home," Tracey told her as they walked through the house. "Would you like a cup of coffee, or breakfast?"

"No, I ate already, but I could use another cup of coffee." Stella followed Tracey into the kitchen.

"Here, why don't you have a seat, and I can tell you what Aunt Flo needs help with." Stella sat in the chair at the table and watched Tracey as she moved about the kitchen.

"That's a nice suit you're wearing, Tracey," Stella said warmly. "Michelle always talks about how nice you dress. I'm hoping she'll become a fine businesswoman like you."

"Why, thank you."

"I appreciate you being so nice to Michelle. She loves working for you."

Tracey smiled as she saw the strong resemblance that Michelle bore to her mother. She also saw where Michelle had picked up her taste in clothing. Stella's skirt was too short and too tight; her purple blouse was too tight across her bust. Her overly made-up face reminded Tracey of a corpse in a coffin. She could be lovely if only she washed her face. Her hair was bleached too light for her dark complexion and stacked too high. Tracey even saw the tracks where it was weaved. Her roots were black; she was obviously overdue for a retouch.

Tracey got down to business. "First of all, my aunt isn't in the best mood these days. She's so used to doing for herself. If you see where she needs help, you will just have to help her. Right now she can barely use her right hand. But like I said on the phone, it may only last for a couple of weeks or it may last a month. Who knows?"

Stella was nodding her head as if she understood.

Tracey continued. "She'll never ask unless she absolutely has to. She's had breakfast already, and you can fix her lunch around noon. There's some baked chicken, rice, and vegetables in the refrigerator."

Stella nodded again.

"You might want to ask her what she wants. She may just want a bowl of soup or something else. You're welcome to eat whatever you want and feel free to call me for anything."

"I understand, Tracey, and don't worry if she's not in a friendly mood this morning. I have a way with people that will make them laugh, good mood or not. My mother always said that I was good with people," she said and crossed her leg. Tracey could see where she had her old-fashioned stocking knotted above her knees. Varicose veins bulged over the twisted nylons. "And girl, I can sure use the money."

Tracey cleared her throat. It worked. Stella stopped talking so Tracey could finish.

Michelle had told her not to talk too much but to listen. Stella knew that there were times that she went on and on without realizing it. She appeared enthusiastic about the job, so Tracey overlooked her tendency to ramble.

"I've already put water and her medication on the night-stand by her bed. Let's see if she is asleep." Tracey beckoned for Stella to follow her. Stella stood in back of Tracey as she looked in on her aunt.

"Aunt Flo, Stella is here," she said in a low tone of voice.

Flora pushed her hair back and straightened her gown. Her edges were beginning to gray. She had made an appointment to go to the beauty shop next week.

Flora heard Tracey say, "Come in, Stella, she's awake."

Stella walked in and looked around the beautiful bedroom before turning to look to Flora. Stella's eyes seemed to savor every detail of the room from the four-poster bed, the matching cherry wood antique furniture, and the soft lavender prints.

Stella sat in the chair by Flora's bed. She smiled eagerly.

"It's good to meet you, Miss Flora. Just tell me what you need and I'll help you. I've taken care of a lady that was ill before, and we got along just great together."

Stella seemed to decide that she had said enough and sat back to listen to what Flora had to say.

"But I'm not ill. I just have arthritis and can do for myself soon," Flora snapped.

Flora looked Stella up and down. What kind of get-up was she wearing? However, her gaze stopped when she arrived at Stella's head. She looked at her face and her eyes, which were soft and friendly. She probably has a soft heart, Flora thought. She smiled and Stella relaxed.

"It's good to meet you too, Stella. I'll try not to worry you to death."

"Miss Flora, that's what I'm here for."

Tracey tiptoed out of the room while the two women began getting acquainted. After fifteen minutes, Tracey returned to the room, kissed Flora on her forehead and said, "Good-bye."

She looked from one woman to the other and seemed satisfied that Flora and Stella were getting along.

"I just love your house, Miss Flora." Stella eyes scanned the soft lavender and floral décor. "I've always wanted a nice house, but with raising the children all by myself, it gets pretty hard sometimes. I don't know what I would do without my Michelle. That girl is going to be somebody one day."

"From what Tracey tells me she is somebody already. Smart and quick. Tracey says that she wants to learn real estate, too. You look young to have a twenty-two-year-old daughter."

"Well, I was only eighteen when I had her. After her, I had the other three and before long my husband was gone and had forgotten about the kids and me. I still don't know where he is today. He was always so wild and never had time for the children."

"Is Michelle the only girl?"

"No, I have two more daughters, nineteen and seventeen. I had one baby right after the other. My son is almost twenty-one. He's a good boy, works after school and comes straight home."

Stella didn't wait for a response, Flora noted. She obviously was on full and she rambled on and on.

"But, that seventeen-year-old girl of mine is boy crazy. Thinks she knows everything and I know nothing at all. I try and tell her to stay in school and learn some sense but will she listen? No, she knows everything. She's nothing like Michelle was at her age. Michelle came straight home from school and did her homework when she didn't have a part-time job. Kids—what can I say?" she complained.

"Can I get you a cup of coffee or a magazine or something?" Stella was now standing with both hands on her wide hips.

"A cup of decaffeinated, please. I don't drink the other stuff anymore."

Stella walked out of the bedroom and Flora looked after her and sighed. "That woman talks too much, and her clothes are much too tight. I'll have to find something for her to do," Flora was thinking when Stella walked back in with a tray and a cup of coffee on it.

"Now, I hope it's strong enough. I've had two cups already. One before I left home and one here with Tracey." She took a seat in the chair by Flora's bed. "Tracey is a good woman for my Michelle to work for, and smart, too. Michelle just loves her. Too bad she lost her husband. A woman gets lonely, too, you know?"

When Flora nodded her head in an absentminded movement, Stella's face screwed into wrinkles of concern. "Am I tiring you out, Miss Flora? You just tell me when I'm talking too much, or when you would like to take a nap."

"I'll do that, Stella. Now, tell me, what do you do with your time all day?"

Stella crossed her legs. "I used to work in the cleaners a few blocks from my house for five years. But a year ago I hurt my back by lifting something too heavy. Can you imagine a forty-two-year-old woman with back problems already? My boyfriend stopped seeing me because I couldn't make love the way we used to," she said and giggled.

Flora's mouth dropped opened. This woman had no sense of morality at all.

"You see, Marvin and I had been seeing each other for five years before he just up and dumped me."

"Well, he wasn't worth your time anyway, Stella. Now, what do you do all day?" Flora repeated herself.

"Oh, I worked in a restaurant until a week ago. A new owner bought it and brought on his own people. The four that were working there, including myself, were laid off with no notice at all. It was pure luck when Tracey called me to take care of you, Miss Flora. I've been out there job-hunting, and it's hard. The older you get . . ."

"Yes, it was luck," Flora said dryly. She was getting tired just from hearing this woman talk.

"Well, there's dishes in the sink that need washing. Can I get you anything? Just yell if you need me," she said and smiled at Flora. She had a sweet smile, Flora noticed. Her round eyes lit up with excitement when she talked.

Flora closed her eyes and fell asleep. When she woke up at noon, she could smell something cooking and heard Stella walking back to her room.

"Are you awake, Miss Flora?"

"Yes, I just woke up. May I have a glass of cold water? I think it's the medication that keeps me so parched."

"Sure, I'll be right back," Stella answered.

Stella came back in less than a minute with a tall glass of water with ice in it and carefully placed it in Flora's hand. "Are you hungry, Miss Flora?"

"Yes, what smells so good?" Flora asked, sniffing the smell, which wafted on the air.

"I saw some carrots, an onion and a chicken in the refrigerator. I added some noodles from your cabinet and made a pot of homemade chicken soup. I cook it for the kids when they have colds."

Stella stood at the edge of the bed and straightened the duvet. "There's nothing like a pot of homemade chicken soup when you're ill. Chicken soup for the soul, they say," she added.

"It certainly smells good. But I'm not ill, Stella." Flora wasn't used to having someone wait on her hand and foot.

She would have to speak to Tracey again about this. She could see that Stella was trying so hard for her approval.

"It would be nice if you ate with me. We can eat in here and watch the TV," Flora said.

"I would love to eat in here with you, Miss Flora. I'll get our lunch."

In ten minutes, Stella was back with the tray in her hand. She had two bowls of soup and crackers and two cups of hot tea.

"That smells good, Stella," Flora said and laughed out loud for the first time that day. She realized that Stella was trying to help her in any way she could.

Stella put her food on a TV tray and stood it next to the bed. Flora sat on the edge of the bed and started to eat while Stella sat in the chair next to her. They ate and watched television together. It was almost four o'clock when Flora looked at the clock.

"I'll be back at nine in the morning, Miss Flora." Stella said as she was walking out the door. Flora had gotten out of bed to see her out.

"Yes, Tracey. Come on in." Flora was sitting on the couch opening her mail when she heard Tracey opening the door.

Tracey smiled. "How was your day with Stella? The woman loves to talk."

"She's interesting, to say the least. But you know there's a kindness about her. I think she has a soft heart. She tries so hard to satisfy you. Robin called a few minutes ago," Flora said. "She had one of her sinus headaches so I told her to go home and go straight to bed. She'll be over tomorrow. Maybe on her lunch hour. I don't know why you girls are fussing so over a little arthritis."

Tracey sighed. "How's Lisa and John?"

"They're all right. Lisa got another good report card. I may buy her a dress that I saw at Macy's a couple of weeks ago. I should be all right by then."

"I'm sure you will, Aunt Flo."

Flora looked at Tracey. "Do you think that you will ever want children, Tracey? You would make such a good mother."

"I did, but Donald said that he was too old. Now, I don't think of it anymore. I don't even know if I ever want to marry again."

Flora saw the sad, faraway look in Tracey's eyes that said she was still hurting. She touched Tracey's hand and smiled. "You never know what can happen in life, Tracey. Your day will come."

"I won't hold my breath, Aunt Flo."

Flora broached something that had been on her mind for quite some time.

"What's going on between Robin and John? They don't seem to be too happy lately."

Tracey appeared relieved. "Nothing that is serious, Aunt Flo. You know how John is sometimes. He's not too happy with Robin getting the promotion to CEO. He feels that she may not have as much time for him. He just can't stand her moving ahead of him, that's all." She patted Flora on her hand. "They'll be all right, Aunt Flo."

"Yes, you're right. All married couples have their ups and downs."

"You look better now, Aunt Flo. How do you really feel?" Tracey's forehead wrinkled with worry.

"I feel better. Didn't you see how good I could open my mail with my right hand?" She held her hand out and flexed her fingers. "Now, I want you to go home and get some rest, Tracey."

Nine

Robin was up at five-thirty and had breakfast cooked by seven. She and Lisa were ready to leave at seven-thirty. John had just finished dressing for work when he walked into the kitchen and saw Robin and Lisa with their jackets on. Robin was picking up her briefcase. He stood in the middle of the kitchen, an angry expression on his face. He looked at his watch and rolled his eyes up at the ceiling.

"What's going on? It's just seven-thirty. Lisa doesn't have to be at school for another hour."

Lisa went to her room to get the new video that Robin had bought her the day before.

"I told you last night that I had a meeting this morning and I'm dropping Lisa off at Karen's house. They can walk to school together. She's going back home with her after school today, too. Didn't you hear me last night?"

"No, Robin, I didn't hear you last night," he snapped.

"Well, I'm sorry, John. Your breakfast is in the microwave, and the coffee is still hot." She wondered why he was so angry this morning. But that wasn't anything new. He had been distant for weeks. She kissed him on the cheek and got no response. "John, what is it now?" She stood in front of him, and it was as if he didn't see her.

"Go on, Robin. As usual, you don't have time," he replied stubbornly.

"Oh, the hell with it," she snarled, and stomped out of the

kitchen before he could say another word. He was impossible, and she was trying her damnedest to make things better between them. Why couldn't he meet her halfway?

Haven't I kept up my duties as a wife and mother, cooked everyday, made sure that my family was comfortable, and done an excellent job at work? What more can he ask of me? she wondered as she was driving Lisa to Karen's house.

"Do you have your homework?" Robin asked.

"Yes, and my videos, too. I'll be glad when summer school is over, but at least we only have to go for half days," Lisa said.

"It'll be over soon. Would you like to see Aunt Flo tonight? We didn't go over last night because of that horrible headache I had."

"Sure," Lisa said. "Will Aunt Tracey be there?"

"I don't know, Lisa. Maybe, since Aunt Flo hasn't been feeling well."

Lisa kissed her mom and jumped out of the car. She stuck her head in the window. "See you later, Mom."

Robin arrived at her office and sat behind her desk. As she listened to her messages, she heard Paul's voice. "Robin, sorry I won't be in today but I will be in first thing tomorrow morning." His voice sounded deep and clear. She stared straight ahead and listened as though he was standing in front of her.

At first Robin was concerned, then she realized she was more disappointed than she was worried. She was so used to seeing him, depending on him to make her feel better and feel the excitement that she had lost with John. She shook her head, hung up, and started to work.

Wendy walked into Tracey's office with a cup of coffee in her hand. She looked stressed out this morning.

"Good morning. How is Miss Flora?" she asked, and sat in the chair in front of Tracey's desk.

"She's feeling better. Fussing about every little thing, so you know she's feeling better. But are you all right, Wendy? You look stressed out already and it's only nine-thirty." Tracey looked at her watch.

"Thanks a lot. I just haven't been able to sleep well lately."

Tracey had two files in her hand. "How's William these days, or is that why you're losing sleep?"

"At least he's working now." Tears were forming in Wendy's eyes and she wiped them with the back of her hand. "We talked about separating last night. It's time, Tracey. We're not even sleeping in the same bed anymore. I fall asleep in bed watching television and he falls asleep on the couch. He'll never grow up. I know that now. He's moving out over the weekend. He doesn't want me anymore. I can admit it now." She held her hands up to her face and sobbed.

"I'm so sorry, Wendy. I thought things were getting a little better with you two." Tracey didn't want to tell her that she should have kicked his ass out a long time ago.

"No, it's only gotten worst. Lately, he feels more like a son to me than a husband. He can't do anything unless I tell him to. I make all the money, pay all the bills. He won't even buy me a dozen roses once in a while," she said, taking a deep breath.

Tracey thought of the marriage she had had with Donald. He gave her all those things: the roses, jewelry, a nice car, and expensive clothes. She had had it all, but now they were just things. Her marriage had been like a mirage. She now realized that she didn't have him. Maybe it was best that she found out after he died. No, she wished that she had never found out at all.

"Look at it this way, Wendy. You're getting slender. Someone who really deserves you will be looking at you, girl."

"Fat chance. I just want to work and clear my head. My

business is doing well since interest rates are dropping so I'm busy enough to keep my mind off him, during the days anyway."

Tracey reached out and hugged Wendy. Suddenly the phone rang. "I knew that you were always too good for him anyway, Wendy. Let me get this phone. Michelle won't be in until one today."

Tracey answered the phone, and it was Robin.

"I'm sorry, honey. I have a client coming in at noon, and Michelle won't be here until one. Maybe we can have lunch later in the week, and Wendy can come along with me," Tracey said and winked at Wendy. She hung up and picked up another call. This time it was Michelle calling to find out if she should bring her some lunch on her way to the office.

"Michelle will pick me up some lunch on her way in. Robin wanted me to meet her, but today I have too much to do."

"I better get back upstairs. I have an escrow to open. I just had to tell you the news. I'm a free woman again," Wendy said sadly. She tried to remain strong, but when she stood up, her legs buckled and gave in. She was certain that Tracey didn't notice.

"Welcome to the free-woman's club. If you need me after he leaves just call me or come over and we can talk again."

"Thanks," Wendy said, forcing herself to smile. She felt as though her whole life was caving in. "Let me know what day we're meeting Robin for lunch."

"I will. Now, try and get some rest tonight, Wendy. You look exhausted."

"I'll be all right. And I have some housecleaning to do. Things to get rid of along with William." Wendy threw her shoulders back and her whole persona changed. "I may even sell my place and buy myself a new one." She tried to smile, but a tear rolled down her face.

Tracey got up and hugged her. "I know it hurts. It still hurts me, too; but I can't let it get me down. I'm not completely happy. That's why I work so hard. I'm not even close to being happy, but one day I will be. One day we both will be."

Wendy let go of Tracey, wiped the tears from her eyes, and pushed a braid back from her face.

"Good thing my assistant isn't here yet. I look a mess today," Wendy said, and blew her nose.

"Go upstairs and put on fresh lipstick before your next client comes in or one of mine and you scare the hell out of her." They both laughed out loud.

"Tracey!" Wendy's words choked up in her throat.

Tracey waved her hand as if to dismiss any special thanks. Wendy went back upstairs to her office.

Robin looked at the small crystal clock on her desk and it was past noon. She sighed, knowing that she should stay in and have lunch at her desk. She looked at the papers piled neatly in her tray. She needed some fresh air.

Robin picked up the phone and dialed her husband's phone number and he answered.

"How about lunch today? I'm buying," she said in a sweet tone of voice. She needed to see her husband and patch things up between them. She needed to feel needed, to feel the love they'd shared for so many years. Robin held her breath, waiting for him to answer.

"Why don't we have breakfast at home tomorrow morning, Robin, like a real family?"

"We never have time to sit down for breakfast at the same time during the week, John. Either I'm running around and can only sit for five minutes or Lisa doesn't want to eat. The weekends are the only time we all sit down at the same time."

"Well, maybe if your job permits you the time, we can start," he snapped at her. "Do you understand what I mean, Robin?"

"You know, John, the sad thing is that I understand perfectly what you mean and I'm not happy with it," she pleaded, gripping the phone tightly in her hand.

"What do you mean by that?" He was beginning to raise his voice.

At first she couldn't answer. She was shaken and taken aback by his tone. The chill in it was cold and dispassionate. He had no concept of what he was putting her through, or what she needed anymore. His only concern was for himself and what he needed from a wife, what he needed for himself.

"I mean that I'm tired, just so tired, John," she retorted at the top of her lungs and slammed down the phone. Robin stalked out the office. She got in her car and drove down La Brea Avenue and made a right turn on Northridge. It was as though an invisible hand guided her. She'd had his address for months now.

When she parked her car, she was in front of Paul's house. She got out and slowly walked up his driveway, feeling her heart beating hard. She had turned to walk back to her car when she heard his voice. He was standing in the door, wearing a dark brown robe and brown slippers. The V-cut of his robe revealed black hair on his chest, and she inhaled, feeling the cool air blow against her face that was on fire.

He looked into her face and took her by the hand, leading her into his house. They stood in the living room looking at each other. No words were spoken between them. He gazed into her eyes and down at her body. Robin looked gorgeous; she was dressed in an orange summer dress that stopped just above her knees. He stepped closer to her, cupped her face with both hands.

Paul ran his hands down her body as she felt his palms burn through her dress.

"I shouldn't be here." Robin pushed his hands away. She straightened her dress.

"Yes, you should. This is where you belong," he whispered in a deep voice that moved her very soul.

"But, I'm married."

"He doesn't deserve you. I do. I know what you need,

what you want, and how to make you feel." He kissed her hard on the mouth and she returned his kiss with a building hunger that was exploding inside her, taking her into a different world.

She slipped easily into his hot, passionate love. Paul led her to his bedroom, and into his bed. He made her forget all her problems. He wanted her, loved and needed her.

An hour had passed and Robin was still lying in Paul's arms. She looked at the clock by his bed, knowing it was time to go. She moved, but he held her tight.

"Do you feel better, now?" he whispered in her ear and kissed her neck.

"Yes, I feel good, but it's time I get back." She turned to face him and he made love to her again and again. He was so kind and so concerned. She used to think that John was that way, too, but now she'd seen an egocentric side of him she had never known before, and wished she had never seen.

Driving back to her office, she felt good, but guilty. How could she feel so good when what she had done was so wrong? She pulled into the drive-through lane at Burger King and bought a cheeseburger and a large diet Coke.

When Robin got to work she had lunch at her desk. Her secretary had left her a message from John, but she tore it up and didn't return his call. Where was he when she needed him? She worked until it was time to leave. But instead of going home, Robin went to Karen's house to get Lisa and the two went to see Aunt Flo. She wasn't ready to go home and face her husband. What was happening to her?

When Robin and Lisa walked into Flora's house, Tracey and Flora was sitting in the living room talking.

"Hi Aunt Flo," Lisa said, and kissed Flora and Tracey on their cheeks.

"There's cake and milk in the kitchen," Tracey told her.

"Good. Just what I need and I'm hungry, too," Lisa said

as she ran off into the kitchen leaving the three women alone.

In fifteen minutes Lisa was back. She wiped cake crumbs and a whisker of milk away from her upper lip. "Who baked the cake?" she asked. "It was delicious."

"Stella. That woman can cook and talk," Flora said, yet smiled warmly. "She loves to cook and bake. Says she cooks for her children almost every day."

Flora and Tracey sat on the couch in front of the coffee table. A large bouquet of roses that John had sent to Flora obstructed the women's view of one another.

"Who sent the flowers, Aunt Flo?" Robin asked. "I keep looking at them. They're beautiful."

"Your husband, Dear. That was so sweet of him."

"Oh," Robin stammered, trying to hide the fact that she didn't know. She felt a twinge of guilt. Here her husband had sent her aunt roses while she was lying in another man's arms.

But just as fast the feeling of guilt disappeared. He had only sent flowers to Aunt Flo to make up for the way he acted this morning. He knew that Flora would tell her. To cover up her conflicting emotions, Robin offered, "Why don't I take you to brunch Sunday, Aunt Flo. I've been so busy lately. Lisa and I would love to take you. Wouldn't we, Lisa?"

"Yes, Aunt Flo," Lisa said and bounced on the couch next to Flora.

"Okay," Flora answered. "What about you, Tracey?"

"Sorry, Aunt Flo. I have lots of work to do at home and at the office."

Lisa sniffed the roses. "My dad did send pretty roses. They're almost like the ones he gave my mom once," Lisa was beaming. She was definitely a daddy's girl.

Lord, Lisa would stay with her father if she ever found out what she had done, Robin thought. The fear of getting caught clutched at her heart. No, she would never find out, she reasoned with herself.

She changed her train of thought and almost laughed out loud. It had been awhile since her husband had sent her flowers or even brought some home to her. She thought that he would have when she was promoted to her new position, but he didn't even congratulate her for that. With that thought in mind, she erased every ounce of guilt she felt.

"Come to the kitchen with me, Robin. I need to show you something."

Robin stood up but she looked concerned and followed Tracey into the kitchen. Just as she reached the kitchen door, Tracey stopped to get a good look at her.

"Tracey, you look as though something is on your mind. Is there something wrong?"

"That's what I was going to ask you. You know that you can talk to me."

"I know, but it's nothing. We can talk when I come back on the weekend."

Nothing, Robin thought. She had slept with another man, and said it was nothing. She blinked the vision out her mind.

Robin could see the concern etched on her younger sister's face. She kissed her on the cheek, waved her hand in dismissal, and spoke in an airy tone she really didn't feel. "It's nothing, really, Tracey. John and I just had a few nasty words this morning. But what else is new these days?"

"I talked to Wendy this morning. She and William are separating. He's moving out."

"That should have happened two years ago."

"They've only been married for two and a half years, Robin."

"Yes I know that. But, she shouldn't have married that good-for-nothing anyway. All he's done is use her. I bet she has credit card bills up her ass from marrying him."

Tracey laughed, shaking her head in disgust. "You're right, and he's going to leave them all for her to pay. Wendy always picks the users. Everyone can see what they are but her."

"You tried to tell her, Tracey. But, she goes from one man to another. She acts as if she has no life unless a man is in it."

"She's got to learn that she's all right without a man. I know I've learned that since . . ." Tracey's voice broke off as if she didn't even want to say Donald's name.

Robin, sensing her sister's discomfort, steered the conversation back to Wendy. "Wendy needs to give herself a chance to get over one man before she jumps in bed with another. She's going to be sorry one day."

Tracey and Robin went back to the living room where Flora and Lisa were watching TV.

"Anyway, I'd better be going, Aunt Flo," Robin said.

"Me, too, Aunt Flo. I'll be up late tonight."

Flora shook her head. "You're going to work yourself crazy, Tracey. Don't you ever think about going out and having yourself some fun?"

"I'm not in the mood for fun these days, Aunt Flo," Tracey said and picked up her purse from the coffee table.

Tracey and Robin left at the same time.

John was sitting in the living room waiting for his wife and daughter. When they walked in, Robin walked past him without saying anything and went to their bedroom. She shut the door firmly. A week ago they had gone to dinner and dancing to entertain Carl, who could help John get the promotion that he was preparing himself for, and someone who turned out to be a real live jerk, as far as Robin was concerned. Now their lives were back as they were before, with them snapping at each other and barely speaking. Robin was beginning to wonder just how long would it go on before the dam burst.

She could hear the drone of Lisa's chatter as she talked with her father for a while. Finally, she heard Lisa's footsteps in the hallway as she walked to her bedroom.

When John walked into their room Robin was already

in bed with her back turned to him. He turned the lights out and kissed her on her shoulder. She cringed, closed her eyes tight, and didn't move a muscle in her body. He whispered something under his breath and turned to his side of the bed.

The next morning was the same. Robin got up first and cooked breakfast while John was in the shower. But, this morning she got up even earlier because she had to drop Lisa off at least thirty minutes earlier and she was glad because she didn't want him to try and make love to her this morning either.

She was so confused, so angry, and she felt guilty for sleeping with Paul, while at the same time, she blamed John. That's right. It was all John's fault, she kept telling herself. He never tried to make things right between them, and he hadn't apologized for not congratulating her. She was always so supportive of him with his success.

Yet, she knew if Paul touched her, she wouldn't be able to pull away. She couldn't. She needed him, and she was so angry this morning because she wanted him again.

Paul came in to work that day. He and Robin drove in separate cars to his house when they left for lunch. And again they made love.

"I thought we were going to have lunch," Robin said, as she held herself up on one elbow and looked down in his face.

"We did have lunch, baby. It was the best I've ever had."

Robin assessed her situation. For Paul, it was the beginning of a beautiful relationship, but for Robin, she knew that today had to be their last. After all, she was married to John and if they decided to get a divorce, she wouldn't want it to be for another man. They had a child, fifteen years together, and there had been some good years.

"This could become a habit, you know," Paul said and held her tighter.

"This can also become a problem, too, Paul." Robin pulled away from him and climbed out of bed. "I'm married. I have a child to protect," she said wrapping the sheet around her nakedness. Suddenly she felt exposed. She shuddered at an invisible wind that pricked her conscience.

"We can talk about this another time. I better take a shower and get back to work."

"Baby, you sound so serious." Paul got up and held her. "Why don't we shower together? And you're right. We do need to talk about this. I'm in love with you, Robin."

Robin froze, and looked at him as though she was looking at a stranger. Oh Lord, what had she done?

Ten

Tracey had a one o'clock appointment to show a house to a Mrs. Coleman. A previous client had referred the new client. On the phone Mrs. Coleman said that she was pregnant and wasn't feeling very well. Tracey offered to make the appointment for the next day, but the woman was too excited and said she'd come that afternoon. So Tracey offered to pick her up, and the pregnant woman accepted the offer.

She arrived exactly at one o'clock as promised. She rang the doorbell twice and a young woman in her middle to late twenties opened the door with one hand on the doorknob and the other on her back. She was in the late stage of her pregnancy and very attractive. Her long ponytail hung past her shoulders. Her makeup was expertly applied.

"You must be Miss Woods?"

Tracey nodded. The young woman showed her in.

"Mrs. Coleman, are you sure that you feel well enough to see the house today? I can come back tomorrow and take you," Tracey offered.

"Please, call me Jennifer. I'm not due for another month. It's just back pains that I've had for days. The doctor says I'm carrying a big baby boy." She smiled as she said it. "Why don't you have a seat, Miss Woods? I'll just get my purse, and we can be on our way."

Jennifer walked out of the room and Tracey looked behind her. She walked unsteadily, shifting her weight from side to side. She held her hand beneath her protruding stomach. She soon returned carrying her purse.

"I'm ready now, Miss Woods."

"You can call me Tracey."

As Tracey was driving she noticed that Jennifer had gotten quiet. "Is this your first pregnancy?" Tracey asked, looking at her large, round stomach.

"Yes, and I'm sure it will be the last. I feel so big that it's as if this baby is outgrowing me."

Tracey turned her attention back to the road. The red light had just turned green. She pushed her foot to the accelerator. Suddenly Jennifer grunted and let out a loud moan. Tracey looked over at her passenger. Right away, she could see that something was very wrong.

"You know," Jennifer grimaced in pain. "I don't think it's a good idea for me to see the house today after all," she managed to say between pants.

"Oh God, are you in much pain? What can I do?" Tracey asked, frightened of what Jennifer was going to answer. Was she going to have the baby now?

"Yes, you'd better take me to the hospital," Jennifer groaned as she bent forward with a pain that took her breath.

Tracey could feel her hands sweating as she held the steering wheel.

"Should I call nine-one-one? I don't want you to have the baby in the car," she said and reached for her cell phone. She saw sweat forming on Jennifer's forehead and felt shaken all over.

"No need to. Just make a left at the corner. The hospital is just five minutes away from here." She moaned again. Tracey was driving and trying to watch Jennifer at the same time. She blew her horn at a man who was driving slowly in front of her and rolled down her window.

"Get out the way," she yelled, as if the man could hear her.

Tracey hadn't been with Robin when John had taken her to the hospital to have Lisa. As a matter of fact Tracey had never been near a woman in labor. She was grateful to see the hospital on the left.

When they arrived at the hospital, Tracey parked the car in front of the door of the emergency entrance and jumped out. "Stay here. I'll run in and get help." She squeezed Jennifer's hand, then ran inside.

Once inside the emergency room, Tracey ran up to a nurse. "There's a woman in my car who is in labor. She can't walk, needs a wheelchair," she said in a rush of words, not realizing that she was yelling and pointing at the door as she talked.

The nurse grabbed a wheelchair and ran outside behind Tracey.

Tracey opened the car door. Jennifer had put her head back on the seat, her face contorted as she moaned.

"We're here, Jennifer," Tracey said in a shaky voice. The nurse took her by one arm and Tracey helped by taking the other. Together they eased her slowly into the wheelchair and the nurse pushed her into the emergency room. Once inside the hospital, Tracey felt as if she could breathe again.

"Give me your husband's phone number so I can call him," Tracey told Jennifer. She wrote the number on the back of a business card that was in her purse and ran to a phone booth.

"Mr. Coleman, please," she said. But it was Mr. Coleman who'd answered.

"This is Tracey Woods, the realtor. Your wife is in labor at UCLA on Wilshire Boulevard. You'd better get here—fast!"

"Is she all right?" he asked, his voice rising.

"Yes, but she's having labor pains."

"Oh, God. The baby is early. Will you stay with her until I get there, Mrs. Woods?"

"Yes, but hurry," Tracey said. She felt herself panicking.

"I'll be there in fifteen minutes. Just stay with her, please . . ." But before Tracey could answer he had already hung up.

Tracey went back to the nurse's station. "Is she all right?"

"Yes, and you were right. She is in labor," the nurse said,

flipping through some papers and barely looking up as she talked.

"Can I see her, please?"

"In a minute. The nurses are getting her ready."

"I can't leave her alone," Tracey said more to herself than to the nurse. Tracey paced the floor in front of the nurse's station, looking toward the doors through which the orderly had wheeled Jennifer. She stopped every time she saw someone coming from that direction. She looked at her watch and saw it was only two forty-five. A nurse came out and motioned for Tracey to follow her. Jennifer was lying in bed on her back, rubbing her stomach.

"Jennifer, are you okay?"

"It hurts. My mother was supposed to be here for the baby's birth. But he's early, about a month too early. Now my mom won't be here in time."

"Where does she live?"

"New York City. My husband can call her when he gets here."

"I'm sure he'll be here real soon. He didn't even say good-bye when I told him. He just hung up. How long have you been in pain?"

"For a couple of days, but it got worse today. I'm so thankful that you came with me, Tracey."

Tracey held Jennifer's hand as she cried out from strong labor pains. "Just hold on, honey," Tracey encouraged. Her hand felt numb from the crushing grip Jennifer had on it.

Jennifer screamed when she felt her water break and she looked up at Tracey.

The nurse ran to her and saw the wet spot on the bed. "It shouldn't be too long now. I'll call the doctor. Miss, you can wait outside for a few minutes."

Tracey patted Jennifer on the hand. "I'll be right outside." When she walked out she ran into Richard Coleman. His complexion was so light that his face had turned a beet red.

"Thanks for staying with my wife, Miss Woods."

Tracey nodded. "I'll wait out here for a while if you need me."

"Thanks." He ran to his wife's room.

Forty minutes had passed when the doctor walked out of the room and saw the woman standing alone looking out the window. She looked lean and elegant in a navy dress that stopped above her knees. He admired her black hair that fell to her shoulders as she pushed it back from her face. She looked at her watch and, as though she could feel someone's eyes on her back, she turned around. When she looked in his face she paused in midmotion as her breath expelled in a rush.

He stepped closer to her and extended his hand. The expression on her face almost made him laugh, but he just smiled.

"Tracey, what are you doing here?"

"Travis Howard?" she murmured.

"Dr. Howard, but you can just call me Travis."

She didn't move, just looked at him, her mouth agape. "You never cease to amaze me, Travis. Where will I meet you next? You didn't tell me that you were a doctor, either."

Travis didn't know if Tracey was mad or what. He still hadn't forgotten how she almost pummeled him on their first meeting.

"Did you deliver Jennifer Coleman's baby?" Tracey looked outdone.

Travis looked relieved. "Yes. He's a big one to be six weeks early. He's all right and so is his mother. The father was the one that you would have thought was in labor."

A slow smile played at Tracey's lips. "I find it hard to imagine that such a big man as Richard Coleman was about to faint in the labor room."

Travis stepped closer to her. "You can't see her right now. Would you like to join me in the cafeteria so I can grab a quick bite to eat?"

She looked at his chiseled face and remembered the picture that she had seen in her husband's office. He bore a strong resemblance to his late sister.

Tracey hesitated. Travis studied her. She seemed reluctant to expose herself to any more hurt.

"No, you go ahead. I'll wait here to see Jennifer."

His smile disappeared and he looked at her for a few moments before he replied. "Why? As I said, you can't see her yet."

"Why do you want me to go with you?" she asked.

Travis remembered the night she'd met him in the hospital. It had been only five months ago, and he remembered how much she'd hated him. But when he came to her house to apologize, the hate she'd felt seemed to have disappeared. What was bringing it all back again? Was seeing him a reminder of her dead husband's betrayal?

He decided to take the bull by the horns and just be upfront with her. "I'd like to know how you have been getting along. I would have called you if I thought that you would have talked to me."

"But, you don't know my phone number."

"I know the name of your real estate agency. Your husband mentioned it once. I can easily get your phone number when I want it."

"How could you remember it? You had no reason to," she said.

"At the time, I didn't. But after I met you, I made it my business to remember. And why are we talking out here when I have to be back soon enough?" He motioned for her to follow him and she did.

Tracey remarked on his height as they walked to the elevator. He was dressed in green scrubs, no different from any of the other doctors that passed them, but she had to admit that he looked good in his. She wondered if he had played football when he was in school. She liked his deep, soft brown eyes. And when he locked her in a direct stare, she turned and looked straight ahead.

They got off the elevator and went into the cafeteria.

"Have you had lunch yet, Tracey?" he asked her as they walked around to see what they wanted.

"Yes, I've eaten already. But I'll have a glass of iced tea."

"Whatever the lady wants," he smiled. "There's a table over there, why don't you have a seat while I pay for this."

Travis gestured toward an empty table and Tracey went over and took a seat. Travis felt her eyes on him as he ordered his food. When he turned around, he saw her watching him closely. He paid the cashier and returned carrying a tray in his hand.

"Penny for your thoughts, young lady," he asked and grinned at her.

"I was just wondering if Jennifer and the baby are all right."

"Are you sure that was what you were thinking? Besides, they're in good hands."

"Yes, I'm sure they are. How long have you been practicing medicine?"

"Eight years: three in San Francisco, five years here. How long have you been a realtor, Tracey Woods?"

Her face lit up and she smiled. He liked the way she smiled.

"Seven years. I started off as a receptionist at a realtor's office and learned from the realtors. But, Donald taught me a lot, too. He had been a realtor before he became a developer."

He watched a dark shadow come over her as she spoke of her dead husband. It was like watching her go from lightness to darkness within a split second.

"I've wondered how you've been getting along, Tracey. I've thought about you quite often. Tell me if you're truly all right. It's only been a few months," he asked with genuine concern.

Tracey looked into his eyes and her gaze was so intense, direct, and intrusive that he felt chills crawling down his back.

"I keep myself busy. My aunt tells me I have no life besides work. And I tell myself it's all I need."

"You really believe that?"

"Yes, for now I do."

"When I got out of a bad marriage, I felt the same way. But, after a while, you need more, Tracey. You'll find that out soon enough."

She looked at him as if she wanted to ask a question but changed her mind. He took the last bite of his sandwich and sighed.

"That was good and I was starved. I haven't eaten anything since nine this morning. Now, we were talking about you. Do you live near your office?"

So many questions, she thought. Finally she spoke up. "Yes, I bought myself a house not very far from the house that I sold."

He sat back in his chair and looked at his watch. He didn't want to go back and leave her. He wanted this woman, had wanted her from the first time that he saw her. He said, "I'd better get back. I'm so glad that we saw each other again today." They walked out and the elevator door opened as soon as they got to it. They rode the elevator without any words between them. But when they got off, Travis couldn't let her go. Not this time.

"I want to see you again, Tracey. I want to see a lot of you." He paused and stood straight with both hands at his sides.

"Do you really think it's a good idea for us to see each other? I mean the way we met . . ."

"What does that have to do with you and me? I know what you're thinking, Tracey. Donald was Donald and Susan was Susan." He gave her a pleading look. When she didn't answer, he went on. "We're not them, and we're not married, nor sneaking around. I want to see more of you, get to know you." His voice softened but she looked too shocked to move.

Of all the people in the city or even in the hospital how

could he have run into Tracey? What a serendipitous turn of events. He'd been thinking about her. . . . He pulled out a pen from his shirt pocket and gave it to her.

Tracey didn't say anything. She wrote her home and office phone numbers on the back of a card. When he flipped the card over he saw that it was her business card. He took it from her and gave her one of his business cards, holding her hand for a few seconds before he let go.

He heard her suck in her breath when he held her hand. She slowly pulled hers away. He kissed her on her forehead.

"I'll call you soon, real soon."

Travis walked away and a nurse followed him, telling him about a new patient.

Tracey was already walking away, her stride lengthening in her hurry for distance. She sat on the couch down the hall and wondered what had just happened between Dr. Travis Howard and herself. Her hand still felt the heat where his hand had burned into hers when he touched her. There was definitely some chemistry there . . . or was it just her?

The next day, Tracey and Wendy met Robin at Teaser's in Santa Monica for lunch. When they walked in, Robin was already at a table waiting for them. Tracey had to adjust her eyes from the sun in order to clearly see her.

"This was a good idea," Robin said. "I needed to get out of the office today. That place is just too stressful for me. I had to fire one of my managers and go to a meeting that lasted two and a half hours," she said and sighed.

"It's been that way for me all week," Wendy said and took a drink of her water. "Boy, I'm tired and parched. Even this water tastes good."

"When I got back to the office yesterday you had already left, Wendy. You two are talking about stressful? I told Michelle about the woman I picked up to show a house. Well, guess what?" Tracey took the appropriate pause to arouse their interest and maintain the suspense.

Both Robin and Wendy asked, "What happened?"

"I ended up taking her to the hospital so she could have her baby. I thought she would have it in my car. We never got close to the house."

Robin and Wendy looked at each other. "You mean she wanted to see a house when she was in labor?" Robin mused, her mouth still open.

The waitress came, and they stopped talking about the woman long enough to order.

Tracey put both hands up. "It was her first baby, so I guess she didn't know she was in labor. Wait, that's not all of it, girl. I called her husband and waited for him because I didn't want to leave her alone." Tracey paused dramatically. "But after he got there and I was in the waiting room, guess which doctor walked out and asked me to lunch with him?" She rolled her eyes to the ceiling.

Wendy and Robin looked at each other with a baffled expression on their faces.

"Well who?" Robin finally asked.

"You won't believe this. It was Travis Howard. That woman that Donald had the affair with, he's her brother. . . . Remember him, Robin, at the hospital?"

"Oh no way, you mean that fool is a doctor? And anyway, where does he live, here or San Francisco?"

"I told you before that he lives here. Remember when he paid me a visit after Donald's funeral?"

"A doctor. All the people in the world and you would have to run into him. I just don't like that man, Tracey," Robin said.

"Why?" Wendy asked. "He made a terrible mistake that night. I'm sure he wouldn't have said anything about his sister and Donald had he known who Tracey was."

Robin exploded. "He's still from that same stock. They say it's in the blood. An apple don't fall far from the tree."

"Oh, Robin, don't be so judgmental. After all, Donald did tell him that he had a grown daughter. The man even went to see Tracey after the funeral to apologize."

Tracey was surprised to see Wendy take up for Travis. "He was upset and hurt over his sister's death, too. He just made a mistake, " Wendy added.

Tracey spoke up. "We went to the cafeteria so he could have lunch. I had already had mine. I really enjoyed talking to him."

"What did he talk about? And, a doctor, girl? I'm telling you, life has all kinds of surprises," Robin said, with a puzzled look on her face. She shook her head in a disapproving manner.

Tracey ignored her. "You know what I like about him?"

"What? Just tell me one thing," Robin asked.

"Yes, I'm listening, too," Wendy said playfully.

"He really cares. He wanted to know how I've been and what I've been doing since we last saw each other. At first, I didn't really want to talk to him, but it was really kind of nice of him to ask." Tracey smiled, remembering every word he had said to her. "He's really handsome, too. I had no idea that he was a doctor. Funny, how I never even wondered what he did for a living. Guess I never thought that I would see him again anyway."

"Girl, you never know. You and that man may get something going," Wendy said. "Why are you looking so shocked, Tracey?" Wendy grinned.

"No, I don't think so. I'm not ready for a relationship now. It's just too soon to even think about one."

"Why not, Tracey? All you do is work all day and take more work home with you at night. You have enough money. It's time you had a little fun," Robin said sincerely. "I'm not saying that Travis is for you, but there will be someone."

"No. I can't. Not now." She still couldn't imagine being with any man so soon after Donald.

They had all ordered salad and iced tea or lemonade. The restaurant was beginning to get busy.

"Did Tracey tell you that William and I are going to get a divorce?" Wendy asked Robin.

"Yes she did. You deserve better anyway. I noticed that you've lost weight. You look good. Someone else will be knocking at your door soon."

"Well, I'm going to sell my house and buy a town house. I want to do something different. Sometimes a change is better all the way around."

Wendy took a sip of water from her fluted glass. "I need to lose about ten more pounds, too. I want to lose twenty all together."

"This cobb salad is the best," Robin said. "Oh, I met Stella when I went over to see Aunt Flo yesterday. That woman sure can talk. And doesn't she know her clothes are too tight? It's not like she's slim or that young, you know? And the makeup is too much." Robin laughed. "But, she seems nice enough and Aunt Flo seems to like her. They seem like old friends instead of Stella working for Aunt Flo."

"They *have* become friends," Tracey said, feeling a little irritated. Wendy was right. Robin sure could be judgmental. "Aunt Flo says that Stella is nice. It's just that she didn't have a mother to raise her. Her mother died when she was young. Michelle is a good girl—smart, too. That's why I'm trying to teach her everything I can."

Robin looked at her watch. "It's time for me to go."

"Yes, it's time we get back, too," Tracey said as she pulled out her wallet. "I'm paying."

The waitress came back to their table. Tracey paid and all three left.

Eleven

Two days later, on her way to her office, Tracey took a loan package to the bank that she and Donald had done business with before and where they had received good service. It was the same company that John worked for but at a different branch. The loan officer that she had given her deals to made sure that the funding of her loans was easy and on time. The particular loan that she was dropping off today would be a good commission for her, and for him.

Tracey was wearing a green pantsuit and matching sweater, her hair was straight and falling over her shoulders. It was a nice warm day and she felt good for a change.

Tracey walked to the counter at the loan department and asked the young lady for Bob, the loan officer.

The young woman remembered Tracey and gave her a warm smile. "Mrs. Woods, he just left for lunch, but if you would like to wait, I can . . ."

"I'll help her Judy," the man said as he walked in back of her.

Tracey eyes widened as she looked into Carl Johnson's face. The gentleman, she thought as anger began to stir inside her.

Judy smiled at Carl and walked off. Tracey's and Carl's eyes locked on one another. As Carl looked at her face, and the way she shifted her weight from one leg to the other, she looked determined to go to battle. The soft smile that she had given to Judy disappeared the moment she looked at

Carl's face. She picked the application up off the counter as though she didn't want him to touch it.

"I just happened to be in LA for a couple of weeks and will be at this office for a couple of days. As a matter of fact, I'll be visiting all the loan offices for the company while I'm here," Carl said.

"Well, I guess that means I should take my business to another company." She said and turned around to walk away.

"If you've already given your client a good interest rate you won't find one as good at any other bank. Besides, I don't mix business with pleasure."

She turned around and looked at him. "Good, because you must know by now that you'll find no pleasure with me, Mr. Johnson."

"Now that we understand each other, why don't we get started. I won't be here from the beginning to the end of your transaction, but I can sure give you a good start," Carl said.

Tracey just stared at him as though she wasn't certain whether she wanted to do business with him or not.

"Why don't I take a look at your application and see what I can do." He held out his hand and Tracey placed the loan package on the counter in front of him. Carl picked up the application and looked at it. "Two million? No, don't take a loan this big to any other bank. Bob will love this one. There's an empty desk over there that we can go to." He motioned for Tracey to come around the back of the counter and she followed him.

Carl pulled a chair out so Tracey could sit. He sat behind the desk facing her and placed both hands flat on the desk in front of him. "Now, first of all we have to get something straight. John didn't tell me anything about you until you had left that night we were out to dinner. I've done business with your husband before. I'm sorry, Tracey, I didn't know."

"And if you had, would that have kept your hand from under my dress? Would it have made you more of a gentleman?" she asked, looking straight into his eyes.

He moved around uncomfortably in his chair. "Yes, it would have. If I had known that you were a widow for such a short time, I wouldn't have hit on you at all. Again, I apologize. I'm very sorry is all I can say." He waited for her response, but she didn't answer and she didn't move.

Knowing exactly who he was, Tracey looked at him. But she had business to take care of and this wasn't the time for any personal dislikes. And he was right, this bank had the best rates. She had already shopped around.

"All right, let's get down to business. I've seen the units myself and I'm sure the appraisal will come in at the sales price that my client is asking for. I'll be the contact person for access."

He looked at her and knew she was as good and as knowledgable as her husband was. When Carl found out who she really was, and that she and her late husband were the best real estate brokers in the business, he had looked at a couple of her deals that she had brought to the bank. They were both over a million and a half. And as he looked at her face, he realized that he was completely captivated by her beauty and her intelligence. And since he had already made a mess of things he could only conduct business with her. Every time he looked in those icy eyes, they reminded him of the dinner and the iced water that had soaked into his trousers.

"If you notice on the purchase agreement my client is willing to make a down payment of twenty-five percent. He needs an approval as soon as possible," Tracey was saying.

"Yes, I had noticed." Carl looked at his watch. "Have you had lunch yet, Tracey?"

She looked as though she was shocked. "Lunch? You're asking me to lunch?" The nerve of this man, she thought.

"Yes. You have to eat, you know. And what better lunch partner than someone you've already had dinner with?" he said and smiled.

Tracey didn't seem to be amused at what he said. "No. I don't think so."

"Look. I want to make it up to you for what happened. I can be a good guy if you just give me the chance."

For a few seconds she didn't answer. And he looked as if he was really sorry. And how could it hurt anything? After all, after today, she wouldn't see him again.

"Okay. But can we go in separate cars? There's a small restaurant three blocks away. It has Mexican food. Do you like Mexican food, Carl?"

"Yes, love it," he said and placed the file aside.

Tracey got up and told him to follow her since he wasn't familiar with the area.

The restaurant was crowded, but Tracey didn't care. This was just lunch, and why was she making such a big deal about a simple little lunch, she wondered. This wasn't really a date. She wasn't ready for dating or getting close to anyone.

They had a small table in the center of the restaurant and ordered two tall iced teas to go along with their meals.

"How long have you been in the banking business, Carl?" Tracey watched him as he looked at every woman that passed their table.

"Eighteen years. I used to live here before I was promoted five years ago. Now I'm all over California. Your husband was a busy man, too, wasn't he?"

"Yes, he was busier than I had realized, but his business only took him to San Diego and San Francisco. I would say that San Francisco was his favorite place," she said, averting her eyes. But from the corner of her eyes she could see Carl watching her. Tracey unfolded her napkin and placed it across her lap. She felt uncomfortable discussing Donald and had to do something with her hands to hide her discomfort.

Sensing that he had pricked at a nerve, Carl switched the conversation. "What do you do for fun, Tracey?"

"Lately, nothing but work. I just bought myself a house

that I'm still decorating and I have some good clients that demand a lot of my time. Some I even meet at night." She sipped at her iced tea and noticed that the waitress kept smiling at Carl every time she passed or caught his eye.

Finally, she brought their lunch to the table. She was Hispanic and had an accent. Her hair was brown, long, and curly and her eyes were round and light brown. She reminded Tracey of a small Barbie doll. And as she walked away Carl watched her as he did every woman that walked into the restaurant.

The air had cleared between them and to Tracey's surprise she was laughing and talking to Carl.

"It's always the silly arguments that cause couples to break up," Carl was saying. "My wife and I stuck it out through the bad ones and managed to forget. But when we decided to go our separate ways it was because of a silly argument that never should have taken place. Too much had already happened between us." He loved watching Tracey's delicate mouth when she smiled, and her eyes light up. He could even fall in love with her if he had the chance, but Carl was smart enough to know that it was too late. Too much wine and music that was too soft, plus the fact that he hadn't had a woman in his bed for weeks had caused him to destroy any relationship that he could hope for with Tracey. If only he hadn't they would not be going their separate ways after lunch. Instead, he would be taking her to his hotel and to his bed.

As Tracey smiled, she examined Carl's face. She knew that he wasn't her type. Sure, he dressed nicely, had a terrific career and a nice car, and he was handsome. But he had already made her mistrust him the first night they had met. Even if she were ready for a relationship with a man, Carl would not be her choice.

When they got up to leave, Carl left a five-dollar tip for the pretty little waitress. "She was good and deserves a good tip," he said.

"Yes, she deserved it," Tracey said. She saw his business

card under the bill as he laid it on the table. No, Carl Johnson would definitely not be her choice of men, if she
wanted one. Suddenly an image of Travis Howard appeared
before her and she pushed his face to the back of her mind.

Carl walked Tracey to her car. "Bob will call you if he
needs any additional information for your client's loan."

Tracey extended her hand to him. "Thanks for the lunch.
I had a wonderful time, Carl."

Carl watched her as she drove off in her black Mercedes.
"Damn, she looked good," he whispered and shook his
head. He started to go back inside the restaurant to have a
word with the young waitress. But Carl Johnson knew
women, and he was sure that she would call him before he
left the office.

Twelve

Robin realized that she couldn't look at another loan and set the file aside on her desk. Today had been a long, tiring day and approving five loans was all she could do on a day when she had so much on her mind. She placed her phone on voice mail and left for the day. She needed some time alone to think, and didn't want to be around Paul or John today. Lisa wouldn't be home for another three hours because she was at her friend Karen's house.

When she got home, Robin went into the kitchen, opened a can of soup, and grabbed a Coke from the refrigerator. She sat at the kitchen table, listening to the quiet around her.

This is what I needed, she thought. "Now, what am I going to do?" she whispered. The question tumbled out of her mouth and seemed to echo out in the air without an answer.

But, she knew what she had to do. She had to stop sleeping with Paul. He was younger than she, but so understanding. He was everything that she needed. But she had a daughter and a husband that needed her more.

Sure, John was egotistical, and a little selfish, but he was her husband and a lot of it was her fault. She should have never started her marriage off that way, giving in to him in every way. When she met John he was so handsome that she often wondered why, of all the women, he wanted and loved her. She knew he still did.

This will be a turning point in our lives. He'll just have to change, that's all. Now, how could she tell Paul that what they were doing would have to stop? She was wrong for him and she couldn't be a part of his life. He was still young enough to marry a younger woman and have a family. No, he knows all of that. She sighed heavily and groaned in frustration.

Robin was almost finished cooking dinner when John walked in. He smiled as he walked into the kitchen to see his wife. He stood behind her and kissed her on the neck.

"Are we alone?" he whispered.

"Yes. Lisa won't be home for another hour."

"Good. I'm glad that I got home a little early." He turned her so that she could face him and kissed her hard on the mouth.

"I'm sorry, Robin."

She pulled her face from him and looked in his eyes. "Sorry for what, John?"

"For being an ass, for not being here when you needed me, for being selfish."

She nodded with tears in her eyes and he wiped them away, then he kissed them away and led her to their bedroom. He undressed her slowly, kissing every part of her body. Robin realized that she had missed her husband and forgotten how good he made her feel. No man would ever know her body like he did. John undressed and lay in bed with his wife. She closed her eyes as he made her moan, twist, and turn to every touch of his hand, and she knew this was where she belonged. As she cried out his name at the height of her passion, she held John tightly in her arms. She was back home. She knew that she had to tell Paul tomorrow.

The next day Robin told Paul, but he didn't let go so easily. They were sitting in a restaurant near their office. Robin asked for a corner table so they could talk without being overheard. She didn't know where to begin but she knew that prolonging it would only make it worse.

She cleared her throat. "Paul, I do care about you, but I

am married. I have a daughter, a home, and a family. I just can't leave all of that. You are younger than I am. . . ." Her voice quavered and broke off weakly.

"You didn't screw me like I was so young, Robin. You made me think you wanted me and it seemed like we were getting closer. He cares nothing about you."

Paul glared at her. Robin had never seen his eyes look so cold.

"Isn't that the reason you came to me in the first place? Am I the first, Robin, or were there others?" he asked her sarcastically.

"I see a different side of you that I don't like, Paul. I wanted to do this and still be friends, but I see that we can't. What we did never should have happened."

When he saw that she was determined, it only made him angrier. The gentleness that he had always shared with her was quickly replaced by contempt and rage.

"Am I the first, or is this what you do every time your husband shows his ass?"

She narrowed her eyes at him. This was getting ugly, she thought. Robin cleared her throat again. The waitress came with their food. She looked at them.

"Is everything all right?" she asked, as if even she could feel the air growing taut.

Robin thought about it. They had seemed to be such a happy couple when they first came in. No wonder the waitress was taken aback. She quickly walked away.

"You should know me better than that, Paul. You are the only man that I have ever slept with since I've been married. How dare you ask me such a thing," she said, slamming her hand on the table and looking around the restaurant, hoping that no one heard. "You are being impossible. You knew that I was married when this thing started." And as she looked at him, she realized that what she had done could be potentially dangerous.

"Did you forget? You knew that you were married, too, but you didn't let it stop you," he retaliated. His face twisted into a scowl and he seemed to enjoy hurting Robin. His chin jutted out with determination.

"I will keep you no matter what it takes, Robin. This isn't over." He gritted his teeth.

"I'm getting out of here." She put her napkin back on the table and picked up her purse.

"But, you just ordered your lunch."

"So, eat it. You can walk back, too. It's only around the corner," she hissed and got up. She heard him call her name and kept walking but she wanted to hear what he had to say. Maybe he had come to his senses.

He got up and walked closer to her so no one else would hear. "I won't let you go, Robin. You can't use me and just walk away. Get used to it, baby," he said with a wide, calm smile and returned to their table.

He stared at her with an intensity that frightened her. He enunciated his words as a father might to a child he was about to spank. She rushed out of the restaurant to her car. Once she got in she locked the door and took a deep breath, closed her eyes.

"God, Robin, what have you done? What have you gotten yourself into?" she whispered.

Paul was back at the office an hour after Robin. He'd had her lunch packaged and he dropped it on her desk and kept walking to his office. They didn't speak for the rest of the day, and Robin wondered what tomorrow would bring.

Tracey was listening to her messages on her answering machine when she heard the doorbell ring. She switched it off and ran to the door and it was Robin. Robin walked past Tracey and flopped down on the couch. Tracey just looked at her, followed her, and stood in the middle of the room as Robin lay her head back and closed her eyes.

"You look like hell, Robin. Didn't you sleep last night?"

"No, not really."

"Is it John or Lisa?" Tracey asked.

"No. None of the above. John and I are getting along a little better. I'm having a problem with Paul," she said and held her face in her hands.

"Don't look so serious. What is he doing, pressuring you to go to bed with him?"

"It's not funny, Tracey. I've already gone to bed with him, twice. And don't give me that look."

Tracey was floored. She opened her mouth to say something, but was stunned speechless. She'd never thought her sister was the type to commit adultery. What had come over Robin?

Robin had obviously read the look of shock in Tracey's eyes. She narrowed her eyes and frowned at Tracey with vexation. Robin stood up and held her hands on her hips defiantly.

"Everyone isn't as perfect as you are, Miss Goody-Two-Shoes. Do you ever do anything that is wrong and even not quite right?" Robin's tone was defiant. "I see that self-righteous look on your face!"

"What look are you talking about? I never slept with another man while I was married. But, as it turns out, I wouldn't have lost anything if I had." Tracey threw her head back, mane bouncing like a stallion's, and laughed in a bittersweet roar. "He slept around on me."

Robin looked surprised at Tracey's laughter. She shook her head in wonder.

Finally, Tracey caught herself before she started into another spasm of hysterical laughter at the irony of the situation. "You're serious aren't you? You've slept with him, twice? Well I'll be damned. Twice you said?" she asked with wide eyes.

"That's what I said. I stopped the affair but he won't leave me alone. He says that I used him, and that he's not going to take no for an answer. That was a week ago. Today he asked me to go to his place again, but I told him to forget it."

Tracey sat on the edge of the chair. "He'll give up when he sees that you really mean it. Were things that bad at home that you had to sleep with someone else? It's never been that bad before, has it?"

"No. But, John chose a bad time, a time when I was attracted to another man. It got worse at home, and there was Paul. John was acting so foolish." She started to cry, and Tracey got up and hugged her.

"At least you and John are getting along again. He loves you, Robin. But some men don't really know how to show it."

Robin agreed. "But, I don't think it's going to be easy getting rid of Paul. I'm afraid that he may call my house or do something crazy, Tracey. You should see how he looks at me."

Tracey could sense how frightened Robin was.

"I know that I made an inexcusable mistake. If John finds out, he'll divorce me." She wiped her eyes with the tissue that Tracey had given her. "I could live through that. But if Lisa finds out why, she'll hate me." She began to tremble and shudder.

"He won't find out. Just give Paul a few days. If he didn't work there, it would be so much easier for both of you. He'll have no choice but to give you up."

"I've never dated anyone on my job before. But, I've never dated a man since my marriage either." She reached for another tissue. "I have a bad feeling about this, Tracey. He may cause trouble for me at work. I'm seeing a side of him that I never saw before, a mean side."

"He's no meaner than we are together, and I'll be here if you need me." Tracey was surprised by the fierceness in her own voice. This was her big sister—her only close family besides Aunt Flo—and she wouldn't put her sister in harm's way. . . . Even if her sister did bring some of this on herself.

"Thanks. And thanks for listening to me. Is Wendy feeling better about that fool, William?"

"I didn't see her today. I was busy this morning. But yesterday she was feeling better—although he's all she talked about. Her business is good, and she's always busy, too. Sooner or later she'll feel better."

"Maybe now that her husband has left, she won't have to work so hard and pay for everything."

"Later she won't, but he left her with some credit cards that were charged to the limit and some medical bills she didn't know about."

"You know, Tracey. I know that Wendy is your friend. But she repeats the same mistakes over and over again." Robin shook her head and clucked her tongue. "I have no patience for someone like that. She's her own worst enemy. Why couldn't she learn the first time?"

The phone rang, interrupting Robin's tirade against Wendy, and Tracey answered.

"It's for you. It's Lisa," Tracey said, handing Robin the phone.

Robin talked and hung up.

"Is she all right?"

"Yes, just wants to know when I'm coming home."

"You might as well go home now and get some rest."

"Yes. I guess I should leave. I've been trying to get home from work at a decent time. John loves it when I'm home when he gets there."

"I told you that he loves you, Robin. And don't worry about Paul," Tracey took her right thumb, put it under her chin, and gave Robin the "keep-your-chin up" sign.

Robin blew her a kiss as she closed the door behind her.

Thirteen

It was a beautiful day, one that made you want to stay outside and feel the sun against your face.

Tracey walked inside her office carrying a box of doughnuts. Michelle was already there and had made coffee. Wendy and her assistant had come down to take a break from their work.

"You had a phone call, Tracey, from a Mr. Carl Johnson. He says he'll call you back later," Michelle said, and sat in the chair facing Tracey.

Tracey frowned. "If he calls back, I'm out of the office for the rest of the day."

"What does that creep want?" Wendy asked. She grabbed another doughnut and refilled her cup with coffee.

"Just someone to sleep with," Tracey replied. "He looks at every woman that passes him by. Girl, he's a real dog in heat."

"That's a good one, Tracey. You couldn't have said it better," Wendy laughed. "Well, we better get back upstairs and do some work. I have two escrows to close today." Wendy's assistant grabbed another doughnut on her way back upstairs.

Tracey and Michelle went back to work, too.

"My mom loves your aunt, Tracey. Mom says she's very wise and kind. She says they sit around, talk, and watch television for hours." Michelle leaned on her elbows and rested her chin in her palms. "So, what do you have going for today?"

"Just a new listing to go over. Escrow should be closing on

the Hawthorne deal in a day or two. You did real well with that one. Have you been studying for your real estate exam?"

"Yeah, but I still need more time. It's not that easy, Tracey."

Tracey laughed. "You'll do okay. I have to go and drop some documents off at the bank so this deal can close. I should be back before lunch."

As Tracey was on the way back to the office she decided to visit Donald's mother. They hadn't talked since Tracey moved into her new home, and Tracey had always like Mildred. Right after the accident it was too painful for her to be around any of Donald's family. But she was beginning to get over the worst of the hurt. It had been well over seven months since his death.

Mildred opened the door and grabbed Tracey by her arm. "You get in here. I was just thinking of you this morning," she said, leading Tracey to the couch. "Honey, I've missed you." Her smile widened.

Tracey felt an urge to cry, but she held it back. She sat on the couch, facing Mildred and held her hand. "I've missed you, too. How is Janet? I haven't seen or heard from her."

"That child is all right. She's in that big house all by herself."

"But I thought that her mother was going to move in with her."

"Norma thought so, too. But she and Janet had an argument and that was the end of that. You know they never got along. She was always closer to Donald, and she blamed her mother for the divorce. As she got older she just kind of grew apart from both of them. I guess she had her own life by then."

Tracey smiled. "Donald was crazy about her. I know she must miss her father. I still do." Tracey said sadly. She looked at Mildred, who looked away. Tracey knew it was because she was trying to hide the tears. They both were. They were silent for a while.

"Can I get you anything?" Mildred stood up, smoothing her skirt.

"No, I'm fine. I just wanted to see you."

"Is there something bothering you, Tracey? I can see something is wrong."

"No, Mildred, just a lot on my mind and I'm still dealing with my new life the best way that I can. Don't worry about me. You just take care of yourself." But she didn't want to tell Mildred that seeing her was breaking her heart in two. She and Donald had sat together in Mildred's living room so many times and had so many happy moments in this house. Three years ago, Mildred had gone out of town and Donald and Tracey had come over to feed the dogs. While they were there they had even made love in the room that used to be Donald's.

"How's Flora, Tracey?"

"She's all right, Mildred," Tracey answered with a far-away look in her eyes.

"Flora is such a dear person. I'll have to drop by and pay her a surprise visit soon."

Mildred's eyes were getting sad as she looked at Tracey. "You know, the first time Donald brought you by to meet me, I thought you were just a pretty young face who infatuated him. It didn't take long to find out that there was so much behind that pretty face." Her gaze was riveted on Tracey. "My Donald was lucky. He always knew what a kind and smart woman you were. You're strong, too, Tracey. You've lifted yourself up again, working and making a life for yourself. Don't ever let anyone take that kind of pride and courage away from you, dear."

Tracey took Mildred in her arms and the two women embraced. She had never told her that Donald was in that terrible car accident with another woman. Mildred didn't need to know that. Tracey wasn't sure if Mildred knew about the other woman, but at least she'd kept her dignity, and hadn't sullied her mother-in-law's memory of her son.

"Donald was a good man. He was always good to me. I was lucky to have a son like him. Even when he was a child, he always tried to help me."

"Yes, you were lucky to have him, Mildred. He loved you very much. He was smart. He taught me so much about life and my work."

"Have you been doing anything except working every-day, Tracey?"

"No, just working. Oh, I did buy myself a nice house. I still have some remodeling to do. It's not too far from you."

As Mildred spoke Tracey looked at the picture of Donald that was on the table by the couch. He looked so much like his mother. His smooth, caramel complexion, the brown eyes. It was almost as if he were in another room waiting to come out and talk to them.

Suddenly, Tracey had to go. She couldn't sit there any longer. Maybe she still wasn't ready to be with so much that reminded her of him.

Tracey looked at her watch. "I have an appointment in less than an hour, but I had to come by and see you, Mildred," she said, getting up from the couch. Mildred didn't mention it, but the corners of her mouth turned down as though she had noticed Tracey's sudden mood shift.

"Thank you for coming, Tracey, but you should come more often. I want to see more of my daughter-in-law. You'll always be my daughter-in-law, you know?"

Tracey hugged her. "I know, Mildred." She walked to her car, feeling the fresh air going down her throat. Once she was in her car, she wondered how much longer her life would be at a standstill. She felt as if she was not moving forward but simply running away from her good and bad memories of Donald.

That evening, Tracey stopped by Flora's house on her way home. Flora was sitting on the couch watching television with Stella. She looked rested and it seemed that she was getting more use of her hands again.

Stella was laughing at something someone had said on the TV.

"It's good to see you two ladies laughing." She spoke to

Stella and kissed Flora on the cheek. Tracey sat on the couch by her aunt.

"You feel better, Aunt Flo?"

"Yes, much better. Stella cooked some of her famous chicken soup today, and I was hungry, too," Flora said.

"She's been busy today, Tracey," Stella said, beaming at Flora.

Tracey noticed the warmth between the two women. The two weeks that Stella was asked to come over and take care of Flora had turned into three. They had really become friends.

"I went by to see Mildred today. She says she's coming over to see you soon."

Flora smiled good-naturedly. "I don't think it will be too soon. She doesn't drive as much as she used to. Last time we talked, she said Janet takes her around and sometimes her nephew drives her places. But, who knows, she may come over. It's not too far."

"It was nice to see her again."

Flora looked at Tracey. "Are you sure it was, honey? You don't look too happy"

"Mildred is my mother-in-law."

"It was nice of you to go and see her," Stella spoke up. "None of my ex-husband's family comes around to see the children or me. Just don't care I guess. But the children ask what their grandmother or grandfather are like."

"That's a shame, Stella," Tracey said, surprised.

Stella got up and picked up her purse. "Is there anything I can get you before I leave, Miss Flora?"

"No, honey. You don't have to come by until tomorrow afternoon. I feel better now. I can do more for myself."

Stella stood in front of her. "Are you sure? It's not a problem for me."

"No, noon is good enough."

"See you at noon then, Miss Flora."

Tracey watched Stella as she walked to her old brown Buick, wearing tight-legged black pants and a sweater. Her hair was pinned back in a French roll. She had taken out the weave and her natural hair looked neater. Since she had come to work for Flora, she was beginning to dress in better fitting clothes and wearing less makeup. She was actually beginning to look like a young "forty." Flora and Stella were good for each other, Tracey mused.

Fourteen

Robin kissed her husband and daughter at the door. "Drive careful, honey."

"I will. You just rest today and get better. I'll pick something up for dinner so don't cook," he said, and kissed her again.

Robin watched them as John drove off, and she went inside to call Flora.

"Aunt Flo, are you feeling all right?"

"Yes, Robin. My hands are not hurting anymore."

"Good. I'm home today with this bug that's going around. "

"Stay in bed, honey, and drink some hot tea. Too bad you're not feeling well enough to come over and get a bowl of chicken soup that Stella cooked."

"Don't worry, Aunt Flo. I'll be all right."

Robin put the dishes in the dishwasher, picked up the magazine off the table, and went to her bedroom. She was going to do just as John told her: rest, take it easy. She was dozing off into a peaceful sleep when the phone rang. She looked at the clock on the nightstand, and it was ten-thirty. Robin answered, still half asleep. The minute she heard Paul's voice she shot up straight in bed.

"What are you doing calling my house? Are you crazy, Paul?" she yelled.

"I'm an employee who works under you. What's wrong with me calling?"

"You're not my assistant. Everyone doesn't call the CEO of the bank."

"Well, it's different with you and me, Robin. We're more than just two people who work together. There's so much more between us."

She lowered her voice into a firm growl. "Paul, we've gone over this before. You've got to stop this. I can't do it anymore."

"Are you ill today, or are you just laying up with another man?" he asked in a hard, cold voice.

"My patience is wearing thin. What do I have to say to make you understand that no matter what you do, it is over, finished." She could feel her hands sweating, her head was pounding. "Please, Paul. Let it go."

"Let me come over to see you, Robin."

"No. Never."

"I know where you live," he said calmly.

"Have you been following me?" she yelled.

"Just once. To find out where you live. Just let me come over to look at you." He began to breath heavily into the phone. He sounded like the perverts and Peeping Toms who would call just to hear the sound of a woman's voice.

Suddenly, his voice took on a lascivious, sultry tone. "My eyes are closed, Robin. I still remember you lying under me naked, your brown skin glowing, and your eyes closed, moaning for more. . . . You loved what we did, didn't you?"

Robin's hands started to tremble. She dropped the phone as if it were a rattlesnake. Shaken, she picked up the receiver and placed it in the cradle. In a flurry of motion, she ran to check the doors, the windows. They were all locked. She got back in bed, wondering what to do. Should she call John and tell him what happened? Would he forgive her?

Never. She knew the answer and she wasn't ready to lose her family. Lord, if only she knew Paul better before she got involved with him. She looked at the ceiling as if she was waiting for an answer, but it was too late. She had done wrong and now she had to pay. She had to figure out what to do about Paul. Just last week he had gotten an offer from a mortgage company. Maybe sooner or later he'd move on. But, in the meantime, what was she to do?

Tracey's office door was open. He walked in, heard some talking upstairs, and stood at the door just watching her. She looked tired, but she seemed to be going over some figures. She was so preoccupied that she hadn't even looked up to see him standing there watching her. He stared at all of the awards hanging on her wall along with her real estate license, the tall plant in the corner.

"You look like you need a friend, Tracey Woods."

Tracey stopped at the sound of his deep voice. When she looked at him, he was smiling.

"Do you always leave your door open for strangers?"

He was dressed in a pair of black slacks and a black shirt. His soft hazel eyes were taking her in, always so intense and intrusive when he looked at her. He bothered her; she had to admit, on some deep, elemental level. Maybe it was his size, the broad shoulders, and large hands, or just the way he stared at her.

"No, I don't usually leave my doors open. A client was upstairs and I guess he didn't close it when he left. Have a seat, Travis. What brings you this way?"

"I was off today and decided to drop by. How can we get to know each other if we don't see each other?"

She pushed her hair from her face and placed both hands on the desk. " I see," was all she could say.

"You look tired. Were you out too late last night?"

She returned his smile. Travis watched as her body seemed to relax. "I wish. I was up until after midnight, working."

"And the results were?" he asked, now beginning to smile.

"I got a lot done. Almost more than I have since I've been here this morning."

"Good, then you can play hooky with me the rest of the day."

"What?" she asked, and looked at him as if he was a complete stranger.

Travis felt his stomach muscles tighten and sucked in his breath. He saw her looking as if she was about to say no, so he spoke in a rush of words.

"You are tired and you work too hard. You won't be any good for yourself if you get sick. Then, who'll do your work? Now, why don't we go someplace quiet for lunch. Where would you like to go?" he asked eagerly. He was not going to take no for an answer. He wanted to get to know this woman that he couldn't get out his mind.

She leaned back in her chair. "My house."

Travis perked up. Here was his opportunity to try to make everything up to Tracey.

"Your house? You're inviting me to your house?" he asked with interest.

"Yes. I haven't had anyone for lunch there since I moved in. Just too busy I suppose. So, we can stop by the store and pick up lunch on the way. Can you handle that, Dr. Howard?"

"Lady, I can handle anything you want. Now, let's go."

She stood up and clutched her purse. "I guess playing hooky is not always a bad thing."

"No it's not, and if you're with the right person it can be a good thing." He followed her outside.

"You want to follow me or ride with me? I'll bring you back to your car when we finish." Tracey asked.

"It's not out of your way?" Travis grinned, amused at this turn of events.

"Oh, no. I have to come back for a while anyway."

"Good. I'll ride with you."

She pulled off her jacket and laid it on the back seat of her car. She drove down Sepulveda Boulevard, turned left on Slauson Avenue.

"What kind of food do you want for lunch? Chinese, Mexican?" she asked as she looked over at him.

"Whatever you like. I'll make the selection next time," he said. She decided on pizza and drove home to have it delivered.

"This is a very nice house, very comfortable," he said and looked around her living room. She had impeccable taste. The walls were balanced with African art. Her bleached hardwood floors glistened and a large oriental rug centered the room. The furniture was an eclectic mix of antique and Art Deco.

"Make yourself at home. I'm going to change." She turned on the radio as she passed by him.

Tracey changed into a pair of blue sweats and a sleeveless blouse. They had pizza and Coke on the patio looking into the backyard. Travis talked about the hospital and she talked about her work. It was awhile before either of them dared to get more personal.

"What was it like when you were a child growing up? Were you in any kind of sports while you were in school? You look as if you could have played football," she asked with interest.

He smiled. "I played a little in high school. Was good, too. But, I always wanted to be a doctor. My father was a doctor and my sister was a nurse."

He looked to see if Tracey's expression had changed when he mentioned his sister, but it hadn't. He would have to be careful about mentioning his sister in her presence. "I had a good childhood. I have an older brother, but he lives in Detroit."

"Is he in medicine, too?"

"No. He's a vice president at Ford Motors. He didn't want to be a doctor, though my father wanted him to. They didn't get along too well, so he would never have listened to my father."

Travis stopped, and took another bite of pizza. "Anyway, he got a good job offer at Ford Motors as soon as he graduated from college and off he went. My mother cried when he left. I'll never forget that week."

He wiped his mouth in the corner with his napkin. "I think she cried every day, but it was what he wanted and my father felt that he was old enough to make that decision. Now, tell me what your childhood was like? It had to have been more interesting than mine," he mused as he meticulously brushed crumbs from his fingertips. He was a neat man by habit.

Tracey propped her elbows on the table, resting her face in both hands. "I don't know if it was more interesting, but it's very different from yours. I only have one sister. My mother and father were killed in a car accident." Sadness crouched in her eyes as she looked directly into his. He looked sad, too, just as everyone did when she told her story.

"My aunt raised Robin and me. She was the only living relative my mother had except for some distant cousins that we only saw every three or four years. At first, I was afraid that Robin and I would be separated and put in foster homes." She laughed for the first time. "I was afraid for a whole year. I was perfect, got good grades, didn't talk back to my aunt, and I kept our room neat and clean. Anything to keep from going into a foster home."

"What made you think it was so bad in a foster home?"

"I went to grammar school with a girl that lived with foster parents. She was always filthy, unhappy, and treated badly. Aunt Flo never had any children of her own."

"What was living with your aunt like? I take it she treated you well, the way you and your sister are so loyal to her now."

"Before we came to live with her, she traveled a lot and was in different women's clubs. She'd always brought Robin and me gifts every time she returned from one of her many trips. I knew she loved us, but I didn't think that she would have given it all up to take us or that she even wanted children. But she's been like a mother to Robin and me. She gave up so much freedom for us."

"You haven't changed much, you know."

"What do you mean?" She shrugged her shoulders, lifted her palms upward, and looked confused.

"You are still the perfect woman. Look around you. There's nothing out of place and it's the same at your office." Travis made a sweeping motion with his hand, pointing inside her house and around the patio. "Even the stacks of papers on your desk were all turned the same way, neat, and in place. I bet you are not off a penny in your bankbook. You can let go now, Tracey."

Seeing her alarmed look, Travis tried to clear up the point he was making. "No one is perfect. Relax. Live a little. I'll bet you were the perfect wife, too."

How many times had Aunt Flo told her the very same thing? Even Donald had told her to loosen up. There was an interminable pause between them for a few seconds. Her eyes flew to Travis's face, and in an unconscious gesture, she pushed her hair away from her face and sucked her teeth.

Travis could tell he had pushed a button that no one had gotten close to, probably not even her late husband, Donald.

She held her head high with a haughty tilt in her neck. She sounded a bit miffed when she spoke again. "I was a good wife, and I'm a hard worker. But, that's just the way I am. I'll give it some thought since I am so transparent. Now tell me Travis, what do you want from me?"

"I didn't mean to offend you. That was just an observation. . . . If we had met under different circumstances, would you have asked me that question?" he asked, looking momentarily crestfallen.

"I guess not, but maybe I would wonder." He held her hand; his hand was strong, warm and gentle.

"I want to get to know you better. If we still like each other, we will see what happens after that. I want to be your friend, Tracey. Now, this is where you say that you would like to get to know me, too."

"Okay, friend." Tracey relented and flashed him a smile.

She gave him her hand and he held it. Travis couldn't believe his good fortune. He loved how her eyes danced when she teased him. He was glad he'd put her at ease.

They chatted and laughed until she took him back to his car. He was whistling all the way back to his Mercedes Benz.

As she drove back home, she smiled as she recounted the afternoon with Travis. It had been a good day to play hooky after all, and she found that Travis intrigued her. She was charmed by his life, his kindness, and the way she felt when she was with him. She didn't feel uptight around him as she had felt when he first walked into her office. Maybe they could become friends, she thought with a smile on her face as she parked her car in her driveway.

"Travis, come on in. I just finished cooking. Would you like some fried chicken?"

"No thanks, Mother. I just stopped by to say hello and to make sure you're doing all right." He followed her into the den and slumped into the Queen Anne chair that had been his father's favorite. He watched his mother as she turned the TV on to listen to the six o'clock news. When Travis's father was alive, he and his mother used to watch the news every evening together. They did everything together. As long as he could remember his parents were close. His father had died five years ago and now his sister was dead. Susan had been the only daughter and the youngest child.

His mother would never be the same. Losing her daughter had hit her hard. It still showed in her eyes. They were weary with grief and not as clear as they were before. If only she would talk about Susan, maybe it would relieve some of the pain, but Travis knew that she couldn't. It was much too painful.

Travis looked around the cozy room at all of the high school and college graduation pictures.

Maureen Howard sat on the sofa facing her son. "You finally got a day off? You're just like your father, Travis. You work too hard." His mother studied him and held his gaze for what seemed like an interminable time. Finally she spoke again. "You need to meet a nice young woman, get married, and have some children to come home to. Give me that grandchild before I die," she persisted. "Oh, did I tell you that your brother will be here day after tomorrow?"

"Yes, Mother, you told me. It will be nice to see my niece."

"What about your brother and his wife?"

"It's always good to see them, too."

Maureen smiled. "I have two good sons. Your father was proud of all three of his children," she said cautiously, trying not to cry. And Travis knew that she was thinking of her daughter. It had been hard on all of them. His brother called home often after his father's and, now, his sister's death.

"Anyway, you should enjoy life more, Travis."

"Mother, helping patients and saving lives is my life."

She shook her head. "You'll feel differently when you meet the right woman and you'll love her more than life."

"Can you really love someone that much? I wonder."

"Oh yes, honey, believe me you can. One day if you're lucky, you will find out for yourself. It was that way with your father and me."

"I know it was. I've often wondered if it would ever happen to me. I've wondered that a lot lately."

Maureen Howard's eyes widened with happiness. "Travis Howard, do you have your eyes on a special lady?"

"Yes, but she doesn't feel the same as I do."

"Son, she's a fool if she doesn't. She'd better open her eyes before someone else with some sense comes along. How could she not?"

She stood up. "Come on and have a piece of chicken before it gets too cold. What you can't eat, you can always take home."

"It does smells good, and no one can fry chicken as good as you do, Mother," he teased, and followed her to the kitchen.

Fifteen

Flora was in the kitchen when she heard the doorbell ring.

"Miss Flora, there is a Miss Mildred here to see you," Stella said, wondering who the well-dressed woman was.

"Stella, please tell her that I'll be right there. She was Tracey's mother-in-law," Flora answered happily.

"Oh, so that's who she is. I'll tell her to sit down." Stella went back to the living room. "Miss Flora is coming, she says to have a seat."

Flora walked into the living room and Mildred stood up and held her arms out.

"You look good, Flora," Mildred said and kissed Flora on her cheek. "I'm glad to see that you are feeling better. It's a darn shame when you can't use your hands. I know how helpless you must have felt," Mildred smiled wryly.

"I do feel better, Mildred. Honey, I can do anything for myself now."

"Excuse me. Can I get you ladies some tea or coffee?" Stella asked.

"I'll take tea with lemon, please," Mildred answered, and took off her gloves.

"The same for me," Flora said. "And get yourself a cup, too, Stella."

"Would you like a couple of slices of the pound cake? I baked it yesterday," Stella asked with pride.

Both women nodded. Stella scurried out of the room.

"Tracey came to see me a couple of days ago. It was

so nice to know that she thought of me. We didn't exactly start off on good terms in the beginning of her marriage to Donald."

"Yes, I remember, but Tracey is a forgiving person." The doorbell rang and Flora got up to answer it. It was Robin.

"Stella, bring in an extra cup for Robin," Flora yelled from the living room.

Stella came in carrying a tray with four cups of tea and a plate with slices of pound cake on it.

"I didn't call you today because I knew that I was coming over. It's good to see you, too, Mildred. How have you been?"

Flora thought Robin's smile seemed a little forced. It looked as if the corners of her mouth quivered in an attempt to smile naturally.

"Pretty good, Robin. I was telling Flora that Tracey was nice enough to come and visit me. You two girls look so good. I see you're keeping your weight down, too, Robin."

"Thank you, Mildred."

"Oh, this is Stella, Mildred," Flora said. "She was coming over to help me out twice a week. But now she comes once a week. I can really take care of myself now, but you know Tracey. She wants Stella to come over for another week before she's convinced that I'm just fine."

Mildred looked at Stella, nodded her head in acknowledgment, and gave her a warm smile.

Stella took a seat in the chair that was next to the couch. Flora and Mildred sat on the couch, and Robin was sitting in the chair opposite Mildred.

"I never had the flu so bad, Aunt Flo. Today is just my second day at work in eight days."

"I know how bad it can be. I had it two years ago. Poor Tracey slept in that chair and took me to the doctor's office just so he could say that I had a stomach virus."

"Tracey is such a good girl," said Mildred. "My Donald knew that he was a lucky man. He always told me that she was the perfect wife."

"Yes, he should have known how lucky he was," Robin remarked sarcastically. She curled her lip up in repugnance and shook her head.

"Robin, I'm sure he did. After all, he was a very good husband and he loved her very much. He said so himself," Mildred said.

"How is Janet?" Flora asked, but Mildred didn't hear her. Flora took a long look at Mildred. She seemed to be puzzling over what Robin had meant.

"You and Donald got along good, didn't you, Robin?" Mildred asked, still not understanding what was going on in Robin's head.

"Yes, we got along well, up until the end. But, of course I didn't know that he had been unfaithful to my sister. Tracey didn't know herself until his death."

"Ladies, why are we bringing this up now? Tracey is getting over it and she has come to terms with it," Flora interjected.

"You're right, Aunt Flo. I shouldn't have said anything."

Stella looked from Flora to Robin and back at Mildred again. It was clear that Mildred had no idea what had happened between her son and Tracey. Stella didn't know either, up until now.

"What in God's name are you talking about, Robin?" Mildred asked impatiently.

"I was talking about the woman that died in the car crash with Donald. But it's over, Mildred. I had no idea that Tracey hadn't mentioned it to you. Why don't we talk of happier times? We have so many to remember," Robin said. Right away she looked sorry that she had gone too far. She put two fingers up to her lips and widened her eyes.

Mildred nervously clenched her slender hands together as if she didn't know what to do next. She couldn't stop the tears that had started to fall from her eyes.

"I don't know what to say, Mildred," Robin said, walking over and taking her hand in hers. "It was so careless of me, but I assumed Tracey or Janet had told you."

"I've got to go," Mildred said, still crying softly. " I didn't come here to hear this. I knew nothing of this. I can't stay any longer."

Flora stood up and went to Mildred. "Mildred, don't go like this. Tracey didn't want you to know. She wanted to spare your feelings." Flora put her arm around Mildred's shoulder.

"What good did it do? Robin didn't seem to have any trouble washing my face in it. And, who was the woman anyway? I never knew of any woman."

"We don't know, Mildred. I didn't mean to wash your face in it, like you said. I just thought that you knew. I'm so sorry that you had to find out this way," Robin said.

Mildred stepped closer to Robin. "Was I talking as if I knew? But you couldn't stop, could you? I think you wanted me to know. You wanted me to hurt because Tracey was hurt." Mildred put one hand on her hip and pointed her finger in Robin's face.

"Well, I never wanted to see Tracey hurt. But you, you told me on purpose. It was no accident that you mentioned it. You are evil, evil," Mildred shouted. "Are you jealous because Tracey had a husband who could give her more?" She grabbed her coat, rushing out as Robin and Flora tried to comfort her.

When Mildred walked outside, Tracey was getting out of her car. She smiled when she saw Mildred, but Mildred just stopped in front of her. She opened her mouth, but no words emerged. She shook her head and ran to her car. Bewildered, Tracey looked at Flora, Robin, and Stella standing on the front steps.

"Mildred, where are you going?" Tracey yelled after her. But Mildred sped off.

"Aunt Flo, what just happened to Mildred? Why are all of you looking as if something terrible has happened?" she asked, looking from Flora to Robin.

"I'm so sorry, Tracey. I just happened to mention that there was another woman in the car with Donald when he had the accident . . ."

"You what? Oh no you didn't, Robin. How did the conversation even come up? And why Robin, why?" Tracey raised her voice.

"I don't know. She said that Donald knew how lucky he was to have you and one thing led to another. I swear, I had no idea that she didn't know. I just didn't think." Robin hung her head.

"It wasn't any of her business to know. Why would I tell her that her son who died was a liar and a cheat? Why would I tell her that, Robin?" Tracey shook her head in disgust and anger.

"Tracey, I'm sorry," Robin explained, following Tracey to the bathroom. But Tracey swore to herself and slammed the door in Robin's face.

Flora was grateful that Stella, knowing that she was in the midst of a family fight, went into the kitchen and closed the door.

"Now, what should I do, Aunt Flo?" Robin asked as she took a seat on the couch. Flora was sitting on the couch with her head back, her eyes closed from the headache that she felt coming on. She could still see the pain on Mildred's face, and she was worried about her. Flora was certain that Robin hadn't known, but the way she handled the situation was very distasteful. After all, Mildred was his mother.

"It's too late. Tracey is the only one who can straighten this whole mess out."

The door to the bathroom opened. Tracey walked out and stood in front of Flora. "Why don't you lie down for a while, Aunt Flo? I won't be gone too long."

"I think I need to," Flora answered. "This is all too much," she said, looking pointedly at Robin.

"Can I get you anything before I go?" Tracey asked with her back to Robin.

"No, honey. You just go and make sure that Mildred made it home all right. In her state of mind, she could have an accident," Flora said, still looking at Robin, but Robin kept her head down.

Robin followed Tracey to the car. "Tracey, I'm so very sorry. I just didn't know. When I found out that Mildred didn't know, it was too late."

Tracey continued to walk and ignore Robin.

"She just kept asking questions. Well, it's your fault you know. Why not tell her what kind of son she had?" Robin snapped.

Tracey stopped only inches from where Robin was standing. "Did anyone ever tell you you're short on sympathy, Robin? It's not any of your damn business why I didn't tell her, and it's my business if I wanted to or not. Not yours, Robin, just like it wasn't my business when you screwed Paul while you were married. What makes you any different from Donald?" She spun on her heels and climbed into her car, never looking back.

Tracey's words were so forceful that Robin could only stand there in the street, where Tracey had left her. Her mouth was wide open, and she didn't know how much time passed before she felt her jaws clamp shut again. She couldn't seem to move. It was like her feet were frozen to the ground. It reminded her of the game "Freeze" she and Tracey used to play as little girls. They seldom had angry words between them, at least never like this. She was hurt, and didn't know how to make it up to Tracey. Robin no longer wondered what her sister thought of her sleeping with another man while she was married. She'd cheated just as Donald had. She walked inside the house, sat on the edge of Flora's bed, and held her face in both hands and cried.

* * *

Tracey rang Mildred's doorbell four times before she answered. Mildred eyes were red and her hair in disarray as though she had been lying down. She fell into Tracey's arms. They both held each other, tears streaming down their faces, shoulders heaving.

"I'm so sorry, Mildred," Tracey said between sobs. "I didn't think it was necessary to tell you about Donald's affair. I didn't know myself until the night he died. There was no reason for you to know."

Finally, they pulled themselves together and wiped their eyes. Both women shook their heads in understanding. The two went and sat on the couch and held hands

"I know why you didn't tell me, Tracey. I'm just sorry and disappointed in my son. All the hurt and pain, the unanswered questions you probably have. Too bad you didn't find out before he died. At least he could have explained why he did it."

"I know. I've wished the same thing over and over again. But even if I had asked him it wouldn't stop the hurt."

"I know, dear." Mildred looked at her. "I don't understand Robin at all, Tracey."

"She's sorry, Mildred."

Mildred nodded her head, but she wasn't convinced that Robin was entirely sorry.

She held Tracey's hand tightly in hers. "I'm all right now and I feel better since you came over to see me. I hope that you will come again soon."

"Oh, you know I will. I'll take you and Aunt Flo to brunch one Sunday."

"That'll be nice," Mildred said. She kept her arm around Tracey's waist as she walked her to the door.

When Tracey got back to check on Flora, Robin and Stella were already gone. She walked softly to Flora's bedroom and looked in on her.

"I'm awake. How was Mildred when you left her?" Flora asked with concern.

"She had been crying before I got there, but we did come to an understanding. It was just a shock for her to hear it for the first time."

"I'm just sorry that she had to hear it the way she did."

"Let's just forget it, Aunt Flo. Now, how's that headache?"

"It's gone. I had a bowl of chicken and dumplings. I hope you're hungry because they're delicious."

"I'll take a bowl with me. Now, I have my own headache. Do you need anything before I leave?"

"No, and if I do, I can get it for myself. You and Stella wait on me hand and foot."

Once Tracey was home, she went straight to her bedroom and lay on her back, facing the ceiling in the dark. She closed her eyes and Donald's face appeared in front of her. When she blinked and opened them, he had disappeared. She was tired of thinking of Donald, tired of trying to figure out why he had been cheating on her and if it was the first time. She wasn't even sure if she still loved him. The love they had shared died the same night that he died, but did she hate him? She wasn't certain anymore.

She closed her eyes again and thought about Travis. She hadn't missed the unsettled expression on his face when he mentioned his sister. Poor guy. He hadn't been sure how she would react. Tracey smiled as she remembered the expression on his face. Would they always walk on eggshells when they talked about their families? How could they become friends with the memories of that night in the hospital?

Tracey turned onto her stomach and sighed. This could certainly complicate a friendship. And she was sure that there could be more unforeseen obstacles if they continued to see each other. She hadn't heard from Travis for two days. In a weird way she was glad, but still a little disappointed. She was so conflicted about Travis, she didn't know how she felt.

Tracey rolled over again and fell asleep. It was midnight when she woke up and undressed. She went into her study and picked up a purchase agreement to go over it, but changed her mind and got back into bed.

At noon the next day the phone rang at Tracey's office and Michelle answered.

"It's your sister, Tracey." Michelle handed her the phone.

"Hello," Tracey answered in a dry tone of voice. "No, but maybe tomorrow. I can't get away today. No, I'm not angry anymore. It was my business and my decision, Robin, it should have stayed that way. Okay, maybe tomorrow."

"That sister of mine can make me so mad," Tracey said after she'd hung up.

"Mine can, too," Michelle said and laughed.

"I have a client to meet at eleven-thirty. Would you like to come along? We can stop and have lunch when I finish with him. Besides, it will give you more exposure to clients and the actual real estate transaction part of it."

"I'd love to. This is the chance that I've been waiting for, Tracey. Have you noticed the change in my appearance lately? I'm trying to look more businesslike."

"Yes, I've noticed and that's a nice dress you're wearing, today. Is Wendy upstairs?"

"I haven't seen her or her assistant yet."

"I guess they're late for some reason. Wendy wasn't in yesterday and it's almost one and she's still not in. That's not like her." Tracey looked concerned.

The meeting with the client went well. Tracey took Michelle to lunch on the way back to the office. "You were very professional today with my client. I think you'll do well in this business. And he couldn't keep his eyes off you the entire time we were there. He's young, single, and very handsome," Tracey said playfully.

"Yeah, right. Those are all the reasons that he wouldn't want me."

"I can't believe you said that. He's older than you are and, when he was your age, he was probably doing the same thing that you are doing now. Which is trying to learn and get ahead. In a couple of years you will have your feet flat on the ground, and with a degree, too. Don't ever put yourself down like that again, Michelle," Tracey said with a serious expression. "You're too hard on yourself."

"I know. But, sometimes it seems so hard and it takes so long to get what you want in life."

"Well, girl, when you finish, guys like Kirk Larson will be running after you. Now, let's eat and go home after this. I'll take you to the office to get your car, and I want to go home early tonight. I'm not even going to do any work when I get there. My hair needs to be washed and set, my nails needs to be polished. Tonight is my night."

Michelle smiled the same smile her mother did. Tracey thought it was like looking at a younger version of Stella. But Michelle would be educated and a businesswoman.

When Tracey got home, Robin was driving up in front of her house at the same time. She followed Tracey inside and waited in the den while she was changing into her bathrobe. Tracey walked out and glared at her, took a seat, and waited for her to speak.

Robin cleared her throat. "Look, Tracey, I know we haven't really talked since I opened my big mouth to Mildred, but I am sorry. I've been wondering why I didn't realize that Mildred didn't know and, when I did, it was too late. And you were absolutely right, it wasn't any of my business. I had no right to say anything to Mildred about your marriage."

Tracey nodded her head in agreement. "It's over now. Just forget it," she said and crossed her arms in front of her as though she felt a chill in the air.

"The only excuse I have is because of the mess I've gotten myself into."

"What now?"

"Paul. Nothing has changed. He's still won't let go. I keep ignoring him as much as possible, but I never know what's on his mind. And I'm having a hard time keeping up this show without anyone on my job finding out what went on between us."

Tracey looked at her face and saw how frightened she really was. "You mean to tell me that he hasn't given up yet?"

"No. And I think that he could become dangerous, too."

"Oh come on, Robin. What can he do?"

"I don't know yet. But, I have a feeling he's going to try and intimidate me into seeing him again. The only good thing about it is he was offered a position in San Francisco. I don't know yet if he will accept it. God, I hope so."

Tracey didn't say anything for a few seconds. "Maybe there is a way that he can be forced to take it."

"What do you mean? He'll only take it if that's what he wants, or if he loses his job here. I hear it's a great position, too, but he's not thinking wisely right now."

"Let me think about this for a couple of days and tell me if he keeps threatening you. There's an answer for everything you know. Donald taught me that much."

"Donald taught you a lot, honey."

"Yes, I guess he did at that. How are you and John getting along these days?"

"Better than ever. It's as if he knows that I'm having a hard time, but he thinks it's the workload at the office. Sometimes I wonder if he senses anything else. If he ever finds out, Tracey, he'll divorce me."

"No he won't. It won't get that far. Now, go home to your family. It'll be over soon," Tracey promised.

"May I come in?" he asked as he stood in the door with a file in his hand. Robin had just finished going over a file with another agent who was leaving her office. She had to go over the budget for the retail department but it could wait until later.

"Yes, come in, Paul. I have time for one more," she said, looking down at her watch.

He closed the door behind the other agent and took a seat in the chair in front of her desk. Paul leaned forward with the file in front of him.

Robin opened the file and looked over the application. "Looks like a good loan, his salary is substantial. What did you want to talk to me about?" she asked, not certain of what he really wanted.

"What are you doing for lunch today, Robin?"

"I'm working straight through my lunch. Now, how can I help you with this loan?"

"I brought in a nine-hundred-fifty-thousand-dollar loan and you won't have lunch with me? Shame on you Robin, I thought you would be proud of me," he said playfully.

"We mixed business with pleasure once, Paul, and I'm paying dearly for it. Now, again, how can I help you with this loan?" she asked impatiently. *Why doesn't he accept the job offer in San Francisco? The opportunity is such a great one.* She looked at him and his smile had disappeared. His jaw had tightened. He didn't like the way she was treating him.

"I need to talk to you alone, Robin, and away from here. It's important, you need to hear my plans. Just one lunch is all I'm asking, one hour." He raised his voice. She jumped, and looked around to see if anyone had heard him.

"What is this lunch all about, Paul? Why can't you talk to me here?"

"One hour, Robin. Maybe we can talk all our differences out, and we both can feel comfortable working together again."

She folded her hands on the desk. "That makes sense. It has been tense lately. Yes, maybe we should talk. But first you have to promise me, we talk and that's it. Clear the air between us and settle it once and for all," she said, with a sigh of relief.

"That's all I ask."

They went to lunch in separate cars. They sat at a small corner table for two. The café was quiet as there weren't very many guests. Robin wondered how much longer it would be in business.

"Finally alone again. Just you and me, Robin. Now, I'm going to tell you what my plans are so you will know what to expect. I know that you are married, but that can be easily eliminated. You also have a daughter and that's all right with me. I've always wanted a daughter of my own. I have one you know, but I haven't seen her since she was a year old. That was five years ago," he said absentmindedly.

Robin looked as if she was going into complete shock.

Paul continued. "All I want is for us to be a family. That's all I dream of, Robin. I know you love me, baby. You're just confused, that's all. If that husband of yours gets in our way of happiness, we can eliminate him, too. Do you understand what I'm saying, Robin?"

She cleared her throat, trying to assimilate his words, her eyes wide with fear. Robin couldn't begin to comprehend what he was saying and to think that he was serious was inconceivable to her.

"Paul, what are you talking about? Just listen to yourself. You can't really be serious about this. It's over between us, has been for some time now. . . ."

"Maybe it is for you, Robin, but it's not over for me. What makes you feel it is over with just because you say so? Who do you think you are?" he said in a hard voice that scared her.

"Paul, can't you understand that I love my husband and he loves me?"

"No, he doesn't love you. He doesn't know you, Robin."

"God, Paul. You can't always have everything you want in life. My daughter has the only father she wants, and I have the only man I want. What I did with you was a mistake, and I take all the blame for it. I shouldn't have been so weak. But, it happened and now it's over." She started to get up and he grabbed her arm.

"Wait, Robin, your lunch is coming." The waitress set their food on the table and smiled at the couple. She walked away and Paul grabbed Robin's arm again.

"We're not finished with this conversation, yet."

Robin placed her napkin in her lap, but she wasn't hungry. She only wanted to leave this restaurant and get back to her office, to safety. She sighed and tried to think of a way to make him understand without getting angry. She tried to reason with him.

"Paul, you are a nice man, a very handsome and smart man. You deserve a woman that is younger than I am. One that can give you the family that you deserve. I'm too old to have another child and Lisa doesn't belong to you. John will never agree to let me take her. You are putting me in a very bad predicament, one that can cause pain for my child." Robin studied his face to see if she was getting through to him.

"You have so much going for you, a new position in San Francisco that any man would die for. Why are you still here as a loan officer when you have the opportunity to manage ten other loan officers? You have a chance to get a fresh start and meet the woman of your dreams," she said, trying to sound encouraging and mask the fear in her voice.

Paul was quiet for a while. He finally spoke. His voice was low, firm. "I have the woman of my dreams. And, yes, I am going to take that position, Robin. Haven't you heard a word that I've said to you? I want you and Lisa to go with me. John can't harass you there." He grinned the smile that used to melt her, but now disgusted her, then held up both hands. "See, I have it all figured out. All you have to do is give me a date, so I can call the company in San Francisco and give them my start date. Maybe you and I can take a trip there on the weekend and look at some apartments. I've even saved enough money to buy a house. I'm going to sell the one I have here and buy you the house that you've always dreamed of." His voice was growing loud in his excitement, and he gesticulated wildly with his hands.

Robin suddenly grew tired of listening to his nonsense. "And what if I don't go with you? What if I tell my husband about the mistake I made and he forgives me?"

"You won't do that, sweetheart. He'll fight and take your daughter away and you know that."

"He'll fight and take her away if I leave with you. So, what's the difference?"

"The difference is he won't get hurt. No one will." He forced a smile.

She put her fork down hard in her plate and picked up her purse.

"I'm going back to the office. I'm going to tell my husband the truth and pray that he forgives me. In the meantime, I suggest you take that position, Paul. I don't love you, and I won't go. Nothing you can do will make me go. Even if my husband doesn't want me after I tell him, I still won't go with you."

"Then, I'll just have to stay here. Sooner or later, you will change your mind, Robin. No matter what you say, I know you love me. Just stop playing games and admit it."

She pushed her chair from the table and stood up. "Go to hell, Paul," she hissed.

He sat back in his chair, smiling smugly at her. She could feel his eyes on her as she stormed out of the restaurant. She walked quickly, breathless, trying to get a distance from him.

When Robin got home, she was still upset. She was standing in front of the stove when John kissed her on the back of her neck.

She jumped and dropped the spoon on the kitchen floor. "John, damn you. I've told you about sneaking up on me like that," she snapped, sorry the moment she yelled at him.

"What's wrong, Robin? I just wanted to kiss my wife like a loving husband." He took her into his arms, and she lay her head on his shoulder.

"I know, and I'm sorry. It's been a stressful day."

"Tell me about it. It's been that way all week in my branch. Since we were robbed last week all the tellers are jumpy, too."

She kissed him on the cheek and turned back to the stove so he wouldn't see that she had been crying.

"Dinner will be ready in about twenty minutes. Why don't you change into something comfortable?"

"Where's Lisa?" he asked.

"In her room doing her homework. Tell her twenty minutes for me?"

The phone rang and it was Tracey. "I've got to tell him tonight, Tracey," Robin whispered into the phone.

"No the hell you don't. Don't be silly. Come to my office in the morning so we can figure out what to do about Paul. Together we can figure out something. If we don't, then we go to Aunt Flo. She has an answer for everything."

"I wonder what she'll think of me, Tracey."

"Nothing. She knows that you were under a lot of stress and John can be stupid sometimes, Robin. Just don't tell him."

"Okay, but I'm having a nervous breakdown."

"No, you're not. You'll be fine."

When Robin drove to Tracey's office the next morning, she was tired and still sleepy. John had made love to her for hours the night before. He was trying so hard to make things the way they used to be. He bought her flowers, took her to lunch, even asked about her new position.

Things were getting good between them again and now there was Paul to threaten it all. She parked her car in the lot and walked into Tracey's office. Tracey was on the phone so she went into the small kitchen and came back with a cup of coffee in her hand.

"Where's Wendy? I didn't see her car outside."

"Her sister is ill so she went home for a couple of weeks."

"Who's running her business?" Robin asked.

"That's something I don't quite understand yet. She said

that she had no more escrows open and wasn't taking on any new ones. But, that was at least a week before she got word that her sister was ill." Tracey shrugged her shoulders, looking baffled. "Her assistant was gone a week before that. I think when she comes back, I'll ask if there's something else going on in her life. Hope it's nothing too serious. She's probably having a hard time getting over William," Tracey added with concern.

"You never know with Wendy. Don't let it worry you too much, Tracey. Have you seen that Travis guy lately?"

"No, but I've talked to him. He's out of town for a few days this week. Something to do with his work. A medical convention I think. "

Robin nodded. "Do you like him, Tracey?"

"I could if I had the time."

"You have the time. You are just too afraid to. Don't rush yourself. Just let it happen naturally, if it's meant to be."

Tracey got up and poured herself a cup of coffee. "I don't know. What if he turns out to be a nutcase like Paul or a cheat like Donald?"

"Believe me, honey, no one's a nutcase like that Paul."

"You look like hell this morning, Robin. Didn't you get enough sleep?"

"No, with John, and then Paul was on my mind, I got no sleep last night. I'm in trouble, Tracey, and I don't know which way to turn." She wiped tears from her eyes. It seemed as though she had been crying a lot lately. "Women do what I did all the time, but I had to do it with a nutcase. I stand to lose everything. But he doesn't care or understand it."

"We've got to put our heads together, Robin. I was thinking about going to him for a home loan. Maybe some way we can start from there. I mean, we never met before. He won't know that I'm your sister."

"Everyone else in the office knows you."

"It doesn't have to take place in the office. We can meet in a restaurant. I take applications all the time in restaurants, or just talk with the client to see if I really want to do business with them or not."

"You're good, girl. You can pick who you want to do business with now."

"It took a lot of work to be in this position," Tracey said.

"Tracey, we have to work fast. Are you thinking of getting him fired?"

"Yes, he'll have no choice, but to accept that other position in San Francisco."

"That worries me. He wants the position, but he wants me with him. Whatever we do may not make him change his mind."

"Well, I have another plan. Tell me how this sounds. I know a guy that used to work for Donald. I ran into him three months ago and he was looking for work. I'll give him a call tonight and see what he says. Maybe he can dig up something on Paul and scare the hell out of him."

Robin looked completely baffled, and placed her cup on the desk. "What can he do?"

"Robin. A man like Paul has to have some skeletons in the closet. We just have to find out what they are."

"Who taught you all of this?"

"Remember who I was married to? He was a tough businessman, but he knew a lot. Now, we have to find something on Paul. Like I said, a man like him has a past. Does he have any children that he may have mentioned?"

"You know, he did say that he has a six-year-old daughter that he hasn't seen in five years."

"That's a start. I wonder why he hasn't seen her in five years?"

"I don't know. He didn't say, and I was too upset with him to ask."

"Maybe the child's mother doesn't want him to see her. I'm sure she's staying away from him for a good reason. Anyway, be here tomorrow morning at this same time. I have an appointment that can be changed to the afternoon. Oh, bring his personnel record with you."

"They're kept in the human resources office, but I can request a copy of his application."

"Good, I'll have Fred meet us here, too."

"Is Fred the friend that owes you a favor?"

"No, Fred's the private investigator. I want him to see Paul's application. He may see something that we won't pick up." Tracey put her finger on her cheek as if she was in deep thought. "He's good. When he leaves us tomorrow we will have a plan to run Paul's ass to San Francisco."

Robin got up and slipped into her navy blazer, picked up her purse and headed for the door. She stopped and turned to face Tracey. "I'll never get myself in this position again."

"I know what it's like to have your life crumble around you. It's not so easy to put it back together again." Tracey got up and walked over to her sister and put her arm around her shoulder. She walked Robin outside and watched her drive off.

The next morning Robin arrived at Tracey's office ten minutes before Fred got there. Michelle had taken the day off to study for her exams. Fred walked in and shook Tracey's and Robin's hands. Tracey poured him a cup of black coffee.

Out of the corner of her eye, Robin examined this private eye. He did not exactly fit her image of an investigator, but she was desperate. She'd try anything to get rid of this fool. Hopefully, John would never find out.

Fred was medium height, had light brown skin, dark slanted eyes, and was holding a pipe in his hand. He was dressed in a pair of brown tweed trousers and a short-sleeve white shirt. Fred took a seat next to Robin and went over the copy of Paul's application, asking questions as he looked it over.

Robin watched quietly and listened to the questions that Tracey was answering. She was surprised as she listened to her sister.

What had happened to the scared girl that Flora had taken in after their parents' deaths? There were nights when Tracey would get out of her bed and get in bed with Robin, crying for her mother and father and afraid that the girls would be separated and put in foster homes. She would lie in Robin's arms and cry herself to sleep. Lying next to Robin gave her the comfort she no longer got from their parents. That girl was gone and replaced with the shrewd businesswoman who was confident and powerful, her head held high while conducting business as she would every day. Robin knew that Tracey was now the strong one.

"How long have you known this man?" Fred asked.

"He's been with the company for almost a year."

"No, I mean how long have you known him personally?"

"Only two months," she answered, not liking the tone of his voice and wondering if he was always so prickly. She closed her eyes against the migraine that she felt coming on from lack of sleep.

"What do you think, Fred?" Tracey asked.

"I think that this time tomorrow we will have enough to run poor old Paul away. I'll bet anything he left Seattle because he had to. Maybe even owes a lot of child support, too." He shifted the application into his briefcase. "Anyway, this application gives his personal business, that's if any of it is true. But it's a start."

They stood up and walked outside. "This is all I need for now. I know someone in Seattle that can give me some answers by tomorrow."

Standing in front of Tracey's office, Fred touched Robin on her shoulder and held her hand. He said, "Don't worry, everything will work out. Before you know it, your life will be back to normal again."

Robin nodded in agreement. "I appreciate anything that you can do for me, Fred. It's been a nightmare."

Sixteen

When Tracey walked in the house, she was mentally exhausted and physically drained. She wanted to take a nap but wondered if Robin was all right. She looked at her watch. It was five-thirty, too late to call. John was probably home with her.

She sat back in her big chair and closed her eyes, and opened them again as she thought of Travis. With Robin and Fred in her office today she had forgotten him, for the moment anyway. She closed her eyes again and could see his face clearly in front of her. What was she going to do about this man? she wondered. She opened her eyes again. Travis's attention was an invasion in her life, but she was beginning to welcome it. She was drifting into a deep sleep just as the telephone woke her. It was Wendy on the other line. Tracey sat up straight.

"Girl, where have you been? I've been trying to contact you for the last two days. Is there something wrong?" Tracey asked, hearing the urgency in Wendy's voice. "I'll be right over."

She hung up, slipped on a pair of loafers and her blue jean jacket, and rushed out the door.

"What is so important?" Tracey asked, as she walked into Wendy's foyer. "Wendy, what's in the boxes? Are you moving, girl?" she asked standing in the middle of the living room. There were no more pictures hanging on the walls and the room looked cold and empty. Tracey stood with her eyes wide, surprised that Wendy was moving and had not mentioned it to her sooner. What was going on here? she wondered.

"Come on in the den so we can talk. Would you like something to drink?"

"Just a Coke. You woke me out of my sleep."

"Sorry about that."

"Don't be. It's no problem. Anyway, I don't like the way this sounds."

Wendy looked back at her but didn't say anything. She was back in five minutes with a cup of coffee and a Coke in her hands. Tracey was already waiting in the small den, and noticed that all the paintings were standing against the wall in a corner of the room. Wendy turned the television off so she and Tracey could talk.

"I've been concerned about you, Wendy. You haven't been in the office for over a week and your assistant hasn't been in either. I came over but you weren't home. I called and got no answer so I couldn't leave a message. I thought you were still in Mississippi."

"I know. That's why I asked you to come over tonight." Wendy looked as though she didn't know where to start.

Suddenly Wendy seemed to switch gears. "You know, for years all I've ever wanted was to be happy with a nice man and to make him happy, too. But everyone I met was a user. Look how William treated me."

"Oh no, girl, you're not getting back with him?"

"Oh no. I've been looking over my life, and I was madly in love with William. Still am. I was sure that he was going to be the last man in my life, and guess what? I was right."

Tracey felt as confused as before. What kind of mumbo-jumbo was Wendy talking about? She was staring at Wendy, puzzled. She saw tears glittering in Wendy's eyes.

"I'm moving back to Mississippi to work with my sister. She's doing very well with her escrow company."

Tracey couldn't believe what she was hearing. Her best

friend was leaving her. "But, you've done well for yourself. Why go all the way to Mississippi?"

"I can't stay here, Tracey. I can't forget William. And I can't sleep or eat. Look at me. I'm losing more weight. I just want to get away and start new." She held her face in her hand and begin weeping.

Tracey felt as if she couldn't breathe. She inhaled deeply and held Wendy in her arms. They cried together, tears sluicing down both of their faces and running together. For a few moments, the room was as quiet as if it was deserted, except for the sounds of their sobs. Neither woman said a word. They just held each other and cried. And Tracey almost wondered if she was still asleep. First she had lost Donald, now Wendy.

"Have you seen William?"

"No. He hasn't even called to see if I'm alive or dead. We broke up, and he didn't look back. My credit cards are at their limit. It's all on me now. After he left I got a bill in the mail where he had used one of my credit cards after he left. Can you believe it? Three thousand dollars on my Visa!"

"I hate him. I think I always have."

"Yes, you always have. Too bad I wasn't smart enough to," Wendy cried.

"So, when are you leaving?"

"Next week. First, I have to clean out my office and get all my furniture shipped back there. Tracey, I'm sorry that I'm not giving you a thirty-day notice. The lease did stipulate a thirty-day advance notice," Wendy said, looking truly sorry.

"Girl, a month's notice is the last thing on my mind right now. I can always lease it out. We've been friends too long."

"I'm going to miss you, Tracey."

"We will still see each other and talk on the phone. I'll come to visit you, and you can come to stay some weekends with me. How did your assistant, Janice, take the news?"

"I didn't tell her what is really going on in my life. I just told her that my sister needs me to work with her. Now she

may start as an escrow officer instead of someone's assistant."
Wendy seemed to cheer up as she thought of her assistant and
how she'd mentored her and made a difference in someone's
life. "She's really good. I gave her a good reference."

Tracey and Wendy sat up and talked for hours, reminiscing
and crying about the good days and bad days they'd shared.
Suddenly Tracey felt as though everything around her was
falling apart. Her husband's death, Robin's problem, and now
Wendy, her close friend, was leaving her.

Tracey looked at her watch. "Girl, it's past twelve. I'd better get home and get some sleep. If you need to stay a few
nights before you leave, you are welcome. And, of course, we
are going to dinner, or maybe a movie or something before
you leave."

Wendy couldn't reply, but nodded her head in agreement.

She walked Tracey to the door, and they hugged again.
Tracey drove off, her heart so heavy and her eyes so full of
tears that she could hardly see her way home. And when she
got home and got in bed, it was impossible for her to get any
sleep. She lay in the dark with her eyes open. What a day it
had been!

"Tracey, Mr. Howard left a message for you," Michelle
said as she handed her the slip of paper. "He sounds nice on
the phone. Is he a client?"

"No, just someone that I know."

"Well, if that's the case why are your cheeks so rosy?"
she teased.

"It's really nothing. But he is a nice guy. How did your
exams go?"

"I think I passed. I studied half the night and every day
on my lunch break."

And then she saw an envelope that was from Travis. It
was a card, and when she read it, her heart started to beat
faster. *He seems to be a romantic man. Just what every
woman needs and wants. But, why me? Should I call him?*

she wondered. Tracey put the card in her desk drawer as her client was walking in the door. Michelle asked him if he wanted a cup of coffee or tea, but he refused.

Tracey extended her hand to the older man. "It's nice to meet you, Mr. Richardson. You said that you were referred by Julia White?"

"Yes, and she was very pleased with the way you do business, Mrs. Woods," he said and smiled. His hair was almost completely white and wavy. His eyes were light brown, his skin the color of light brown sugar. He was medium height, well dressed in a navy suit and light blue shirt. He looked to be in his sixties.

"Miss Woods, I have a thirty-unit apartment complex that I would like to sell. After I was referred to you, I found out that it was your husband that built it. Isn't that a coincidence?"

"Yes, Mr. Richardson, that is quite a coincidence. Where is it located?"

"West LA, in the Palms area."

"That was work he did before we met, but I know the ones you're speaking of."

"You know, I met your husband before. Nice fellow he was, real businessman, hard, but good. My wife was still alive at the time. She was with me when I met your late husband."

"Yes, he was that, too. He taught me a lot. Now, why don't I get a contract out, and we can get to work?" She couldn't bear to speak of Donald today. "I know someone who is looking for a large unit in that particular area. Will the appraiser contact you for access?"

"Yes, I'm always available. He can contact me anytime."

"Okay, Mr. Richardson," Tracey said, as she consulted her notes. "I'll take all the information I need to get started with and give you a call tomorrow after I have a talk with the client that may want to buy."

Mr. Richardson stood up. "I'll look forward to your call, Mrs. Woods."

* * *

It was three o'clock, and Tracey was still working. She thought of Mr. Richardson and smiled. He seemed to be a nice gentlemen. Without thinking, she pulled Travis's card out of the drawer again and read it, seeing his face float in front of her as she read. The phone rang and she was so surprised to hear Travis's voice that she could hardly speak. Talk about coincidences, this day was full of them.

"I received your beautiful card today, Travis," she smiled as she heard his smooth voice through the phone.

"I would love to see you tonight, Tracey."

"I'll be home by five."

"Okay, see you then."

She sat at her desk, savoring their conversation. She realized something. Travis had the same rich, deep voice Donald had possessed. But that's not why she felt herself tingling inside when she talked with him. Travis was Travis and Donald was Donald. The two men were so different.

"So, he's just a friend, huh?" Michelle interrupted her reverie with her teasing. "Your face is on fire, Tracey."

"Okay, okay, I like him a little. We had lunch together one day, and that's all."

"That was all, but it won't be all for long."

"What do you mean?" Tracey laughed.

"By the sound of your voice, the dreamy eyes. Must I go on?"

"Clean up and go home. You're finished here today."

Michelle laughed, and cleared her desk. "Have fun, Tracey," she said as she rushed out the door. Tracey put the files in the file cabinet and was locking the door when she heard the phone ring. She started not to answer, but decided that she should. *What if it's Aunt Flo?* she thought, racing back to her desk.

It was Travis. He asked if she wanted to go out for dinner since they had lunch at her house the last time they were together, and she accepted. Now she had to think of something to wear. She wanted to look fresh, not in a suit for a change.

It was four o'clock when she got home. Tracey went straight to her bedroom and opened her closet. She pulled out a red dress and held it against her in front of the mirror. It was too fancy. Next, she pulled out a pair of purple slacks and purple silk blouse. Better, she thought. She grabbed a shoebox with her purple pumps and took a quick shower. She had worn her hair up and decided to let it fall to her shoulders. After she was dressed she turned on the radio. Ten minutes later, her doorbell rang. She felt her stomach jump, and smiled, feeling like a sixteen-year-old going on her first date.

Tracey opened the door and smiled, and he looked at her from head to toe. He had one hand in back of him and when he stepped closer to her, he gave her a dozen roses.

"Thanks. They're beautiful, Travis."

"So are you, Tracey Woods," he said with a warm smile.

"Come in and have a seat. I'll put these in some water." She went to the kitchen while he walked around her living room looking at the African paintings on her walls and stopped in front of a portrait that was hanging over her fireplace. When she walked in, he turned to face her.

"Is this your family?" he asked standing in front of the picture.

"Yes, it's my aunt, my sister, and me, of course. I had it blown up as big as they could get it. I was only fourteen, Robin was sixteen."

"You haven't changed very much—just prettier."

She felt heat in her cheeks, but there wasn't anything she could do to stop it. She moistened her bottom lip. "Thank you."

"Are you ready?"

"Yes, I'm ready."

But, she wondered if she was really ready for this, for dating, for starting all over again.

After they got halfway to the restaurant Tracey started

to relax. She was beginning to enjoy talking to him, sitting near him in the same car, and anticipating the rest of the evening. She realized that she needed to get out and live it up for a change. The news of Wendy's departure had depressed her.

It was a beautiful night and they ended up in a restaurant in Malibu, off the coast. The restaurant was a two-story mansion, and they were seated on the second level. It was quiet and Travis asked for a window table facing the pier.

"How's your aunt?"

"She's feeling much better. No one has to stay with her every day anymore. I have a lady that comes in once a week. My sister and I still stop by and check on her. But, she's well. How's your mom?"

"The last three weeks, she's been having herself a ball. My brother and sister-in-law are in Miami on vacation with friends. My niece is staying with my mom."

"How nice. How old is your niece?"

"She's ten. My mother takes her someplace every day. Yesterday, it was Disneyland, the day before it was the movies. I had dinner with them last night. She's such a smart kid, and well trained, too. I think she reminds my mom of my sister." He stopped suddenly, wondering if he had said too much.

Tracey smiled. "I'm sure your mother will miss her when she leaves. Does she visit them often?"

"Not very often. Maybe twice a year. Usually they make a quick run here to see her. My brother comes more often since my dad died. And now he tries to get her to visit him more. She may after my niece leaves."

The waiter brought their food and a bottle of wine. Travis couldn't keep his eyes off Tracey.

The dinner went well and it was still early when Travis brought her home.

"Would you like to come in? It's still early."

"Yes, I'd love to. I'm not ready for this night to end," he said, following her inside.

"I have some wine, or would you like a cup of coffee?"

"Coffee, please. If it's no trouble, that is."

"Good, I'd rather have coffee, too." She went into the kitchen, and she came back into the living room. He was looking through a stack of CDs and handed her the one by Barry White.

"So, you like him, too?" she said and looked up at him and smiled.

"Love him," he answered.

"Well, I'll play it." She put the tray on the coffee table and played the CD.

The music was soft and slow. When he held out his hand, she followed him to the middle of the floor and fell into step with him as he held her close. As he felt the heat from her body rise he held her even closer. He kissed her. She returned his kiss by wrapping her arms around his neck. All the frustration she had held inside about Wendy leaving and dealing with Donald's death began to slowly disappear. It was replaced with a desire that she had never felt before, a desire that burned deep in her heart. She felt weak and leaned all her weight against his strong, hard body.

While they were dancing, Travis felt he could explode. All night he had been watching her closely. She was sculpted like a goddess, beautifully curved, and her brown skin looked as smooth as silk. Her exotic eyes and the scent of her perfume were driving him crazy. She was simply irresistible.

If Travis had held her a minute longer, he would have had to take her to bed. But, he didn't want to ruin their relationship and frighten her away. After all, they hadn't met on good terms. His sister was "the other woman," and he could see by the expression on Tracey's face when he said her name that she hadn't forgotten. He sighed and gently pulled away from her. She opened her eyes and looked at him questioningly.

"I need you, but not now, not like this," he whispered. She nodded her head and pressed it against his chest. They stood there just holding each other, not speaking. Travis took her hand and walked to the door.

"I had a great time, and I would like to see more of you," he said still holding her hand. "I think you know how I feel about you, Tracey." He cupped her face in his hands and kissed her tenderly. "I sure wish we could have met under different circumstances."

"I'm still trying to find a way to handle it. It's not our fault, we just fell in the middle of it."

"I know, Love. But, remember what you just said, 'It's not our fault.'" He walked out the door.

Tracey sat on the couch and closed her eyes.

Couldn't he say anything without that sister of his coming out of his mouth? Would she eventually get used to it? Travis loved his sister and she couldn't ask him to never mention her again. That wouldn't be fair, she knew.

But was it fair that she had to be reminded of Susan's and Donald's infidelity every time they saw each other? She wasn't even sure if she should see him again. She needed a fresh start, not someone to remind her of a painful past. She turned out the lights and went to bed.

She lay awake in the dark and jumped when the phone rang. She looked at the clock beside her bed, but it was only nine.

"Hello," she answered.

"Hi, Tracey, were you asleep?"

"No, I wasn't asleep, Robin."

"I was thinking of dropping by for a while tomorrow. That's if you're not working at home tomorrow evening. You know how hard you work, girl."

"I should be home tomorrow around four. Come on by."

The next day, Tracey and Robin drove up at the same time. Tracey got out of her car and unlocked the door. "Come on in."

Robin came in and placed her jacket across the arm of

the couch. She walked around and looked at the paintings on the walls.

"I'll be right back. Make yourself at home."

When Tracey returned, she had changed clothes. "We haven't had a chance to talk since we met with Fred. Are you all right?"

"I'm coping the best I can. He calls me at home now. It's getting to be a nightmare, Tracey. He leaves me messages on my phone at work, telling me how unfair I am and how much he loves me, how he envisions me naked in front of him, and then he goes on to tell me all the things he wants to do to me. Girl, can you imagine anyone leaving a message like that at your place of business? I can't take this shit much longer."

"Fred called me this morning. He says by the end of the week, he should have enough to run that silly ass idiot to San Francisco."

"End of the week? I can't wait until the end of the week, Tracey," Robin said, looking frightened.

"Okay, okay, Robin. I'll give him a call again tonight and see how much faster he can do this," she said with a worried look. "How is John? He doesn't suspect anything does he?"

They were sitting in the den, and Tracey was facing Robin as she sat on the edge of a chair holding a Coke in her hand.

"He's all right. He thinks I'm stressed out because of my job. Anyway, I stopped by Aunt Flo's before I got here. She says that Stella will be over tomorrow." Robin grabbed her purse and pulled out her checkbook. "I forgot to leave a check with Aunt Flo. It's my week to pay Stella. Aunt Flo really enjoys having her over."

"I'm going to stop and see her on my way to the office tomorrow. I'll take the check with me. Now, when can my niece come over and spend the night with me?"

Robin smiled. "She asked the same thing when I told her you were home last night." Robin got up and picked up the Barry White CD. "This is a good one. You were playing music last night?"

"Yes, Travis and I went to dinner and came back here."

"Travis—that woman's brother?" she asked, lifting her eyebrows the way she did whenever she didn't think something was proper etiquette.

Tracey rolled her eyes up at the ceiling. "Do you have to say 'that woman's brother'? Just say, Travis, please."

"I'm sorry, Tracey. But, it's just the circumstances under which you two met. I'll never forget that night. Doesn't being with him make you remember it?"

"Yes, and no. It's not something that I would like to remember. Hell, I'm still trying to forget, but he's a nice man, Robin. Sometimes when I'm with him—well actually it's only been three times—I forget for a while."

"But, Tracey, you shouldn't have to have someone to make you remember. You need someone to make you forget."

"I like him, Robin," she said with a straight face. "I like the man. What can I say?" She was getting exasperated with the conversation.

"Okay, Tracey. I just want you to be happy. Don't be foolish like me," Robin said and touched Tracey's hand.

"Don't worry, I won't." They both laughed.

"Okay, I deserved that one." Robin looked at her watch. "I better get home before John calls to see if I've left already."

Tracey walked her outside. "Have you talked to Wendy, today?"

"No, but, I'll call her later."

"Poor thing. Maybe she needs to go home and get a fresh start."

Robin drove off and Tracey walked back inside, changed into a long green bathrobe, and curled up in her large chair in the den to watch the news. She was tired and had had a long day. She closed her eyes and fell asleep in the chair.

Travis was sitting alone in the hospital cafeteria when Sharon took a seat next to him. Sharon was sixty-five and ready to retire from nursing. She had worked with Travis's father and now with Travis.

"I noticed you've been awfully quiet today," Sharon said, sitting down at his table. "Penny for your thoughts, good-looking?"

He looked at her and smiled. She always made him laugh and he could talk to her. It was odd the way she sensed his moods. He suspected that she was once in love with his father from a conversation they had when they first became friends.

"I'm not thinking about much, Sharon, just tired today, that's all. It's been a busy morning, wouldn't you say?"

"Yes, but we've had them before," she answered, looking at him with her glasses resting on her nose. "So, what makes this one so different?"

"It's just the Brown girl that I bandaged up today. I don't believe for a minute that she fell and broke her arm again."

"I don't either, but believe me, honey, Dana in Social Services will get to the bottom of this. She always does. Now, what else has you in such a blue mood?" She put her coffee cup down and waited for him to answer.

He looked at her and smiled again. She reminded him of his mother in some ways. The way she wore her hair up in back, her wise eyes that were never fooled. "I was thinking about a girl I met."

Sharon took her glasses off and laid them on the table. "Well, why are you looking so sad about it, baby?" she asked in a most serious voice, but wanted to laugh because he always got whatever nurse he wanted. Now, it seemed that the table had turned for Travis Howard.

He folded his hands in front of him and smiled at the doctor who passed their table. "She doesn't feel the same as I do, Sharon."

"How do you know? Have you asked her already?"

"No, for the first time I'm afraid to ask." He moved around in his chair and sighed in annoyance and Sharon looked as if she didn't quite understand.

"She's so independent, so unreachable, and it's hard to

know what she is feeling. I mean, I know she likes me, but that's not enough."

"Is that all?" she asked.

"No, not quite. Her husband was killed in a car accident. She found out that he was cheating on her with my sister. That was how we met."

Sharon rubbed her tired eyes. "Now that's deep, really deep, but with love and understanding, it can be forgotten. It may just take a little time, Travis. Don't give it up."

"That's what I keep telling myself. She's so pretty, Sharon, and so smart. She's kind and considerate. Everything that I want in a woman."

"I can see that," she mused. "And there's still no reason to sit around and look sad about it. Is she pleasant when you two are together?"

"Very. But, she wasn't comfortable at first. The last time we saw each other she was very pleasant." He remembered the kiss between them. Travis looked at his watch. "We'd better get back." As they walked out of the cafeteria, a pretty young nurse smiled at him.

"Now, that one's been hot in the pants for you for some time now."

"I know. But I know who I want."

Seventeen

"What's wrong, John?" Robin asked, as she walked in the door. John slammed the receiver down hard and cursed. He stood facing Robin, one hand in his pocket.

"Some damn pervert has called for the second time. Every time I answer he tells me my wife wears black panties, or that she's good in bed. People are sick these days, Robin."

Robin glanced at John. He twisted his mouth and wrinkled his nose as if he'd tasted something bitter.

"I just don't want Lisa to answer. He's just sick enough to say something dirty to her."

Robin felt faint and shuddered with fear as she thought of Paul's derisive sneer at their last luncheon. He really did plan to make her pay. "What else did he say?" she asked as she sat on the arm of the sofa for support. Lifting her eyebrow, she tried to freeze her features into a casually indifferent look. Did John suspect that this man knew what he was talking about? Oh Lord. What was she going to do if John found out? Should she tell him?

Tracey's admonishment returned to her. *Don't get stupid, now.* No, Tracey was right. She'd better not confess to John. Some things had to be carried to the grave. Committing adultery was one such thing.

"Believe me. You don't want to know. That bastard is sick and he has a dirty mouth."

"He didn't give his name? Maybe we can have our number changed," Robin said, trying to keep her hands from trembling.

"You know, I was surprised when he mentioned his name. He said it was Paul. If he calls again I'll have the number changed tomorrow. Now, don't worry about it, Robin. Go change clothes and eat dinner." John kissed his wife on her forehead and went to the kitchen. "I bought some pizza on the way home. Lisa and I ate already."

Robin watched John's retreating back. He seemed to not be suspicious of her. Well, why should he be? In fifteen years of marriage, she'd never given him any reason to distrust him.

She went to the bathroom and sat on the side of the tub, with tears streaming down her face. She felt as if Paul was closing in on her and she didn't know what to do about it. She would call Tracey tomorrow and tell her that they had to work with whatever Fred has found out. She couldn't wait any longer. Time was running out. . . .

Robin was approving the new loan program that the bank had to offer when Paul walked in and took a seat at her desk. She looked up and dropped her pen on the desk.

"How dare you call my house. What if my daughter had answered? What if there's a tape playing here while you're talking dirty on the phone?" Her eyes squinted in rage and she curled her lips into a snarl. She tried not to get loud or draw attention to her office, but still she wanted Paul to know his behavior was reprehensible and had to stop.

"Don't get so sanctimonious with me. It's time your daughter got to know me, Robin. But, I would have never said anything to her like I had said to your husband." He paused, closed his eyes as if he could feel her, and licked his lips in a suggestive manner. "Besides, your husband knows how good you feel." And he paused again, remembering how good she felt.

Robin swiveled around in her chair. The side of her office was all glass. She was getting panicky and looked around to see if anyone was watching them.

"What do you mean it's time she got to know you? I want you out of my life, Paul. What will it take to convince you of that?" she asked with tears in her eyes. She was so tired of fighting with him. So tired of jumping every time her phone rang at her house. And so afraid that one day John would find out she had cheated on him.

Paul pulled his chair closer to her desk. Robin looked around to see if anyone in the office was watching, or could see how upset she was.

"I love you, Robin," he whispered as he stared at her breasts. "I need to be alone with you—to feel you under me. . . ."

Robin jumped from her chair and ran to the restroom. She washed her face in cold water and looked in the mirror. She had dark circles under her eyes. Her face appeared thin and gaunt.

"Robin, are you all right?" asked Latasha, one of the loan processors.

"Yes. Thank you. I think I ate something that made me ill. I'll be just fine in a little while." Latasha walked out of the bathroom and left Robin alone. She wiped her face before anyone walked in on her again. *How long will I be able to take any more of this,* she wondered, and felt as if she was on the edge of cracking up.

She went back to her desk, but Paul had left. He was nowhere in the office. Maybe he had left for the rest of the day.

Robin tried to keep her mind on her work, but to no avail. Her stomach was upset and she tried to stop her fingers from quivering every time the door to her office opened. She couldn't concentrate and when she looked at the clock thirty minutes later she hadn't accomplished anything since morning.

Robin picked up the phone. "Latasha, I'm going to lunch. Please be sure and take a message if my sister calls."

She had no idea where she was going, but she needed some air. She needed time to herself to think and she still hadn't heard any word from Fred.

* * *

"Robin, where have you been, Girl?" She looked around, surprised to see Larry.

"Larry? I can't believe it's you. I haven seen you in about five years now. What's going on in your life?" Looking at Larry, a former classmate, she noticed that he had aged tremendously. Even though he wore a pair of dark glasses, she could see the lines of dissipation gouged in his skin. The last time she heard about him he was on drugs and had gone to jail.

"What's going on in your life, baby? And why are you standing in front of a pawnshop like you don't know where you're at?" he asked, staring her up and down. "You looking good, too, baby."

Robin didn't know how to ask him, but she had to. "I need a gun, Larry. Do pawnshops carry guns? I mean, is it easier to buy one at a pawnshop than it is at a gun store?"

Larry eyed her long and hard. "What do you need a gun for, Robin? Oh, don't tell me your old man is playing around with some chick and you want to shoot her?"

"Boy, no. I just thought I would get one for protection, that's all."

"Yeah, right. But, you came to the right place. My cousin owns this place and I can talk him into helping you," he asked, looking at her as if he was undressing her. "Now, what's in it for me?" He peered over his sunglasses in a lascivious manner.

"I can pay you extra, Larry. I need a gun right now."

"Right now, you say?"

"Yes, Larry. Now, are you going to help me or not?" she snapped, and looked at her watch as if she was getting impatient. "I've got to get back to my office. And it ain't that kind of party, here."

"Okay, okay. Hold on baby. I'll hook you up." He crooked his finger for Robin to follow him inside. "You know Old Larry will help you."

Robin followed him inside the pawnshop. The man behind the counter was huge. A cigar dangled dangerously out of the corner of his mouth. The cigar smoke made her stomach quiver. She paid Larry one hundred dollars and gave the man one hundred dollars for selling it with no questions asked. Larry strutted alongside her when she walked out, but she scurried away from him as fast as she could.

Robin went back to work and locked the gun in her car. As she was closing the door Paul walked up in back of her and put his arms around her waist. She jumped.

"What in hell are you doing? Don't you realize someone could have easily seen you?"

"I don't really care what anyone thinks, Robin. And anyway, where have you been?"

"That's my business, Paul." she said with a confidence that he hadn't seen in her before. He grabbed her arm but she shook loose and gave herself some distance between them. And then she remembered the gun and started to unlock the door.

"Hi, Robin, Paul." Robin jumped and turned around to see Latasha smiling at her as she walked past them. *Lord, what had just come over her.*

Robin pulled the key out of the door. She had never believed in carrying a gun and would never let John have one in the house. What had she become? She had to protect her family, had to protect herself, and she was now afraid of her own shadow.

"I said none of your business. Go away, Paul. Go to San Francisco before someone gets hurt," she shouted, with a flick of her wrist—a wave of dismissal that was so direct and so uncompromising that Paul just stood there looking after her.

Paul was dumbfounded. It was as though she was no longer afraid of him and he didn't like it. He was in control of their relationship and he didn't want to have to prove it to her by hurting her like he had the others. The last few days he had been following her, but today she left the office before he returned and he had missed her. In the end he knew that he would have her. He just needed a chance to catch her alone where no one would see. He was in control and would have his chance, soon. This week, he had made plans. By Friday, he and Robin would be in San Francisco.

The next afternoon Robin met Fred at Tracey's office. Michelle had left early for the day since she had final exams. Robin started to take the gun out of the trunk of her car. No, she didn't need it yet. But she knew that soon she would. She stood at the door of Tracey's office to make sure Paul hadn't followed her. She couldn't trust him any longer.

When Robin walked in, Tracey was sitting at a small round table looking over some papers with Fred.

Tracey looked up. "Looks like we have something."

"Hi, Fred. It sure is good to see you," Robin said.

"How's it going, kid. You look tired."

"I am. I even bought myself a gun yesterday."

Tracey jumped from her desk. "Are you crazy? You may shoot the wrong person with that thing. Where is it now?" she asked in horror.

"It's in my car. Don't worry. I don't carry it on me."

"Is it getting that bad?" Fred asked.

"Yes. You don't know just how bad. I think he has something on his mind. He even called and talk to John on the phone."

"Oh, Lord. What did he say, Robin?" Tracey asked.

"John says he did a lot of dirty talking. But he never did connect the two of us together," Robin said and sighed. She took a seat at the table with Tracey and Fred.

"He owes over one hundred fifty thousand dollars in child support payments. And he's also wanted for beating a woman in Washington, and he lied on his application of employment. I called the lady that he beat up and she's going to turn him in to the authorities now that she knows where he is." Fred beamed as though he was proud of his job. He continued, "She says he stole seventy-five thousand from her and she knows someone who will testify on her behalf. I should be getting a call soon. The cops are following him, so he'll be picked up any minute and taken to jail."

"I hope he gets what he deserves. For the last few weeks I've been going through hell," Robin said.

"He's a *scary man*," Tracey said. "He needs to be locked up. And Robin, you can take that gun back."

"Not until I know he's locked up and gone for good."

"They will arrest him now that the criminal check has revealed outstanding warrants. Well that wraps this case up," Fred said, interrupting Robin. He picked up his briefcase as he got up to leave.

Tracey walked Fred and Robin out the door.

Robin hugged Fred. "I appreciate everything you've done for me Fred—"

"You two-timing bitch! Take your hands off that man."

Suddenly, they heard a man's voice and all three looked across the street. The man was running across the street with something in his hand, waving it in the air.

"Oh my God, it's Paul! He must have followed me and my gun is in the car!" Robin yelled.

"What's in his hand?" Tracey shouted with fear in her voice. The high noon sun was too bright and Tracey couldn't see clearly. She squinted, using her palms to shield her eyes from the sun's glare.

Suddenly, a metallic glint flashed in the sunlight.

"My God, he has a gun," Tracey screamed hysterically.

Paul was in the middle of the street, brandishing a gun. He pointed it in Robin's direction. Tracey screamed and grabbed her sister by her arm. She pushed her to the pavement and covered her with her body.

* * *

At first, Paul was planning to take Robin away with him, but after he saw her with another man he decided to kill her. *How dare that bitch play him for a fool?* She was cheating on him with another man. So that's why she left her house so early this morning.

Infuriated, he took aim and fired. The gun went off but he missed, and before he had a chance to shoot again, he heard a siren, and a voice shouting for him to drop the gun.

"I said drop the gun. . . ."

Paul looked at Robin, then stopped for a few seconds and looked in back of him, the gun still in his hand. He saw two police officers with their guns pointed at him. The siren stopped, and two more policemen jumping out of the black-and-white squad car were also pulling out their guns. He looked at Robin again and pointed his gun at her.

Robin heard voices that seemed far away, but at the same time sounded so close. She heard the gunshots. Everyone seemed to be moving in slow motion. Suddenly, Paul's body dropped slowly to the ground as bullets tore into his chest. Tracey's hands were covering her face, and Fred was covering both of them with his body. All three were on the ground, waiting, waiting.

Finally, Tracey and Robin looked at each other to see if one of them was hit, but no one was. The gun was on the ground just two feet away from Paul's body.

Robin became hysterical, crying, pointing, jabbering in senseless language.

"Get hold of yourself, Robin," Tracey said as she and Fred pulled her into Tracey's office. "You've got to get a hold of yourself and go back to your office even if it's just for a while."

"I can't leave him here," Robin sobbed. Suddenly she felt sorry for him.

The police had shot him repeatedly. His bullet-riddled body looked like a punched-out, bloody dummy. Blood ran from the sidewalk into the streets, where his body was slumped.

"Oh yes the hell you can, and you will. The paramedics are already on the way. I can hear them. He's not your responsibility." Tracey spun her around and looked directly in her sister's eyes. Robin was too hysterical to think clearly.

"Didn't he try to shoot you? Nobody knows that he was shouting at you. For all we know, he's a stranger. He could have been shouting at anyone." She shook Robin hard. "Pull yourself together, girl."

"She's right, Robin. You have to go back to your office and act as if you know nothing about this. When you get the news, of course you will be as shocked as everyone in the office. Look at it like this. He solved your problem."

Robin looked at Fred as if she couldn't believe what he was saying. *Paul was dead. Didn't anyone care?*

"I know how cold it seems, but remember, he was going to kill you," Fred said.

"You're right, I know. I just hate it had to happen this way," Robin said, holding her face in her hands and sobbing. "I just need a minute to wash my face in cold water." She went to the rest room and Fred was standing at the window. People were standing in the streets as Paul's body was being carried away.

"His face was covered, he must be dead," Tracey said, looking at Fred.

Fred shook his head in disgust. "It looks that way. He's been a dog, and this is a case of comeuppance."

Relieved, Robin walked back in. "I don't think that I can go back to the office. I'd better go home. This is just too much for me." She slumped down in the chair again. "I feel ill. I didn't think it would have ended this way." She looked up somberly at Fred. "Why didn't he listen to me?" she asked as if she was waiting for an answer. But no one had one for her.

"I'll tell you what was too much for me. Not knowing who was going to get the bullet was too much!" Tracey said, throwing her hands in the air. Tracey walked over to a cabinet and pulled out a bottle of brandy and three glasses.

"Just what we need to calm our nerves," Fred said, as he handed a glass to Robin. She took a long swallow and sighed, wiping the tears from her eyes.

Robin put the glass down and picked up her keys and purse. Tracey stood in front of her.

"Perhaps you need to go home and get some rest, Robin."

"I'm going out to talk to the police," Fred said, as he set the glass on Tracey's desk. "We don't want them questioning Robin. I'll do everything I can to keep her out of it."

"Please do what you can, Fred," Tracey said.

Tracey stood in front of Robin. "You need to go home and get yourself together, Robin, before John or Lisa gets home."

Robin held her head down. "I know. I need the rest of this day to myself."

"Are you sure that you can drive?" Tracey asked with concern.

"Yes." She held her hands in front of her. "No. My hands are shaking."

"I'll drive you." Tracey turned off the coffeemaker and took Robin's arm to lead her outside.

"No, Tracey," Fred spoke up. "You drive your sister's car, and I'll follow you in my car and bring you back to your office. Give me a few minutes to talk to the police officers and we can leave."

"Thanks Fred. We'll wait in here."

Eighteen

It was Saturday morning and Tracey was leaving the mall after doing some shopping to decorate the second bathroom in her house. She was dressed in blue jeans and a white shirt. It had rained earlier, and the dampness lingered; the air was raw on this chilly Saturday afternoon in March. The sky was overcast and a drab gray. She was walking to her car when she heard a man's voice calling her name. She looked around and saw that it was John carrying two bags from Macy's.

"What are you doing out here?" she asked him.

"Well, Robin and Lisa left the house early, so I decided to do some shopping for myself. Here, let me hold your bags while you open the trunk."

She gave him her large bags. He helped her arrange them in the trunk.

"Thanks, they were heavy."

"You can say that again. You women shop like the stores are going out of business."

"No, not all the time." John held the car door while she got in and fastened her seat belt.

"Tracey?"

"Yes, John, what is it?" she asked cautiously.

"I know that you and Robin are pretty close. One of her employees died, and she's been a little under the weather. At first, I thought her new position was too stressful, but I'm sure it's the death of the guy that she worked with."

Tracey studied John closely to see if he suspected what the truth was. She didn't say anything and held her breath.

John continued, "I realize that I acted like a jerk when she was first promoted and I'm doing all I can to make it up to her. Robin and Lisa mean everything to me, Tracey. Has she said anything to you?"

"Everyone takes death differently, John. She hasn't really said much to me about it. She did mention that a guy had died." Tracey tried to hide her sense of relief. "I'll tell you what. I'll call her and Aunt Flo and have everyone over for dinner at my house tomorrow. We can laugh and talk the way we used to. We haven't had dinner together since Donald's death. We need to get together and have a good time."

"That sounds great. And don't forget to fry some chicken, too."

"I won't. I know you love fried chicken. Tell Robin that you ran into me, and I invited you guys over for dinner tomorrow. I'll call her when I get home."

"Thanks, Tracey. Maybe she'll feel better."

"She will, John."

Tracey drove off and turned into Lucky's Market in Culver City to shop for Sunday's dinner. She decided that she would get Robin in the kitchen with her and talk to her. She had to go on with her life and stop blaming herself for Paul's death.

On Sunday, Tracey had a glass of wine as she cooked dinner. It was odd, but she was in a melancholy mood. Or was it so odd these days? The last time she'd had her family over for dinner was the day that Donald died.

She played some jazz, which usually uplifted her and had another glass of wine. Nothing seemed to help her mood, which matched the cloudy weather outside her kitchen windows. She looked at her watch, and it was almost two. They would be arriving any minute, she thought.

She went to the living room and back to the kitchen to

check and see if everything was all right. The fried chicken was a golden brown, the greens and candied yams were all ready, and she'd even gone to Marie Callender's in Marina Del Rey and bought a lemon pie, Lisa's favorite.

As she walked out of the kitchen, she wiped a tear from her eyes. "Good job, Tracey," she whispered. She was supposed to make Robin feel better and she'd put herself in just as blue a mood as her sister's. She slumped down on the couch and jumped when the phone rang. She sighed, wondering who it was. When she answered, Travis's voice was like music to her ears.

"I'm just waiting for my family to come over for dinner. Oh no, it's not a bad time. Actually, it's a good time. Your day off and you have nothing to do?" She smiled as he talked to her. "Why don't you join us? Sure, it'll be fun."

She hung up, not entirely sure why she felt so nervous when she heard his voice. Well, everyone would be surprised. When Robin saw him, she'd be so surprised that she may even forget her own problems, she thought as she laughed at the idea. She picked up the crystal decanter and put it down again. She didn't need any more wine.

The doorbell rang, and Lisa and her friend, Karen, were the first to come in. She kissed Tracey on the cheek.

Robin's face looked gaunt; she'd lost almost fifteen pounds in a month. Aunt Flo's coloring was coming back.

"You look very nice today, Aunt Flo. Come and sit in my big leather chair so you can be comfortable." Flora followed Tracey to the den and everyone else went along, too.

"You mind if I turn your television on to see some sports?" John asked.

"No, of course not. In a few minutes, you will have a gentlemen here to watch some sports on television with you." That got everyone's attention.

"Who's coming over?" Robin asked in surprise.

"Travis. I told you about him," Tracey answered.

"And he's coming over to meet the family?"

"No, Robin. He called and I invited him to come for dinner. I told you that we're friends."

John and Flora looked from Tracey to Robin.

"Well, who is this man?" Flora asked.

"His sister is the woman that Donald was with at the time of the accident, and we have become friends, Aunt Flo." Tracey waited for a reaction. For a moment, the room was silent. Everyone seemed to stop whatever they were doing and the only sound was their breathing.

Flora waved her hand. "Honey, I guess there's nothing wrong with that. He doesn't have to be a bad person because of Donald's and his sister's mistake. Now, Lisa, go and get me a glass of water."

"Okay, Aunt Flo."

"Aunt Tracey, do you have anything else to drink?" Lisa asked.

"Get a can of punch for you and Karen. It should be cold enough by now. John, would you like a glass of wine?"

"Sure."

"I'll get it, Tracey." Robin poured a glass for John and one for herself. Tracey started back into the kitchen but heard the doorbell and turned around. "All right everyone, he's here," she said as she walked toward the door.

When Travis stepped into the den he was exactly as Robin remembered: tall, well dressed, and serene. Tracey introduced him and John shook his hand.

"This is my Aunt Flora, and you've met Robin, already."

"Nice to meet you, Miss Flora. And yes, Robin and I have met."

He sensed that Robin was embarrassed about their exchange during their first meeting. That night at the hospital was uncomfortable for everyone.

John and Travis started to talk about sports, and Flora was laughing and talking with them while Tracey and Robin went to finish in the kitchen. Robin set the table while Tracey baked the cornbread.

"Looks like John likes him, Tracey," Robin commented,

watching the two men in the den. Tracey had had the wall knocked out between the kitchen and the dining room and den, and the house had a spacious, airy design.

"Yes, they do seem to be enjoying each other's company, not to mention Aunt Flo. She hasn't stopped talking since Travis got here. But, it seems strange that he's here with the family."

"If he was another date, would it seem strange to you?"

"I don't know, Robin. It seems strange that I even have a date. I was glad when he called." Tracey picked up a potholder and took the cornbread out of the oven.

"Are you all right, Robin?"

"Sometimes I am, and sometimes I can see the police shooting Paul just like it was yesterday. I'm trying so hard to live with it and act natural around John."

"You had better try a little harder."

Robin put her glass on the sink. "What do you mean?"

"I'm having this dinner because John is concerned about you. I ran into him at Manhattan Beach Mall yesterday. But don't tell him that I told you that he's worried about you."

Robin sighed. "Guess I'll have to try harder. I didn't think he had noticed."

"It's over, Robin. Let it go. Pray, do whatever you have to, but let it go." Tracey took Robin's hand and talked to her as though she was the big sister. "No one forced anyone to do anything they didn't want to. It's not your fault that he went crazy. He was already crazy, Robin. He didn't just get crazy when he met you." Lisa walked in and they changed the conversation.

"I think the men are getting hungry, Tracey."

"I'll take this vegetable tray out. You know Aunt Flo loves that. And hand me those crackers on the table."

"I'll take them," Robin said. "We better go back before they wonder what we're doing in here."

"Yes, and I want Travis to feel comfortable, too. After all, he hasn't been around my family before. We've only been together three times."

"And he already wanted to meet your family? You'd better watch out, Tracey. You may have another husband soon," Robin joked.

Tracey fluffed her hair. "Come on, girl. Where do you get such crazy ideas?"

They went to the den and Tracey took a seat on the couch next to Travis. He gave her a conspiratorial smile, and she blushed all over. He had such chiseled good looks and a distinct cleft chin that almost took her breath away. She looked at Aunt Flo and was sure that Flora knew what she was thinking.

Dinner went well, and Tracey was amazed at how comfortable it was for everyone. Flora and Travis talked about his family and childhood and everyone listened with interest.

John looked at his watch. "It's past six, we'd better get ready to go home, Robin."

"Yes, we were up late last night watching television and got up early this morning."

John shook Travis's hand. "It was nice meeting you, man. Hope we do this again."

"I hope so, too, man," Travis said and smiled. He helped Flora put on her coat and walked her to the door where they said their good-byes. Tracey and Travis went back to the den and sat on the couch.

"You have a nice family, Tracey, and I had a nice day," he said, kissing her on the cheek.

"I'm really glad that you called me." They were sitting close together on the den's sofa when he took her hand in his. Before she realized it, their lips had met and he kissed her so tenderly that she felt as if she were dreaming. She wrapped her arms around his neck, feeling the need to be held. Tracey felt dizzy as he kissed her again and again. She felt the need to be close to him, to feel wanted, and she was surprised at how much she really needed him, wanted him.

"Do you realize how I feel about you?" he whispered near her ear.

She kept her eyes closed, her arms around his neck. "Yes, I think so."

"Love me back, Tracey," he whispered.

"I want to, I mean, I do . . ." Tracey murmured. "But, I'm so afraid to let go and love again."

"Don't be afraid of me. Trust me. Love me." Travis hands gently massaged the small of her back as he kissed her down her neck. "Let me show you what it is to really be loved by a man, a man that you can trust your life with. Love me, Tracey," he whispered over and over.

Her skin felt like it was on fire, and she wanted him. She knew that deep in her heart, she loved him. He got up and pulled her up with him and she followed him to the door of the den, then she led him to her bedroom.

Travis held her against the bedroom door and kissed her until she felt weak with a desire so strong that she couldn't control it, and didn't want to. Her heart ached to be touched by him. She arched and pressed her body into his. Slowly, almost like an underwater ballet, she felt her blouse fall from her arms, then her bra and slip fell to the floor.

He lay her on the bed, gently pulling her skirt off. She lay there, unable to move as she watched him undress. Terrifying thoughts spun around in her head. *What are you doing? You don't want to get hurt again.* But, at the same time, her body ached inside. *I need him, I want him.*

Travis never took his eyes off her. He lay next to her and kissed her beautiful, satin brown shoulders, her neck, and lips. He gently cupped her breasts and kissed them until she was under him. When she felt his hot tongue against her stomach, she moaned and pulled him closer, feeling the length of his long, hard body covering hers. Her soul and body opened up for him, welcoming him, touching him. He took such insatiable pleasure in it.

Making love with Travis was better than she had ever remembered. Slowly, he raised her higher into a blue sky which opposed the gray one outside. Her soul felt replenished. When they reached the height of their passion at the

same time, they simultaneously cried out each other's name.
Spent, they fell asleep in each other's arms.

The next morning she opened her eyes and he was there,
holding her in his arms.

"Did you sleep well, love?" he whispered in her ear.

"Yes, very well." She kissed his hairy chest.

"Are you still afraid, Tracey?"

For a second she didn't say anything, and then she looked
him in the face and smiled. "Yes, but I'm willing to take the
chance and see how it works out."

"That's fair enough. I won't disappoint you and soon you
won't be afraid any longer," he said and looked at the clock
on the nightstand. It was five-thirty.

"Are you on duty today?"

"No, but I know that you have to go to your office."

"Not really. My receptionist won't be in because she has
a class that will last all day. I was planning on staying in
today, but I wasn't sure what I would do at home all day."

He held her close. "I'll give you something to do," he
whispered kissing her again until she climbed on top of
him. They made love until they were out of breath. They
lay in bed and talked about their lives. She talked about
her marriage and he talked about his, which hadn't lasted
long. Travis told her that he wanted to take her to meet
his mother, but he didn't want to take her too fast. Being
together was more than she had dared imagine.

At noon, they took a shower together, and Tracey made
lunch. The weather was cloudy, and they stayed inside until
he left her at five that evening.

After Travis left, Tracey changed into her long green
bathrobe and curled up in the large leather chair with a book.
She read, but his face kept appearing in front of her. She lay
back and closed her eyes, but when she thought of Donald
and Susan, Travis's sister, her eyes opened. She sighed in frustration. Tracey closed her eyes again, her set features relaxing.

"Some day I'll stop thinking of them, and at least then, it
won't hurt," she spoke out loud. She cared about Travis,

maybe even loved him. And she knew she had to forget about his sister, stop wondering if her husband had really loved her, or if he would have left her to marry Susan. If she and Travis were to have any chance at happiness, she had to forget. The phone rang and broke her train of thought. She welcomed the interruption.

"Tracey, what's going on?" Wendy asked.

"What's going on with you? I was going to call you this week."

"I'm all right. Oh hell, no I'm not, at least not yet. I miss LA, and I miss talking with you when I'm feeling low. But I can live with it. My family is treating me wonderfully. They are so happy I'm home to stay."

"You have to give yourself time, Wendy. You've only been home three weeks."

"I know, and being around family and old friends seems to help take my mind off William."

"Did you start working last week?"

"Yes, I started right on schedule. My sister thought I should take it easy for a while. But I wanted to get started right away. If you want to start new, why wait? Damn, I wish I was there."

"Oh, Wendy. Listen to me. You have to stop feeling that way." Tracey stood up and walked about as she talked, the phone propped between her ear and her shoulder. "After awhile you'll wonder why it took you so long to go back home to your family. You had no family here, except me," Tracey said.

"I guess you're right. You were my family, Tracey. When are you coming to visit me?"

"Soon, real soon. I just have to close the deals that I'm working on. And remember, you always have a place here, too."

"I know. I really needed to hear your voice. We've been friends for so long."

"Always will be, girl. Just call anytime you need to talk. You know where to find me." They hung up.

Tracey wanted to tell her about Travis but decided to wait until Wendy felt better. She turned off the lights and went to bed. But once she had covered herself with the blanket, she could still smell his cologne and it made her long for him.

Two days later, Travis and Sharon had lunch in the cafeteria together.

"Dr. Howard, you seem to be full of smiles today. What happened while you were off? You've even got a spring in your step now."

"I saved a life today, Sharon. That's enough to make me happy."

"Is it? It wasn't two days ago. Don't you know that I know you better than that? I knew your father and I know you," she smiled and looked suspiciously at him.

Travis grinned and took a bite out of his turkey sandwich. "All right. I got my girl. I told you I would, didn't I?"

"You sure did. Has your mother met her, yet?"

"No. I don't want to take her too soon. Besides, my mother doesn't know that she's the widow of my sister's lover." He paused when he saw Sharon's confused look. "The problem is that I didn't even tell her he was a married man. My sister told me he was divorced. She didn't tell me he hadn't even told his wife that he was leaving her. She didn't tell me the whole story about their relationship." He put his sandwich down as though he had lost his appetite. "I just can't tell my mother about it. It would hurt her deeply to know my sister was involved with a married man. You know, Sharon, after I met Tracey, I realized that he had no intention of leaving her for my sister."

"How do you know that?"

"Because Tracey had no idea that he was cheating on her. The day of the accident, she was home hosting a dinner party for their anniversary. And he was trying to get home to be with his wife." He pounded his fist on the table and sucked his teeth. "Now, how can I tell my mother that?"

"If you and this woman get really involved, will she tell your mother?"

"I don't know. I just don't know. She may think that by not telling her I'm making my sister out to be a saint." Travis put his elbows on the table and put his head down in his hands. He was in a moral quandary. He went on. "And she may not ever believe my sister was a good person who just fell in love with the wrong man. She was a good woman, Sharon."

"I know she was. Besides, your girl may fall so much in love with you that it may not matter if your mother knows or not."

"That's what I'm hoping for. I want to marry her, but I haven't told her, yet. I met her family last Sunday."

"Oh, and how were they?"

"Nice, friendly people. Her aunt is like a mother to her and I had already met her sister the day of the accident."

"What about her parents?"

"They were killed in a car accident when she was a child. Her aunt raised her and her sister."

Sharon nodded as she listened. "I don't want to have to worry about you, Travis. I want to retire knowing you're happy. I also hope to have a wedding to look forward to."

"I want the same. But, for now we had better get back. I just had to get a bite to eat. We almost didn't get a chance to." Sharon smiled at him and finished her meal.

"I'm so excited about my new job, Miss Flora. It's not much, but every dollar will help," Stella said. "Four kids and no husband is not easy. Now, I'm going on about myself and I haven't even asked how you're feeling? You look good."

"Stella, I'm doing fine. But I do miss having you around."

"You gave me such a good reference, Miss Flora. That's why I was able to get this job."

Flora heard the teakettle whistle. "You just make yourself at home. The water is ready for the tea, and I want you to try my lemon cake."

While Stella was waiting for Flora to finish, she heard a car pull into the driveway. The door opened just as Flora was coming back with the tray in her hand, and Tracey walked in.

"Sit down and I'll get another cup, Tracey."

"Thanks, Aunt Flo."

"Tracey, I came to visit for a while. I wanted to tell Miss Flora that I found a new job. They called her for a reference and, after they finished talking to Miss Flora, I was hired," Stella said proudly.

Tracey sighed, holding her hand over her heart. "That's good news, Stella. Now, tell me more about your new job."

Stella looked from Tracey to Flora. "It's a large convalescence home that's not too far. It's in Downey and will only take me about thirty minutes to get there. I'll be working with the patients." She sipped her tea. "This cake is so good, Miss Flora. You see, my job isn't much, but it will help keep a roof over my children's heads, food in their mouths, and clothes on their backs."

"I understand that, Stella," Tracey said.

"Michelle has helped me so much. But, I don't expect her to always have to help me. I want her to finish school. She's changing her style of dressing now, too. She dresses more like a career woman. Just listen to me. I'm talking too much as usual."

"No you're not. You're just excited, and I don't blame you. And, your hair looks good. You are right about Michelle. Did she tell you that she wants to be a realtor?"

"Yes, she told me. She said you would teach her all she needs to know. I appreciate that, Tracey."

"I know you do, Stella."

"I didn't have anyone to teach me anything when I was Michelle's age. You see, my mother died when I was only ten years old. I had two younger brothers.." Stella's eyes crinkled in the corner with the threat of tears. As I said before, I left home when I was sixteen and got married." She inhaled and shook her head in a rueful manner.

"Where is your husband now?" Tracey asked.

"Honey, I don't know. Might be dead for all I know."

"And your two brothers?" Tracey asked.

"The youngest was shot when he was seventeen, and the other one went to jail when he was twenty. When he was released, he never came around. I don't know where he is. Might be dead, too, for all I know." She paused. "My father died of liver disease before he was forty years old. So you see I'm not making excuses, but I had no help, no one to teach me anything or encourage me to get a decent education. That's why it hurts so bad to see my seventeen-year-old daughter's stomach grow everyday."

She wiped a tear in the corner of her eye. "It's like history repeating itself. I wanted to break the cycle."

"At least she has you and Michelle, Stella. She's young and can still finish school," Tracey said.

The doorbell rang again. "Now who is this?" Flora asked. "I'll say, I'm popular today." Flora opened the door and it was Robin.

Robin stepped inside and looked around the room. "Hi everyone. Just thought I would spend a few minutes with Aunt Flo. I left early for lunch today," she said looking at Tracey. "How about you, Tracey? Were you on your way to the office?"

"No, just leaving a meeting. It is good to see Stella again. We haven't seen each other since Aunt Flo got better."

"Yes, it was nice of you to come over, Stella," Robin said. "Did Aunt Flo need some help with something? Are you here to work?"

"No. I missed seeing Miss Flora." But Stella didn't believe that Robin was glad to see her for a minute. She always sensed that as far as Robin was concerned, she was only good enough to work for Miss Flora, but not to be her friend. Funny, she didn't seem to be as snobbish the first time she met her and she wondered why she had changed.

Stella stood up. "Miss Flora, I just wanted to tell you about my new job."

"Oh, you've found someone else to take care of, Stella?" Robin asked.

"Yes, but this time I won't be working in the home." She kissed Flora on the cheek. "Now, you take care of yourself, Miss Flora. I'll be checking up on you."

"I will, dear," Flora said as she walked her to the door. "You just stop by anytime you want. It's always nice to see you, Stella. And remember what we just talked about. Your children will turn out just fine. They have you for a mother."

"I'll remember, and I'll call you when I get a chance to tell you how the new job is going." Stella left and Flora sat back on the couch and finished her tea.

"She's a nice woman. She tries so hard to take care of her family."

"Yes, too bad she waited so long," Robin answered.

"What do you mean, Robin?" Tracey asked, putting her hand on her hip.

"She should have had a job a long time ago. She dresses like she's working the streets. What kind of mother is she?"

"One that didn't have the chance in life that she deserved," Flora snapped.

"I'm sorry, Aunt Flo. I know that she's your and Tracey's friend. I didn't mean to upset you."

"You didn't upset me. But, you can't always judge a book by its cover. You don't really know her, Robin. You're really being a snob."

"I'm not a snob," Robin's voice became high-pitched. "Whatever. Of course, you're right. I don't know her." *And don't really want to,* she thought.

"Tracey, how is Travis? He seems to be a nice man and you two look good together."

"Travis and I have been seeing each other, Aunt Flo. I care a lot for him."

"Don't forget who he is, Tracey."

"What's that supposed to mean, Robin?" Tracey asked, head tilted to the side, an edge of irritation in her voice.

"I mean, just remember who his sister was. Make sure he isn't anything like her."

"You mean because she had an affair with Donald?"

"Yes, just be careful, honey. You don't know anything about him, yet."

"You don't either, Robin. So maybe if you don't have a word of encouragement, you should keep your damn mouth shut." Tracey turned her back to her.

Robin jerked her head around. Aunt Flo looked confused, but she agreed with Tracey.

"I'm sorry, Tracey. I was just trying to help."

Flora went to take the tray back in the kitchen and left them alone.

"You sounded so angry, Tracey."

Tracey turned back to face her. "You deserved it, and I'm tired of it. You may be going through a hard time now, but you brought it on yourself. I don't think you're in a position to judge Travis or his dead sister."

"I know, and I'm sorry."

Flora walked back in the room and looked from Robin to Tracey.

"I have some work that I have to finish, Aunt Flo. Michelle should be in the office by now." She kissed Flora on the cheek and walked out without saying good-bye to Robin.

"Are you girls all right, Robin?"

"Of course, Aunt Flo. You know how sensitive Tracey can be sometimes. I didn't think that I had said anything wrong."

"Well, apparently you did. It was obvious, too."

"When I get back to my office, I'll call her. Now, it's time that I go back and get some work done." She kissed Flora and walked out to her car. But she felt bad. She had gone through so much in the last few months. But Tracey was right—she had brought it on herself.

Nineteen

Tracey walked into Travis's apartment, and he wrapped his arms around her as though he hadn't seen her in years, instead of days.

"I'm glad you decided to spend the night with me. I can't get you out of my mind, Tracey. You're like an itch that I can't scratch."

As she pulled away, he held her hand. "I love your apartment, Travis," she said, sinking her feet into the thick, brown carpet. She gently pulled her hand out of his, went to the glass doors of the patio, and peeked out. "It's such a beautiful night. I've always loved the marina and the view of the pier." She looked in the corner, and saw that Travis had built a fire in the fireplace.

"We'll keep each other warm," he said, walking up behind her, circling his arms around her waist. "Come on, I'll show you where you can put your bag." She followed him to his bedroom. It was nicely decorated for a man's room, in all blacks and varying shades of browns. His bathroom was large, in black and white.

"Would you like to go to a movie or somewhere?"

"No. I just want to be here alone with you."

"That's my girl. Would you like a glass of wine?"

"Sure, I could use one," she said and followed him to the kitchen. It was small, but adequate. Tracey sat at the counter and he placed a glass in her hand.

"Come on, let's go to the living room where we can see

the view of the city. Are you sure you don't want to go out anyplace?"

"You'll be working next weekend, and I've decided to go to Jackson, Mississippi, to visit Wendy. I just want to be alone with you now."

"Good, because it's what I want, too. So, you decided to go after all?"

"Yes, she has called me twice this week and each time she cries on the phone. I made reservations today."

They were sitting close together on the couch, and he took her hand in his.

"Will you stay with her or in a hotel?"

"With her. Wendy and her sister live in a large house that was passed down to them by their parents. It's large enough so we can talk without anyone else around. I'll only be gone for three days," she said and laid her head on his shoulder.

"That's three days too long, baby. But, I have to work anyway."

"I know, and I'll miss you, too."

Travis got up and turned on some soft music. "Why don't you get comfortable, Tracey, and I'll refill our glasses."

She went to his bedroom where she had left her overnight bag. The bathroom was large with large white and black towels hanging on every rack. Travis's brown slippers were in the corner next to her overnight bag.

Tracey came back dressed in a short black satin bathrobe and black satin slippers with her hair hanging to her shoulders.

When Travis came out of his bedroom, he gasped. Every time they were together she looked more beautiful than the time before, and he noticed something new about her. Travis pulled her next to him and he couldn't keep his eyes off her.

This time he noticed a mole on her right thigh. He gently raised her hair from her shoulders and let it fall through his fingers. He traced her face with his index finger, and her smooth ebony skin felt like silk. At that very moment, he decided that he wanted Tracey to have his child, their child.

"I've made a decision today," he said.

She looked up at him and kissed him on his neck and brushed her lips against his cheeks.

"What decision have you made?" she whispered.

"I went to medical school with a friend of mine. He has a practice here in LA and asked me to join him. That was a month ago, but every time we talk, I tell him that I need more time. Today I decided that I want to join him. For one thing, it will mean that I won't be on duty at night. The office closes at five weekdays and on weekends."

"That's very good, Travis," she said, sitting up straight, giving him her full attention. "What made you decide to accept his offer?"

"You did. I want more time with you. I want to plan weekends away with you. Every minute I have, I want to spend with you."

Tracey held her breath and squeezed her eyes shut, trying to hold back the tears and keep her emotions in check. Looking in his eyes, she knew that he loved her and she had fallen in love with him, too. She wasn't ready to say it yet, but she did want to spend every spare moment she had with him. "I want the same, Travis," she managed to say.

"Good." He held her face in his hands. "And I don't want to date anyone but you, Tracey," he said it so sincerely that she could only hold him tighter.

"I don't want to date anyone else but you, either," she whispered, breathless, and he took the glass from her hand and held her tightly. She felt as though she was in another world.

An hour later, they were in bed and he was making love to her so gently, so tenderly, he had to restrain himself. He wanted to be sure she was pleased, too. She was such a piquant lover—so eager and so giving, he found it difficult to hold back.

But his only desire was to satisfy her, so he stopped several times and shifted positions. He breathed deeply to maintain his control. Finally, he heard Tracey's breathing speed up as she cried out his name, her body quivering in spasms. Then, at last, he let go and began to climb, higher, higher, until he felt himself cresting, soaring, exploding into the universe. Afterward, he lay in her arms, shuddering, panting, for the longest time. He knew that this was where they belonged—together.

The next day, they showered and cooked breakfast together. They laughed, kissed, and talked, and she helped him clean the kitchen. Tracey had planned to spend Friday night with him and go home on Saturday morning, but it was Sunday morning when she finally left him.

When she got home and was settled in, she thought of him and wondered how they had gotten so close, so fast. She packed some of the things that she would take to Mississippi. She was so worried about Wendy.

Monday morning, Tracey walked into her office at eight. She needed to get an early start since she wouldn't be doing any work over the weekend. She checked her messages, and Mr. Richardson had returned her call. As she listened to him, she took notes. He talked slowly and clearly, pronouncing each word perfectly. She called him back and asked if he could come to her office. He said that he would be there around one.

The phone rang and it was Travis. "Were you tired today, love?" she asked him.

"No. But I wish you were there with me. I thought of you all night, Tracey. I missed you."

"I missed you, too."

"We'll have to figure out something to do about that."

She smiled into the phone. "It was thoughtful of you to call and tell me. I can't wait to see you either. I'm going to miss you just as much next weekend."

She hung up beaming, then wondered if it would always be this way between them.

Michelle had called and said she would be a little late. It was nine-thirty when she walked in. She looked at Tracey, who was working furiously with a contract.

"Hey, you."

Tracey jumped, and dropped the paper on her desk. "Hi yourself. You scared the life out of me. I was just trying to get some figures together for Mr. Richardson. He's coming in today at one."

"I think I'll get a cup of coffee before I get started. What flavor is it?"

"French Vanilla. Smells good, huh?"

"Yes. I was up late last night, and I need a cup to wake me up this morning. I had to get up early enough to take my mom to work."

"Is she having car trouble?" Tracey asked, looking up from her work.

"Yes, but my brother says it only needs a battery."

"I think Mr. Richardson will be happy with this offer. He's such a nice man, but he seems so lonely to me."

"How can you tell?"

"I don't know. It's just that he lost his wife three years ago. He looked so sad when he told me that. Tracey pushed her hair back from her eyes as she scanned the figures one more time. "Anyway, I think he'll accept this offer. The buyer is almost willing to give anything he asks for."

She looked at her watch and saw that she had time to go over a new listing that was faxed to her from another realtor. Every time she looked at it, Travis would appear in front of her. Going to Mississippi will be best. She needed to get away from him for a weekend, even though she would miss him terribly. She placed the contract on her desk and went to the window.

Why couldn't she just enjoy him and not worry about getting hurt? But she knew Donald had disappointed her. She'd trusted completely and he'd cheated on her.

"Tracey?"

"Oh, I'm sorry. I was just thinking of something. What were you saying?"

"I said the escrow company called and said the Hawthorne deal is closing tomorrow."

"Good. It took long enough."

Michelle and Tracey worked straight through until twelve-thirty. "I think I'm going to lunch now. While I'm out, I have to go to the bookstore to buy a book for my class. We need more stamps, too," Michelle said while putting on her jacket.

"Already? I go through stamps like crazy." Tracey opened her desk and pulled out her purse to give Michelle money. "Take as much time as you need. Mr. Richardson will be here for a while anyway."

"Do you want me to bring you some lunch back?"

Tracey didn't answer for a few seconds. "I don't know what I want. When I get hungry I'll run out and pick something up."

At exactly one o'clock, Mr. Richardson was walking in, dressed in a pair of nice black slacks and sweater. His white wavy hair was neatly combed. He smiled when Tracey stood up behind her desk and held her hand out.

"Have a seat, Mr. Richardson. Can I get you a cup of coffee?"

"No, I've stopped drinking the stuff. It keeps me up all night. But I'll have a glass of water if you don't mind, Mrs. Woods."

"Of course, I don't mind," she answered, and walked to Michelle's desk to put her calls straight to voice mail.

Tracey sat at her desk and handed Mr. Richardson the purchase agreement and counteroffer for the property that he had for sale.

"I think you will be pleased with this offer. Just take your time and go over everything carefully."

He grinned, then read the agreement. After a few minutes passed, he put the papers on the desk in front of Tracey.

"Perfect. I accept."

"I thought you would. The buyer was looking for some units in that area."

"Have you had lunch, Mrs. Woods?"

"No. I'm leaving Thursday evening to go and visit a friend of mine. So I was planning to grab something quick and keep working."

"No, you must eat. You are thin and can stand to eat a good meal."

Tracey laughed. "Not too thin, I hope."

"No, I didn't mean that you are too thin. But you have to take care of yourself. Have you had breakfast today?"

"No, I only eat breakfast on the weekends."

"That does it. Let's go to lunch. I saw a little Italian restaurant around the corner on my way over." He got up and waited. Tracey sighed and got her purse and jacket. Just what she needed, she thought. Someone to stop her from finishing her work. But he was nice to work with and she couldn't refuse.

When they arrived at Giovanni's Restaurant, Mr. Richardson got out and walked around the car to open the door for Tracey. The perfect gentlemen, she thought. She closed her jacket, feeling the cold air blowing against her. The sun was out and the air felt nice, and clean.

Mr. Richardson pulled the chair out for Tracey to sit down. They were seated in the back and the lunch crowd was still clearing out of the restaurant. He ordered linguini served in a clam sauce. Tracey ordered lasagna.

"My wife and I came here to eat once. If memory serves me correctly, the food was good."

"How long were you married, Mr. Richardson?"

"We were married for thirty-five years. She died six months after our anniversary. She was a great woman." He smiled as if he was remembering something pleasant about her. "We have a son that I'm very proud of. He lives in New York with his wife and two children. Every year if they don't come out here, I go there."

He twirled his linguini on his fork and balanced it with

his knife. "When he goes on a business trip, he sometimes surprises me and drops in. Now, have you met a nice man since your husband died?"

The question threw her completely off guard. She didn't expect him to ask about her personal life, even though she had asked about his.

"Yes, I have. He's a doctor. He's very nice."

He looked at her. "Where is that glow that women have when they talk about the man they love?" he asked cautiously, hoping that he wasn't getting too personal.

This time she was taken aback; she didn't know how to answer him.

"There are still a few issues we have to work out. But he's a very nice man. As a matter of fact, he reminds me of you in a way."

"I do hope that's a compliment."

"It is. A sincere one, too."

"Have you always lived in California, Tracey?"

"Born and raised in Los Angeles," she answered as the waitress refilled her glass with iced tea.

"I lived here until I was twenty-two. I met my wife in Dallas. But, before I left Los Angeles I met a nice girl, fell in love, and thought she would be the woman that I was going to marry." He stopped talking and took a sip of his water. "We were so much in love. She was a pretty girl, too, my first love. We went to high school together and went on to college. We were going to get married after we finished school."

"What happened?" Tracey asked between bites.

"When I finished college I was looking for a job that would support a family. To me, she deserved the very best of everything, including a husband with a good job. I loved her so much that I didn't want her to work, just have my children and stay home." He paused. "But, my father died, and me being the only child, I was all that my mother had. I went back to Dallas and stayed with her. She was so afraid that something would happen to me, too, that she didn't want me out of her sight. My father had a small business of his own and I had to keep it running."

"What kind of business was it?" This story was getting interesting to Tracey.

"He owned a small real estate management company that handled several apartment buildings in Dallas. He had his own staff. Two of the buildings were seventy units, some were twenty or thirty. It was a big responsibility. After my father died, my mother wouldn't go outside. She didn't really want me to go out either, but I had to run the business.

"When things got too hectic I stopped writing to my girlfriend. It was always so much to do. My mother died the year after and I came back to LA., but my girl had moved and no one knew where her family had gone. I went back and started running the streets, drinking, and coming in all hours of the night. And one day I was sitting in my father's office, wondering where my life was going.

"I got a contract for more buildings, found a sweet woman, and got married. A year later, I had a son. But, all the years that I was married, I never forgot my first love, never stopped wondering if she was with someone that was good to her. I prayed that she was happy."

Tracey looked in his light brown eyes. She was so intrigued, she knew instinctively what she was going to do. She wanted this man to meet her aunt. When she came back from Mississippi, she would invite Mr. Richardson and Aunt Flo to her house for dinner. She wasn't sure yet how she would do this, but she would. Maybe Robin could help her figure out a way without an argument. *She's so disagreeable these days,* Tracey thought.

He walked her to the door of her office.

"Lunch was great, Mr. Richardson. When I get back we'll have to do this again."

"My pleasure, but please call me Eric."

"All right, Eric." She said good-bye and walked inside, closing the door behind her.

"Did you go to lunch?" Michelle asked, when she walked back in the office.

"Yes, but I didn't plan on it. He was so pleased about the offer, he wanted to take me to lunch."

"He reminds me of one of those older men from the south that has money. You know, the ones in the movies who all wear white suits." Michelle said.

"Yes, I have an idea of what you're talking about and I agree. Did you find your book?"

"Yes, and I got the stamps, too."

Tracey finished going over her new listing and Michelle finished all the filing, typing letters, and mailing flyers by five.

"Let's call it a day. I have a few things to do before I get here tomorrow so don't expect me until ten or ten-thirty. After tomorrow, I'll be in Mississippi," Tracey said, and made sure the coffeemaker was turned off.

Twenty

When Tracey got off the plane, she didn't see Wendy waiting for her anywhere. Maybe she was late. *She said that she would be at the gate,* Tracey thought.

"Hey, you, don't you know me?"

Tracey turned around to face her and hooted with laughter. Wendy looked like a different woman than the broken, dejected person she'd last seen.

"Girl, you look good. I like that haircut." She rushed toward Wendy with her arms out and they hugged each other tight. Tracey pulled away so she could get a good look at Wendy.

"And that body. Have you been working out at the gym or something?"

"Yes, I had to lose weight and exercise because my cholesterol was too high. The doctor's orders. Let's go and pick up your luggage. You didn't bring ten pieces with you, did you, Tracey?"

"Girl, no, just one suitcase and an overnight bag, one pantsuit just in case I find myself a date out here."

"Yeah, right. You'd better keep who you have."

They got to baggage claim and had to wait fifteen minutes before Tracey's bags appeared.

"What do you do on weekends?" Tracey asked.

"Nothing much. I looked up a couple of girls that I went to school with and go to church with Donna."

"How is Donna?"

"She's all right. I'll be glad when I find a place of my

own. She worries the shit out of me sometimes. The plan was that I stay with her in the house that my mother left us, but I can't take too much more of her being an old mama hen. 'Did you eat breakfast, Wendy? Don't you think you need to wear a sweater? You're not used to this rainy weather anymore and it rains one day and is still warm. You may get sick.' That's every day." Wendy rolled her eyes to the sky and sighed. "Here's the car."

They got in, and she turned out of the parking lot. "How's Robin?"

"She's doing all right."

"And Miss Flora?"

"You know Aunt Flo. She bounces back like a ball. As a matter of fact, I have a man that I want to fix her up with."

Wendy looked at her and laughed. "How cute. It's always good to have some kind of companion to go to dinner or a movie with, someone to talk to. I think that's a good idea. Where did you find him?"

"I'm selling some units for him. We talked and went to lunch together, and he's a nice man. His wife died three years ago." Tracey looked out the window as the passing scenery unfurled outside the car. "Sure are a lot of brick houses out here. You see so few in LA."

"So few? You hardly see any in Los Angeles. Well, here we are." She drove down the long driveway and parked the car. Wendy opened the trunk and Tracey took the suitcase out. They had started to the door when Donna came out.

"It's been years since the last time I saw you, Tracey." She kissed Tracey on her cheek and took her suitcase. "I sure hope you're hungry. Girl, I baked a ham, made some potato salad, and cooked some greens."

"If I wasn't hungry, I am now."

"Tracey, you're too skinny. I'm sure glad I cooked," she said looking Tracey up and down.

Tracey looked at Donna from head to toe. She couldn't believe how much weight she had gained. She was still pretty at forty-two, was 5' 3" and at least two hundred pounds.

"Follow me, Tracey, and I'll take you to your room. We've got four bedrooms here and before Wendy came back home, I was staying in this big old house all by myself. I had a roommate once, but it didn't work out. This is your room."

Tracey followed her in and Donna dropped the suitcase in the middle of the room.

"Take your time and unpack. I know you and Wendy want to be alone for a while so you two can catch up on things. I'll put the cornbread in the oven, so don't take too long." She walked out and closed the door.

"Now, Wendy, this house is big enough for both of you. It doesn't make any sense to move out and pay rent. Anyway, I like this room, the flowered drapes, the bedspread, and it's big, too. Are all the bedrooms this big?"

"Yes, this is a big house, Tracey. Every room in this house is big." Tracey admired the high ceilings and the old-fashioned wainscoting.

"Here's the closet." Wendy opened the closet door and hung up Tracey's suit. "I'll show you the rest of the house. Tomorrow we can go to lunch at Perkin's Family Restaurant and do some shopping if you like. It's not cold out, but I know you are tired."

"I am tired. And it's cold because I'm not used to this weather. It rains too hard and yes, it's cold enough to me," Tracey said and pulled her coat off.

They went to the living room where they could be alone. Donna was in the kitchen cooking and talking on the phone. They sat on the couch.

"Aren't you glad to be home again, Wendy?" Tracey asked her.

"I feel better, but I miss you and the weather. It doesn't rain this time of year in LA."

"We will always see each other, honey. And you can come to LA anytime you want and stay with me. You know that."

"I will, Tracey. I feel so alone here sometimes, but I

couldn't stay in LA either. I needed the change. In time, I'll adjust."

"What about the rest of your family? I bet they were happy you came home."

"They are. Do you want a Coke or tea?" Wendy asked.

"I could use a Coke."

Wendy left the room. Tracey sauntered around the large living room with her hands behind her back. She looked at the pictures over the fireplace where a collage of family portraits formed a circle. The furniture was outdated, too, covered in yellowing plastic, but well kept. She went to the window and looked out. It looked like it would rain.

Tracey heard Wendy come in, and she sat back on the couch.

"So, are you going to give it a try and stay on here? It's a nice house, Wendy. You can decorate your room the way you want it. And just think how much money you'll save."

"I'll give it some thought. Like you said, the house is large. I can always hide from Donna in my room. Now tell me about your love life. I know something must be going on with you and the doctor by now."

"We're seeing each other. I like him a lot, maybe even love him. Girl, we spent last weekend together. It was so nice, so peaceful and so . . ."

"And so hot?" Wendy teased.

Tracey laughed, and felt heat in her cheeks. "Yes, that, too. He's just everything a woman would want."

"But?" Wendy lifted her eyebrow, waiting for more.

"You know me too well. Okay. You don't think it's too soon after Donald's death?" Tracey held her knuckles to her mouth. She couldn't help the giddy, insecure sound in her voice. She was like a teenager on the brink of a dangerous, yet new thrill.

"After what he did to you? Are you kidding, Tracey?" Wendy waved her hand. "Pshaww!"

"Well, sometimes I get completely confused about Travis

and myself. Like what do I say when I meet his mother? What if she asks me something about Donald?"

"Honey, I doubt she wants to know anything about Donald. She probably hates him if she knows he was a married man."

"I think that Travis is serious about us. I want to be, but I'm still afraid, Wendy. Sometimes, I don't think I'm even ready to be with a man; other times, I get lonely for one."

"Just take it slow and easy. It'll work out. And if he makes you too angry, you can always come back and spend the weekend with me."

"Dinner is ready. The table is set." Donna interrupted their heart-to-heart chat.

"Are you ready, Tracey?"

"Yes. It smells good."

"Come on. You two can talk later. I'm hungry, too."

Wendy crossed her eyes for Tracey to see and made circles around her ears as they followed Donna into the dining room.

Just as they sat at the table, the doorbell rang. Donna got up to answer it and Wendy's brother walked in.

"Tracey, is that you?"

Tracey got up and ran into Jerry's arms. "I was hoping you would come by before I left."

"I called to check on my sisters and Donna told me you were here." He touched Wendy's shoulder. "You still look good, Tracey. You ready to marry me now?"

"How many women do you have?"

"Only two, but I'll replace one with you."

"Only one? No, thanks. You will never change," Tracey said, fanning off his advances.

"Want some dinner, Jerry?" Wendy asked.

"No, I was on my way home and stopped to say hello to Tracey. You didn't tell me that she was flying in, Wendy."

"Well, now you know."

He kissed her on the cheek. "Sis, I don't see you everyday.

But I love you, too," Jerry teased. And then he kissed all three and left.

"That brother of mine will never grow up," Donna said, shaking her head.

After dinner they sat in the living room and talked until almost midnight.

"I'm tired," Tracey said.

"And I'm tired from all the excitement," Wendy said. "Tomorrow I'll take you by the office so you can see what it looks like. Then we'll go to lunch."

"After a good night's sleep, I'll be ready." All three got up and went upstairs together.

After Wendy left, Tracey undressed and got in bed, wondering what Travis was doing tonight. She thought of him until she fell asleep.

The next morning Tracey awoke with a start. It was eight o'clock, or so she thought. She looked at her watch again, and as she got out of bed she looked at the clock on the dresser and saw that it was three hours later.

Had she really slept this late? She heard a knock on the door. "Come in," she answered. It was Wendy, already dressed.

"Why did you let me sleep so late?" she asked while pulling her robe around her.

"It's the time difference. Plus the flight, and getting ready for the trip. All of that can make you tired. Now, today you only need some kick-around clothes. I'll have breakfast ready by the time you're dressed."

"Where's Donna? Has she left already?"

"Yes, Lord. We won't have the pleasure of her company today after we leave the office."

After breakfast, they were ready to start their day. But when Wendy opened the door to go outside, Tracey jumped behind her, holding her arms and shivering.

"Oh, hell no. I have got to wear a sweater, and a hat so

my hair won't get wet. Just wait right here." She ran upstairs and Wendy's laughter followed her. When she came back down, Wendy was still laughing.

"I think we can go now," she said, walking fast behind Wendy. "Are you used to this warm, rainy weather yet?"

"Not like I was before I left to live in LA. And it's cold out here during the winter months and hot and muggy as hell in the summer with lots of rain." Wendy backed out of the driveway. The ride to the office only took them twenty minutes. They got out in front of a tall, brown-brick building.

"No earthquakes will shake this down," Tracey said while looking at the building. "But I like the brick. It gives the building more character and style. Don't you think?"

After they left the office they had a full day of shopping and sightseeing downtown. They had a late lunch and got ready to go back home.

Once they were home, Tracey ran upstairs and hung up her coat and changed into some comfortable shoes. When she came back down the stairs, Wendy was sitting in the living room on the couch.

"I should take you out. I haven't been going out myself since I've been here."

"I just came to visit you. I can go out when I go home. Now let's just relax and talk, but first turn the heater on. This house does get cold at night."

Wendy laughed. "If you come in the summer when it's even hotter, you'll appreciate this big old cold house. Now, for real, tell me what's bothering you about Travis. You're not saying much, but you are afraid."

Tracey shook her head, bemused. "I should have known that I can't hide anything from you. It's his sister and Donald. I can't get them out of my head. What do I say when I meet his mother? Will Travis and I start to fight every time he brings his sister's name up?"

"Tracey, that was between Donald and Travis's sister. It has nothing to do with you and Travis. You'll have to forget about that part of it in your relationship."

"I know, but I can't." She sounded sad but managed to smile.

The weekend was over and Wendy waited with Tracey at the airport.

"Now, remember what I said. Just take it easy with Donna."

"And you remember what I said. Take it easy with Travis." They hugged, and Tracey boarded the plane.

Twenty-one

"You have got to be kidding, tell me you're kidding," Robin said as she took a step closer to Tracey with one hand on her hip.

"No, I'm not kidding. I'm serious. This will be good for Aunt Flo. You said yourself that she was depressed when you saw her yesterday. Having someone to admire her will make her feel better."

"Tracey, you're stepping out of line. She's pretty enough to find a man of her own, that is, if she wants one. I don't even think she's interested in a man. She's sixty-something, for Pete's sake."

"He's a nice man, a southern gentleman. He'll like being with Aunt Flo."

"I'm not worried about what he'll like," Robin snapped, still not believing what she had heard.

"They can do things like go to church and dinner together. He'll be good company for her, Robin."

John walked into the kitchen where they were arguing. "I couldn't help but overhear you two. I think it's a great idea." He rubbed his hands together and gave Tracey a conspiratorial grin. "Flora could use some company, and she's still young enough to appreciate the attention of a gentleman."

"Aunt Flo got a boyfriend? My friend's grandmother got a husband. Maybe Aunt Flo will want to marry again," Lisa said with wide, excited eyes.

"See what you guys have started? No, Aunt Flo doesn't

have a boyfriend. And, Lisa, go to your room and finish your homework."

"Oh, all right. I never get to give an opinion around here."

"Yes you do," Robin and John said in unison. Lisa left the room.

All three sat at the table. "Now look, you guys, I don't think that we have a right to get into Aunt Flo's life this way. She knows if she wants a boyfriend," Robin said, not believing that they were actually having this conversation. "Like I said, we don't have the right to get into her business."

"Well, Robin, actually we are," Tracey said. "I've decided to do this with or without you."

"Come on, Robin. What could it hurt?" John asked.

"Look, all you will have to do is show up for dinner. I'll do the rest."

"You just had us over for dinner," Robin protested.

"Then let's have it over here," John suggested.

Robin gave a long deflated sigh. "Well, I guess if she gets angry, we can always say it was your idea, Tracey."

"I'll take the blame. Now when is it?" she asked, anxious to make plans.

"What about Sunday afternoon?"

"I'll call Eric tomorrow."

"Great, all Aunt Flo needs is a lonely old man. Now, tell us about your trip. Is Wendy getting along all right?"

"She looks good. Her doctor put her on a diet." Tracey's face lit up.

"I feel sorry for her. Too bad it took leaving her business, paying bills that her husband left for her to wake up. She always seems to make the same mistakes." Robin sucked her teeth. "Maybe this will teach her a lesson."

"You're all heart, Robin," Tracey said sarcastically and started to put on her coat.

"What did I say? I feel sorry for her. But she's her own worst enemy."

Tracey was standing with her coat on, purse and car keys in her hand. "What do you need me to bring over Sunday?"

"I'll let you know."

"Okay, I'll see you then."

"Let me walk you to the car, Tracey. It's dark out there," John suggested.

When John came back inside, Robin had just finished clearing the table.

"I wonder why Tracey got so uptight?" she asked. "And I hope Aunt Flo doesn't get angry with us, but it's Tracey's doing, not mine."

"Are you finished in here?" John asked.

"Almost. Why don't you see if Lisa needs help with her homework?"

"How are you, Aunt Flo?" Tracey asked as she walked into Flora's house.

"Good, Tracey. I just got home a few minutes ago. I went to church and after church was over, Sister Mary and I went to lunch. Robin came by yesterday. Come on in the kitchen with me. I was just making myself a cup of herbal tea. I'm hooked on that stuff now."

Tracey followed her and took a seat at the table as she looked at her aunt. Flora's hair was combed back from her face. She was still a pretty woman.

"Did you have a good time in Mississippi?"

"Yes, it was nice. But, it's too cold out there for me. Next time, I'll wait until April or May."

"Did you guys go out dancing or anything?" Flora asked and sat at the table opposite Tracey.

"No. We went to her office, shopping, and downtown. Most of the time we stayed at home and talked a lot. She needed someone to talk to." And so did Tracey, but she didn't say that to Flora.

"Robin invited me to dinner on Sunday. She'll probably call you tonight or tomorrow. I think she's feeling better now." Flora sipped her herbal tea and looked into the cup as if she'd find answers. She looked at Tracey for her response, but when she didn't, Flora continued to talk.

"I don't know what it was, but she had a problem that was making her unhappy. She would never talk to me about it, so I wouldn't ask. But I know that something was very wrong in her marriage." Flora wrung her hands. "She seems so bitter sometimes and it's not like her at all. She disagrees with everyone." Flora had noticed that Robin had been uncharacteristically short tempered and disagreeable about everything lately.

"Aunt Flo, it may have been some little problem that wasn't as bad as it seemed. You know that Robin can make something worse than it really is."

"Oh no. I know you girls too well. You can't hide anything from me. I'm not asking you what it was. But, it had her very unhappy there for a while," she said with certainty. Tracey couldn't say anything. She just looked into Flora's wise eyes.

"I wonder, will anyone else be there on Sunday?" Flora asked.

"I don't know. But why don't you wear that pretty blue dress you bought the last time we went shopping?"

"That's too fancy to just sit and have dinner in. No one will probably be there except us, Tracey."

Flora looked at Tracey with a strange expression. "I'll ask Robin if someone else will be there. But, I don't know if I will wear my blue dress. I have other dresses, you know."

"The color looks so good on you," Tracey said trying to convince her. Flora always dressed nicely, but this was special. She sat back down and put her glass in front of her.

"Are you all right, Tracey? You look tired."

"Yes, Aunt Flo. I am a little tired. I was up late every night in Mississippi."

"How is Travis? He seems to be a nice fellow."

"I talked to him today. I think I'll invite him to dinner with us Sunday."

"That's a good idea, Tracey. I like him."

Tracey got up. "I think I'd better be going before I fall asleep in this chair. I'm going straight home to take a hot shower and go to bed."

Flora walked her to the door. "Drive careful, child."

"I will, Aunt Flo."

As soon as Tracey got home, she looked in her briefcase and pulled out her phone book. She kicked off her shoes and dialed the number.

"Mr. Richardson, it's Tracey Woods."

"Hello, Tracey. How are you?"

"I'm fine and yourself?"

"Good. I'm doing just fine, and it's good to hear from you."

"The escrow will close as scheduled. The reason I'm calling is to invite you to dinner at my sister's house on Sunday. I hope you don't mind my asking, sir. I know you have a lot of spare time on your hands. I was telling my family what a nice gentleman you are."

Mr. Richardson hesitated for a few seconds before he answered. "I accept your offer, Tracey. Can you hold on for a second so I can get a pen and paper for directions to your sister's house?"

"Sure," Tracey answered.

"Okay, Tracey, what is the address?" Mr. Richardson listened as Tracey gave him the address.

"Dear, I'm very familiar with the neighborhood. I know exactly where your sister lives. It's just so nice of you to ask."

"Good. You can meet me there at three. And thank you, sir, for accepting."

That was easy enough, she thought and smiled. *I just hope that he and Aunt Flo hit it off. If not, I'll never hear the end of it from Robin.* She changed into her bathrobe and lay across her bed. Travis was on duty tonight, but he said that he would call when the emergency room wasn't so busy. The phone rang and she answered. It was Michelle. She sounded upset and asked Tracey if she could come over. Tracey was tired, had planned to go to bed early, but she told her to come on anyway.

Twenty minutes later the doorbell rang. It was Michelle and she had been crying. Her makeup was smeared under her eyes.

"Honey, come in. Are you all right, Michelle?" she asked and led her to the couch.

"Justin dropped me for another girl. His mother never thought that I was good enough for him. And now that I think about it, he was always looking for someone he thought was better than me." Michelle's tears flowed freely.

"We've been together for two years. I loved him. His three sisters have degrees. His parents even have college degrees. I just wasn't good enough for him," she said and fell into Tracey's arms.

"What exactly did he say to you?"

Michelle held her head up and wiped her eyes with the back of her hand.

"He called me on the phone. I knew he sounded remote and dry as if he was stalling for time. So I asked if there was anything wrong or if I had done something?"

"And—?"

"He said that there wasn't anything wrong, that he just couldn't see me anymore. I asked him if he was kidding with me, but somehow I knew that he wasn't." She cleared her throat.

"He said we're just not compatible. I asked what he was talking about. We've been going together for over two years." Shoulders heaving, Michelle tried to muffle her sobs. "Then he said that we were too different, from different backgrounds. It felt as if someone had thrown cold water in my face. It really woke me up, and I knew what he meant. 'Anyway, I've found someone else,'" he said. She struggled to regain her composure.

"Tracey, I couldn't stay in the house for another minute. At first I started to go to his house and tell him off. But I changed my mind and came over here." Tracey looked so sorry for her.

"I don't even know if I can concentrate at school tomorrow and I've got to take a test in one of my classes. Maybe I should stay home tomorrow. Maybe I'm going to school for nothing anyway. I mean, look what happened." She got up and started to pace the floor.

"Come back here and sit next to me," Tracey said and gave her the box of tissues that was on the coffee table. When Michelle sat next to her, Tracey grasped her shoulders with both hands.

"You listen to me, girl. Are you going to throw everything away for him? You're going about this the wrong way, Michelle." Tracey shook her.

"It's better that you know how he feels about you now, rather than later. You don't give up. This should make you want to finish even more. All the hard work you've done, I'm surprised that you would even think of dropping out of school," she said in a sardonic voice. Obviously, Michelle's interest piqued, because she stopped sniffing. She still hung her head, though.

Tracey was genuinely worried as she looked at Michelle, who looked defeated.

"You are going to do even better than before in school and I'm going to teach you to be the best damn realtor in the business. You'll see. And believe me, Michelle, you'll run into him again, and he'll be sorry that he was such a fool."

Michelle looked up and wiped her eyes again. "Do you really think so?"

"I know so. You are intelligent. And the man that you are going to marry will put Justin to shame." Tracey took her in her arms. Michelle was taller but she laid her head on Tracey's shoulder.

"I feel better already. But, it still hurts. I had to leave home, Tracey." Michelle shook her head. "I needed some space, and I guess some encouragement. I didn't want my mother and sister asking any questions. I'll be glad when I can get a place of my own."

"This is your last year in school. It won't be long before you can afford your own apartment. But, if you like, you can stay here tonight."

"Can I really, Tracey?" she asked as her round eyes lit up.

"Yes, call your mother and let her know where you are. But, one thing."

"What's that?"

"If you're hungry, you can go to the kitchen and fix what you want. If you want to watch the television you are welcome to. But I'm going to my room and get in my bed. I'm tired. I had a long day. Now, remember what I said. Forget him, finish school, and be the best that you can be."

Michelle smiled. "You're a good friend, Tracey."

"Good night, Michelle."

Twenty-three

The week went by fast and Tracey and Robin discussed the dinner plans for Sunday. Every time they talked Robin reminded Tracey that if Flora got angry, it would be her fault.

By Saturday, Tracey wasn't so confident that she had done the right thing. And Flora wasn't in the mood to be around any strangers. She had made it clear to Tracey that she didn't really want to go to dinner. But Tracey seemed to think that she should get out of the house and start going out more.

She arrived at two and Flora opened the door wearing her blue dress as Tracey had suggested.

"You look beautiful, Aunt Flo. That color looks good on you, too. And your hair is beautiful. I like the cut. The short hair shows the shape of your lovely face."

Flora turned around to look in the small mirror that hung on the wall. "Do you really think that I should always wear it like this?" she said, touching the sides. Her look was tentative, unsure.

"Yes, I think so."

Flora walked to her room to get her coat. When she came out, Tracey was on the phone. "I called Robin to see if she needed me to pick up anything on our way."

"I'm ready. But, I feel so overdressed. I'm not in the mood for all this dressing up just to be with my family." Flora began fussing. "Goodness Tracey. We just had dinner at your house. Why is Robin having us over so soon? It's not like she doesn't see us much. Well, come on. I don't want to stay too long. Will your friend Travis be there?"

"Yes, I invited him. We both have been so busy that we haven't seen much of each other. Guess, that's the life of a doctor. Though he did mention that he's going into practice with another doctor."

"That's a big step. I wonder what made him decide to. But if it's what he wants, I hope he gets it."

"I think once he makes his mind up about what he wants, he doesn't give up," Tracey answered.

"You seem to care about him a great deal." Flora couldn't see the expression on Tracey's face as she spoke of Travis, but Flora was sure that she cared a great deal for him. Her niece might even be falling in love with him. At least Flora hoped so. She liked Travis.

"Well, we're here," Tracey said, as she parked the car and saw Lisa running out to greet them.

"I've been waiting for you guys," Lisa said. "I even helped my mom bake the lemon cake that you like, Aunt Flo." Lisa's face lit up.

Tracey kissed her on the cheek. "It seems that you are getting taller every time I see you."

"I'm the same height as my mom," Lisa said, and held her head up.

"Come on. No use standing out here going on and on," Flora said.

"Good luck, Tracey," Tracey whispered under her breath. She couldn't remember when her aunt was in such a disheartened mood.

"Are you feeling all right, Aunt Flo?" John asked.

"Yes, I'm getting better every day. What smells so good?"

"Your niece has been in that kitchen all morning. Now, I guess Tracey will be in there for a while, too." John took Flora's coat. "You just make yourself comfortable and I'll get you a glass of apple cider," he said, trying to coax a smile from the unusually stern Flora.

John walked into the kitchen as Tracey and Robin bickered about Flora's mood.

"This was not a good idea, Tracey. I never should have let you talk me into it," Robin said, while washing a pot in the sink.

"Why don't you just wait and see what happens. It may turn out better than we think."

"You don't even look too convinced about it now," Robin answered.

"It's just that she's feeling a little depressed right now. Mr. Richardson—I mean Eric—will be good company for her," Tracey said and fluffed her hair.

"Look you two, it's too late to think of that now. She's here, and he will be any minute now. I'm trying to get her in a good mood." John took the apple cider out of the refrigerator and poured a glass for Flora. "Now, you two finish and get out there." He walked out of the kitchen.

Suddenly the doorbell rang. In the kitchen, Tracey and Robin stopped what they were doing and looked at each other.

"Oh, it's Travis. I guess Eric will be here any minute now." The doorbell rang again. When Tracey turned around to finish placing vegetables on the tray they heard a loud clamor.

"Did someone drop a glass?" Robin asked. Robin and Tracey ran out of the kitchen at the same time. Flora and Eric were facing each other. John and Travis just stood watching them. No one said anything, no movements, or sounds. The room was quiet. Flora's hands were at her sides and the broken glass of apple cider was on the floor in front of her. Tracey's mouth was open.

What in hell happened? she thought and turned to Robin who was scratching her head.

"Oh my God, Eric. Is it really you?" Flora asked.

"It's me," he said and held his arms out. She fell into his

arms and he held her tight for moments before they spoke again

Tracey walked over to Travis and stood next to him.

"You two know each other?" Tracey asked, dumbfounded.

"Flora was my first love. The girl I was telling you about last week," Eric said, never taking his eyes off Flora. They both seemed locked into each other's eyes. "We have a lot to talk about. I can't believe it's you Flora, really you." He stood back and looked at her.

"You mean that you know each other?" Robin asked, still not entirely sure of what had just happened. *Is this possible?* she thought.

Tracey remembered the conversation that she'd had with Eric a week ago. So Aunt Flora was the first love that he spoke of! But it was so hard to believe. Looking into Eric's eyes, Tracey knew that it was true. Could the love they had forty-odd years ago be rekindled?

Looking at them, Tracey had a feeling that those years could still be bridged. And how wonderful they looked together.

Finally, Flora's breath expelled in a rush. She and Eric looked at each other and for a few seconds silence fell between them again. He sat on the sofa and Flora sat beside him. He held her hand in his. Flora's cheeks reddened.

Tracey stepped forward. "Eric, let me introduce you to the rest of my family." She introduced him to everyone, including Travis, whom she called her "friend."

"Now, would you like a glass of wine?"

"Yes, I sure could use one," Eric answered.

"And you, Travis?" Tracey asked.

"Yes, I could use one, too."

"Let me help you, Tracey. We all could use one," Robin said.

Tracey and Robin walked back into the kitchen.

"I can't believe what just happened. Can you, Robin?" Tracey asked as she took a bottle of wine out of the refrigerator.

Robin was putting the glasses on a tray. "I don't know if this is good or bad. Did you see the way Aunt Flo looked at him? I was certain that she was going to faint or have a heart attack or something, girl."

"It's good, of course. I think it's so romantic. Aunt Flo isn't too old to go out and have a little fun in her life."

"Just what kind of fun are you taking about, Tracey?"

"What kind of fun do you think I'm talking about? They can go to dinner together, to church, the movies. He's someone that she can talk about old times with," Tracey answered with excitement.

"Well, let's go in and hear the whole story," Robin said.

Tracey gave Travis a glass and took one for herself. They sat together on the love seat. John and Robin sat next to each other in the two tall chairs.

"I'm so happy to be here today," Eric said to Flora. "I've thought of you so many times over the years. I still remember the first time we saw each other."

Flora grinned. "So do I. My mother had sent my sister and me to the supermarket where you were working. You got our bags mixed up with someone else's. My mother made us go back to the store to get what she wanted," Flora laughed.

"Yes, and Old Man White was angry at me for making the mistake. The next time you came in the store, I was just getting off work and walked you home."

Robin looked at Tracey. "Aunt Flo looks so content with him," she murmured under her breath. Travis looked content with Tracey, too. But, most of the time, all eyes were on Flora and Eric.

"You guys, why don't we go into the living room and gave them some space?" John suggested.

"Good idea," Tracey answered.

Once they were alone, Eric decided to talk about their long ago separation.

"Flora, we've talked about everything except why I

stopped writing you," he said, and saw the sudden change in Flora's expression. He wondered if he had hurt her.

"I often wondered. I just took it for granted that you had found someone else. Years later I heard that you were married. But by that time I had already gotten married, too."

"After my father died, my mother had no one else but me. I had to take over his business and take care of her. Whenever I mentioned coming out here, even for a visit, she would get ill. She didn't want me out of her sight." He stopped and took a deep sigh. "I wrote letters but after awhile I just couldn't mail them."

"But, why Eric? I looked in the mailbox everyday. After the first month, you just stopped writing." He moved a little closer to her and was happy for the privacy. Now, they could talk and get to know each other again.

"My mother lived for a year after she lost my father. I came out here to ask you to go back to Dallas and marry me. I asked everyone that we both knew. No one could tell me where you and your family had moved to. I was so disappointed. I went back." He paused. "I met Claudia and we got married. After a few years, I sold my father's company and came back here to live. One month after my return, I was told where you were.

"But, like me, you were married, too. I used to look for you in crowds, but it's funny how you can live in Los Angeles for years and never see someone by chance. Anyway, my wife died three years ago. I guess God sent Tracey to me," he said and held her hand in his.

"My husband was still a young man when he died."

"You never got married again?"

"No, but I could have. A couple of years after my husband's death, my sister and her husband were in a car accident. Both were killed. I got custody of Tracey and Robin. I missed my husband, and they came along and changed my life," she explained, and he could see that she was sincere and proud of her nieces.

"Tracey is a smart woman. I know you must be proud of her."

"Yes. I'm proud of both of them. They have never given me a minute's worry."

He touched Flora's hand again. "Flora, I hope we can be friends again. I don't expect anything more. We were once such close friends. You can't find that every day, you know."

She looked at him and nodded. "Now, I guess we should join the others. They were kind enough to give us this time together."

"They sure were," he answered, and followed her to the living room where the others were laughing, talking, and drinking wine. Flora smiled as she walked in and saw that Travis was holding Tracey's hand and looking at her as if she were the only person in the room.

"Is everyone ready for dinner now? I'm starved," John said.

Everyone got up at the same time. Flora looked at her watch, now realizing how long she and Eric had been talking in the den.

"Everyone sit tight. Robin and I will have dinner on the table in no time," Tracey said, and followed Robin into the kitchen.

"This has been quite an interesting day, don't you think, Tracey?" Robin was pouring the corn into a large bowl.

"Yes, but somehow I knew it would be. I must admit, I was getting a little worried this morning. Aunt Flo really didn't want to come. She wanted to stay in all day. So, if this didn't go right, she probably would have been ready to kill me."

"Here, you can put the chicken on this platter. I'll take out the pot roast." Robin sat the platter in front of Tracey. "Now, tell me, how are you and Dr. Travis getting along?"

"To tell the truth, I don't know. This relationship hasn't gone to the next step, yet." Tracey stopped, knowing she was telling a white lie. Their steamy, passionate moments together flashed across her mind. "He works all hours and

I'm still not certain if I want to get any more involved than I am," she said, her expression flickering with indecision.

She hadn't told Robin that they had slept together. But still, she wasn't sure where they would go from there.

"To tell you the truth, I didn't want you to be involved with him. But he seems to be nice and very taken with you, girl. Maybe you better think about it."

"So did Donald."

"I know. But he isn't Donald. Donald was everywhere, all the time. He probably had more than one woman when you first met him. But you were younger, and he wanted you."

"He wanted me to show off and prove to everyone that he could get any woman he wanted, young or old."

"Travis doesn't seem to be anything like Donald was, Tracey. Let it go and start over again."

"You didn't sound this positive three weeks ago, Robin."

"I know. I've been under so much pressure. Now, we'd better get in there before John comes in here to see what's taking dinner so long."

As Tracey walked into the living room, Travis was watching her. Her blue skirt was short enough to show her well-proportioned legs, and her blue matching sweater showed the voluptuous swell of her breasts. She was a stunning woman.

He looked at Robin and saw the resemblance between the two sisters. Tracey had long hair and Robin wore hers cut short, but both had the same smooth brown skin. Tracey was about a foot taller, a size eight, and he loved to watch her walk, loved watching her hips move slowly from side to side.

"It's ready, everyone," Robin announced.

Flora and Eric blessed the food. The dinner went well and the conversation kept everyone laughing and happy. Eric and Flora told everyone what they did together when they were younger.

Tracey was sitting next to Travis. She glanced at him out of the corner of her eyes. He was impeccably dressed, manicured, and groomed. He looked good in his black shirt and trousers. His black hair was cut close and combed back. His dark, intelligent eyes always made Tracey nervous, as if he could see something in her that no one else could.

When dinner was over, Tracey and Travis went outside and sat on a bench in the backyard.

They sat spellbound as they gazed at the new Calla lilies that were blooming in the flower garden.

"It's always so peaceful out here. Now that I've planted flowers, I sit in my backyard sometimes, too," she said.

"You don't look like a woman that works in a yard," he answered looking at her manicured hands.

She smiled. "There's a lot you don't know about me, Travis."

"I know. But, I know all that I need to know to care for you. Sometimes it's better to find out as you get to know the person. And sometimes I think I know all about you, Tracey Woods."

She was surprised to hear that. "How is that?"

"It's easy. You care for a person, and you know just enough to want to know more about them. And each time you see that person, you learn something new." He looked into her eyes.

"Today for instance. I found out that you are a romantic. You set your aunt and Eric up, right?"

"Yes. But I did it for both of them. My aunt has been a little under the weather lately."

"She'll be all right, baby."

"Today, she seems to be much better. I had no idea that they knew each other. Aunt Flo never told us about any of the guys she dated before she was married."

Travis picked a lily from the bush and placed it in Tracey's hair and traced the side of her face. She couldn't move, or say anything. He kissed her on her lips as if he couldn't help himself.

Tracey wondered why he made her feel something that

no other man had ever made her feel before—not even Donald. It bothered her a bit, she had to admit. She was mesmerized with his touch, with his kiss. He made her feel the urgency to be loved, the excitement that built so deep inside her. And he was so handsome, so perfectly built and gentle that she couldn't get him off her mind.

"I want you to be my girl, Tracey," he whispered so softly that she trembled as she heard the words against her ear. "I want you to be mine, only mine. Forget everything that has happened and pretend that we just met in a supermarket, a shopping mall, anywhere, except the night that we really met."

He brushed his lips down her neck. "Can you do that, Tracey?"

He was still holding her close in his arms. "I want to, but it's so hard to forget," she panted back into his ear, feeling herself becoming aroused.

"You've got to live again, love again. You have to try, Tracey."

"I know. I'm trying, Travis. God, I'm trying."

"Tracey."

The spell was broken. She heard a voice that sounded far away; it was Robin standing near the deck. Tracey wondered how long she had been there. Knowing Robin, she had been watching and eavesdropping.

"Eric wants to say good-bye."

Tracey sighed, but was grateful for the interruption. "I'm coming," Tracey said. She turned to Travis. "I guess we'd better get back inside." She shivered, feeling a chill in the air that she hadn't felt before.

"We'll finish this conversation another time. You won't get off this easily, baby."

Travis followed Tracey inside and decided that it was time for him to leave, too. He had promised his mother that he would drop by on the way to his new partner's house. They had to discuss their partnership and when he would join the practice.

When Eric and Travis had left, Tracey helped Robin clean the kitchen while Flora, John, and Lisa watched television in the den.

"Are you ready, Aunt Flo? I bet you're tired from all the excitement you had today," Tracey asked.

"Yes, it has be an exciting day." When they slipped on their coats, Aunt Flo asked her, "How long have you known Eric?"

"We met about two months ago. A client sent him to me. We started talking and he told me that Donald built the building that he sold." Tracey gave Aunt Flo a wide smile. "He still has three other minimalls that he's keeping but he didn't want any more apartment buildings. He was such a nice man and I sensed that he was lonely. I hope you are okay with what I did, Aunt Flo," she said tentatively.

"Actually, I was against it, Aunt Flo," Robin said. "So if you are unhappy with it, it wasn't my idea. It was Tracey's and my husband's."

"Thanks for your support, Robin," Tracey snapped. "Are you ready to go home, Aunt Flo?"

"Yes. It's been a long day, but a good one. It's good to see someone with whom you can talk about your past and they know what you're talking about."

"Good, Aunt Flo," Tracey said as she looked in Robin's direction. They said good-bye, kissed Lisa, and walked out.

On the way home, Tracey was quiet. Flora broke the silence. "You can't pay any attention to Robin. You were only trying to make me happy, and I appreciate that. You are always trying to be perfect, Tracey. Don't try so hard. Now, it's time to make yourself happy, honey."

"What do you mean, Aunt Flo?"

"You know what I mean. Travis is in love with you. You care a great deal for him, too." Tracey opened her mouth to say something and Flora stopped her.

"If you didn't like him, you wouldn't have him over. If you do, then it's time for you to admit it to yourself and do something about it. He's a good-looking, eligible man."

Flora's tone became serious. "Other women see it just as you do. Don't take too long, honey. Good men don't come around everyday, you know. What his sister and Donald did is not his fault."

Tracey knew that Flora was right, but it kept eating at her. She had loved Donald so much and Travis was a constant remainder of what Donald had done to her and of the horrible night she met him in the hospital. It was all so complex. She was sure that she was in love with him. But she couldn't get his sister out of her mind. The night of the accident when Tracey met Travis in the hospital, she'd hated him. Now she couldn't remember when she'd stopped hating him and started loving him. She turned the corner still listening to her aunt.

"I know that you are right, Aunt Flo. But, I just don't know what to do about it. I don't know how to forget."

"First, you stop thinking that life has to be perfect. You've been thinking that way for so long it's become a way of life for you. After your mother and father died, I understood. But, now it's different. Nothing is perfect, Tracey."

Aunt Flo's voice dropped. "Take it from me. Eric hurt me terribly many years ago. You have to forgive and forget, child. You are going to make yourself miserable for no reason at all." Tracey parked and walked Flora inside.

She drove home and thought of everything her aunt had told her, but she had the same thoughts so many times herself. When she walked in her house, the phone was ringing. It was Travis.

"Are you at the hospital?" she asked, glancing at her watch.

"No. I just left my mother's house. I promised her that I would stop by."

"Do you always keep your promises?" She sat on the edge of the sofa.

"Yes, I always keep my promises, darling. If I can't, I'll let you know. What are you doing Wednesday evening?"

"That all depends on what you have in mind."

"Will you go to dinner with me?"

"Yes, I'd love to."

"Good. By the way, it's at my mother's house."

At first there was silence. "Your mother's house?"

"Yes. Is there a problem, Tracey?"

She hesitated before answering. Remembering Aunt Flo's words, she answered,"No, no problem. What time?"

"I'll pick you up at five. That will give you enough time to warm up and get comfortable. Remember what I asked you? I want you to be mine."

She didn't know what to say. She wanted to say that she was, but she couldn't. She was too afraid to trust and love again. Wednesday was only three days away.

"I remember what you asked. We can talk about it Wednesday," she answered in a soft whisper, her heart pounding hard. She sat on the couch, closed her eyes, and after he hung up she let out a long sigh.

The next morning at work nothing went as planned. Michelle called in and said that she would be an hour late. The client she had scheduled to see at nine called and said that he couldn't see her until eleven. And to make matters worse, he wanted her to drive to Riverside to meet him. "Hell, what's next?"

At nine-thirty Michelle arrived at the office. She said, "I'm sorry. I had to stop and buy a book for my class tonight." She looked around and saw only one coffee cup. "Where's your client? I know he didn't leave already."

"He wants me to meet him at eleven, and in Riverside. If this wasn't a good commission I would tell him to go to someone else," Tracey said, frowning. "Would you like to come along?"

"Yes, of course I will. I need all the experience that I can get."

"You're doing pretty good, Michelle. You finish school

and we can share this office. Who knows, you may want to lease the office upstairs. It's time we got started. I don't want to rush and get lost."

"Let me comb my hair," Michelle said. She started to walk away and stopped. "You like my new dress?" She turned around in front of Tracey so she could get a good look.

"I love it. This was a good day to wear it, too." Tracey looked Michelle in the eye "Are you feeling better lately? I know how hard breaking up can be."

Michelle leaned against the desk. "I just try and think of something else when something reminds me of him. I still can't believe we're not together. I don't even know what to do to keep him off my mind, Tracey."

"You keep pushing ahead, keep busy. You'll get over it." *Yeah, right,* thought Tracey. *Who am I to give advice? I'm still jealous and angry over a dead woman.*

The drive took forever. The San Bernardino Freeway was busy and Tracey wasn't familiar with the city of Riverside. She got off two exits before she was supposed to and was lost for fifteen minutes before she found the place.

"I was so sure that I had missed the exit. I should never have gotten off. But, thank goodness we found it," she said. "Next time he's going to drive to LA, no matter what. Goodness, I'm hungry. Well, this is it," Tracey said. The building was tall and white.

They got out of the car and walked inside. Mr. Gross met them at the door.

"I'm sorry to put you through so much trouble. It was a mad house here earlier when I called to tell you that I couldn't go to your office."

Michelle couldn't take her eyes off him. He was much younger than she had thought he would be. He looked to be about thirty, dressed in jeans and a white T-shirt.

"Do you ladies like pizza? I can order one while you're here." he said and led them in the back to a large, round table.

"Sure, we love pizza," Tracey answered. All three sat at the table while Mr. Gross called and ordered pizza. He talked on the phone but he was watching Michelle and she gave him a sweet smile. Tracey didn't miss the look that passed between them.

Larry Gross and his brother were developers who had built apartment buildings from Riverside to Los Angeles. Tracey had met him five years ago when he did some business with Donald. They had taken over their father's business when he became too ill to continue working. His brother was only a couple of years older than he. They both had homes of their own, but his brother was married. Larry wasn't married and devoted all his time to the business. He was good-looking, smart, and easy to do business with.

"We want to buy a twenty- or thirty-unit building in Inglewood. Since we are so far away, we need someone who knows the business, Tracey. We know that you will get us the best deal." He sounded older than his years to Tracey. "You know what we're looking for. I have a name and phone number of a man that may want to sell."

"Have you talked with him at all?" Tracey asked.

"No. We would like you to talk to him. If he doesn't want to sell, then, there are others." He stood up. "Excuse me, I think the man is here with our pizza."

"He's so cute," Michelle whispered. "Is he married or what?"

"No, he's not married. He keeps looking at you. I think he has a crush on you already, honey."

"You really think so?" she whispered.

"Yes, I do."

Larry came back with pizza and salad. He sat it on the table and went to the small kitchen to get some plates, forks, and Cokes. "I hope this is all right with you ladies. I was just too busy to take you to lunch."

"This is great, Larry," Tracey answered. "How's your dad?"

"He's good. He just can't work the way he used to. He

and my mom travel more now, and he stays close to home." He turned to Michelle. "How long have you worked with Tracey?"

Michelle smiled. "For a year now."

"I'm teaching her the business. She's going to be real good, too."

"I know she will. She's learning from a professional, Tracey. You're the best. I hear that you're really in demand now."

"I do get a lot of business. That's why I need someone like Michelle to learn it."

"Thanks, Tracey," Michelle said with a girlish giggle.

"Michelle, I could take you to see some of the buildings that my brother and I have built. I'm not working Saturday. Not that you want to know how to build, but I could show you around."

Tracey wanted to laugh. Was that the best he could do by way of asking for a date?

"I'm free on Saturday," Michelle said, looking astonished that he would ask her. She wondered what they would talk about, what she would wear. God, she was excited.

After they finished going over prices and ideas of what Tracey needed to look for, she and Michelle left. When they got in the car, Larry told Michelle that he would call her at the office on Friday.

"You know that Saturday is really a date, don't you?" Tracey asked her as she was driving back to LA.

"I hope so. But, what does he want with me? He has money, everything."

"I've told you about talking like that. The man likes what he sees. You're smart, intelligent, and young and so is he. Now, why wouldn't he ask?"

"It's just that he's so smart. He has so much to offer, and I have nothing."

"You have much more than you give yourself credit for.

Go out with him and enjoy yourself. Maybe you'll forget that fool who thought he was too good for you. The truth is, you were too good for him," Tracey said and smiled at her.

"Maybe you're right. Maybe I was too good for him after all. I have no parents with money, but at least I work and do for myself. His parents give him everything."

"He'll never be any good for anyone. You're lucky that he's out of the picture."

Twenty-three

Wednesday came soon, too soon for Tracey. She was standing in her closet trying to decide what she was going to wear to meet Travis's mother. She pulled out a purple dress, put it in front of her, and hung it back up. She grabbed the green one and hung it up. She sighed, standing with one hand on her hip. Finally, she decided on the new mustard-colored dress that she had never worn, and the stiletto-heeled shoes and Donna Karan purse, the same color as her dress.

Perfect, she thought. She put her hair up and pulled the pins out to let it fall back down. As she was standing in front of the mirror, the doorbell rang. She looked at the clock on the nightstand and it was five. Must be Travis, she thought. She went into the living room and opened the door.

"You look lovely, Tracey." He kissed her on the cheek. He wanted to pick her up and take her to bed and make wild, hot love to her, but it would have to wait.

"I'll get my purse. It will just be a minute. He walked around her living room and stopped in front of a painting on the wall that was painted in black and white.

"You like it?"

"Very much. Did you pick it?"

"Yes, I fell in love with it the first time I saw it." She turned out the light and they left.

The ride to his mother's house only took fifteen minutes. "I didn't realize that your mother lived in the View Park area."

"Yes, this is where I grew up." Travis rang the doorbell and his mother opened the door. She was tall and attractive with a warm smile. Her short hair was frosted with streaks of gray. He kissed her on the cheek.

"Come in. I've been expecting you. You must be Tracey."

"Yes, and it's nice to meet you, Mrs. Howard. Thank you for having me over for dinner." Tracey held out her hand and shook Mrs. Howard's.

"My pleasure." They followed her to the living room. "I was pleased when Travis told me that you could come."

"Tracey, would you like a glass of wine?" Travis asked.

"Yes, that would be nice."

"You, Mom?"

"Yes, I'll take one, too. I have a bottle chilling in the refrigerator," she said as he headed into the kitchen.

"Travis tells me that you are in real estate," she said, turning back to face Tracey. "My brother used to be in real estate before he retired."

"Yes, I have been for almost ten years now." She looked around. "You have a lovely house. I only live fifteen minutes from you."

Travis walked in with long-stemmed glasses. "Here's the wine," he said, giving them their glasses. "It smells good, Mom," he said and sat on the couch next to Tracey. His mother was sitting in the chair opposite them.

"Your brother called today, Travis. He'll be here Saturday."

"That's good news. How long is he staying?"

"Just two days. He'll be on a business trip and has to stop here. Do you have any sisters or brothers, Tracey?"

"Yes, I have one sister and no brothers, though I've always wanted one."

"I have two sons. My youngest was a daughter, but she's deceased," she said sadly, and looked at her daughter's picture that was hanging on the wall.

"I'm so sorry." Tracey was certain that Travis hadn't told his mother who she was or that his sister had been dating a married man, her husband.

Maureen told Tracey about her husband, her son's work, and how she spent her time. "Your aunt's name sounds familiar to me. I've lived in this neighborhood for a long time. My children grew up here and went to school here.

"We used to lived in the house next door. My husband had this house built and sold the one next door." She told Tracey all about her family, her children, husband, and two sisters that she only saw twice a year. Tracey noticed she was loquacious, but at the same time, she seemed eager to let Tracey know about the family.

"Are you ready for dinner, Travis? I could sit here and talk all night."

"Yes, Mother. I'm starved and it smells delicious."

"And you, Tracey, are you ready?"

"Yes. I agree with Travis. It smells wonderful."

They had dinner in the dining room. On the wall facing Tracey was a painting of Mr. and Mrs. Howard and their three children. It seemed as though the young girl who later became Donald's mistress was looking straight at Tracey. Tracey tried to eat without looking at the picture. After they finished, Mrs. Howard went to the kitchen for cake and coffee. And when she returned she started another conversation about her husband.

"My husband loved the boys, but you know how father's are about their daughters. Susan was his heart. She was so perfect, so beautiful. She was a child who did nothing wrong in her life. My husband adored her. Isn't that right, Travis?"

Travis cleared his throat and looked at Tracey. "Mother, all children do some things that they shouldn't. Remember the time Scott and I took the bus to San Diego and you and Dad were worried out of your minds?"

"Yes, I remember. But, Susan never did anything like you boys." She looked at Tracey. "Are you all right, honey?"

Tracey felt sick and she realized that coming here was a mistake, seeing Travis was another mistake. It would never work.

"Tracey?" Mrs. Howard sounded concerned.

"Oh, I'm sorry. I was just looking at the painting of your family. Your daughter is beautiful," she said, clenching her hands together in her lap. She felt a migraine, and the pain in her left temple, and wondered why had she ever come here. She looked at Travis and he looked so tense and uncomfortable.

"Mother, as always dinner was good, but I think it's time to take Tracey home. Besides, I have the early shift in the morning," he said, getting up from the table.

Tracey stood up, too. "It was really nice meeting you, Mrs. Howard."

Travis's mother got up and touched Tracey's hand. "I hope that you will come back again. I would like to see more of you." She looked at Travis. "You'd better bring her back, son."

"I would love to, Mom." He kissed his mother and they left.

The ride home was quiet. The fresh air felt good against Tracey's face but there was an intense strain in the air that Tracey and Travis felt.

They arrived at Tracey's house and Travis parked the car in the driveway and turned to face her.

"Tracey, I'm sorry about tonight. Mother misses my sister and father very much. She was the only daughter and her youngest. It was hard enough when she lost my father, but when Susan died she was devastated. You know, ironic as it may sound, tonight she talked to you about my sister more than she has since the accident. I've been trying to get her to talk about Susan, but she never does. Tonight was just as strenuous for me as it was for you."

Lucky me, thought Tracey. "I can't do this anymore, Travis."

"Do what, baby? We are just getting started. I want you forever. I want to do more with you. Pretty soon I will be at an office and can spend more time with you. That's what I want for us, Tracey."

She was shaking her head from side to side. "You're not listening to me, Travis. There will always be your sister and Donald between us. I can't handle that. Your mother thinks that Susan was a saint. But I know better."

"She didn't do it alone, Tracey. Donald was there, too."

"That doesn't excuse anything and it doesn't make it any easier, Travis," she retorted.

"No, it doesn't. But, they're dead; we're not. Why can't we be happy and enjoy life? I want to marry you, Tracey." He kissed her hard on the lips.

When Tracey realized that she was responding to his kiss, she gently pulled away. "I can't do this, Travis. I can't have a conversation with your mother about Susan knowing what I know. I can't blame you for not telling her."

Her eyes watered, and she stared straight ahead like a zombie. "But it's no good. Please don't call me anymore," she said, thankful that it was too dark for him to see the tears rolling down her face. He reached for her again but she opened the door and got out of the car.

"Wait, let me see you in."

She waved her hand. "No, you can see me from here." She ran to the door before he could say anything else.

Travis sat in the car for ten minutes after she ran inside. He sighed, shook his head in frustration. This was supposed to be another step forward for them tonight, but it was two steps backward. He drove off and went home. But when he got there, he couldn't sleep. He tried phoning Tracey but she hadn't turned off her answering machine.

Tracey took off her clothes and hung them in the closet. She made herself a hot cup of tea, took two aspirin, lay across the bed, and closed her eyes.

She tossed and turned all night, seeing the painting of Travis's family in front of her. The painting was so large, the colors bright. They all were smiling as if they were the perfect family.

The phone rang again and she looked at the clock. It was only eight and Tracey turned up the answering machine. It was Wendy. She quickly picked up the phone. "I'm here, Wendy, don't hang up."

"I called you earlier, didn't you get my message?" she asked in an excited voice.

"No. I came home with a headache, took two aspirins, and lay down. You sound great and happy, too."

"I am great and happy. I'm getting married next month. Can you believe it, Tracey? I had to travel all the way to Mississippi to find a good man?"

"Did you say next month?" Tracey asked in surprise.

"Yes. James doesn't want to wait. We are both sure of this. He's the right man, Tracey. He's a good, hardworking man. I want to be happy before I roll over and die," she joked.

"How can you joke about a thing like that?" Tracey wasn't in a joking mood.

"Oh, stop being so prickly. Impropriety and what is politically correct is no concern for us. We're in love, honey. You should be, too. What's the matter with you?"

"Nothing. This headache, that's all. I'm happy for you and James. Will you guys be coming to LA any time soon? I wish you were moving back."

"I know, honey. James has been on his job for more than twenty years. Our family and his daughter is here." Wendy was absolutely cooing in the phone.

"LA will no longer be my home. But, we will visit. Are you coming for my wedding, Tracey? It's going to be small and simple, just family, and you, my best friend."

"You know I'll be there. But, I have three real estate deals going at once. I'll only be there from Friday to Sunday." She knew that she needed to get away for her sake as much as Wendy's. Would she ever be happy and in love? she wondered.

"That's good, it's better than not coming at all. It will be on a Saturday. Tracey, I'm so happy that I could die. I keep waiting to wake up and find out that it's only a dream. Maybe you'll be next, Tracey."

"I don't think so. It doesn't look too good for me. Besides, I'm not sure if it ever will," she said, feeling sorry for herself. *Damn, why was she crying?*

"Don't let a little argument come between you and Travis, Tracey. James and I just had an argument last week and we're getting married."

"Yes, but you and James don't have the excess baggage to bring into your marriage. Travis and I do."

Wendy's voice raised so loud, Tracey had to pull the phone away from her ear. Then Wendy lowered her voice.

"Look, all I'm saying is don't walk away because of something that two dead people did. We'll talk about it when you get here."

"Okay. How is Donna taking all of this?"

"You know Donna. She always has something to say. She's kind of like Robin."

"Yes, I know. I'll call you over the weekend, and we can make plans."

"Tracey, I wish you were here with me now."

"Me, too, girl." Tracey hung up and the phone rang again, but she didn't answer it. She turned over in bed and closed her eyes, but she couldn't sleep.

Twenty-four

Travis was glad that his brother had arrived. When he got off duty he and his brother, Scott, met at a bar in Santa Monica. They ordered two beers and took a table near the poolroom.

"We haven't done this in a long time," Scott said.

"How did you get away from Mom?" Travis asked.

"It wasn't easy. Hey, she told me about this beauty that you are dating. You guys were over for dinner, huh?"

"Yes, but it didn't go too well. She won't see me or return any of my calls."

"Everyone has their ups and downs in a relationship, Travis. It'll pass and you'll be lovers again."

"Not that simple."

"Why? This sounds serious."

"It is."

Travis told his brother how he met Tracey and about Susan's and Donald's relationship. Scott listened with disappointment written all over his face.

"I had no idea, Travis. Dad must be turning over in his grave."

"I was going to tell you, but I was waiting until we were alone. Man, you looked just like Dad when you said that. The only thing I can do now is let her go. She's never going to forget. Or forgive. I thought that everything was going good between us. But Mom kept bringing up Susan and that did it."

"You mean she talked about Susan?" Scott asked, just as surprised as Travis was.

"That's what got me. We've been trying to get her to talk about Susan. She wouldn't say her name to me, but she opens up to a complete stranger."

"I wonder why that is?" Scott asked, as if Travis knew the answer.

"Maybe it's some woman's thing. I don't know. She went on and on about how perfect Susan was, how pretty she was." Travis looked as though he was still flabbergasted.

"You wouldn't have believed it unless you were there. I thought that Tracey would throw up at the table. Finally, she couldn't take anymore and said she had a headache. That was my cue to take her home."

Scott just sat and listened to his brother. He sensed that Travis was very much in love with this new woman. "She must be special for you to take her to meet Mom. It must be love. Mom told me the same thing.

"The only way I know that you can solve this is to tell Mother the truth. Maybe she should know about Susan and the woman's husband. It'll be better that she knows it now than to find it out later. Everyone will be more comfortable that way, Travis."

"Why should we tell her that?"

"No, little brother, not we, but you. It's your girl, remember?"

"Thanks a whole hell of a lot. But, I don't see why she needs to know because of Tracey's hang-ups. I wonder if his mother knows."

"Ask her. If she doesn't, you can use it to fight with. Maybe she'll listen to reason." Scott motioned for the waitress to come over and ordered two more beers. He watched her walking away in her short shirt until she was out of sight. "Cute; nice legs, too. You were saying, Travis?"

Travis sighed. "I was saying that I don't know if her mother-in-law knows or not." The waitress came back with two beers and Scott gave her a five-dollar tip.

"Are you paying attention, Scott?" Travis asked, sounding annoyed.

"Of course, I'm listening. Find out if his mother knows. If she doesn't, then ask why. Maybe she hasn't even thought of telling her because she doesn't think that she needs to know. Ask her why. Make her see that you don't think that Mother needs to know either. If that doesn't do it, strip her clothes off and take her to bed," he said diabolically. They both laughed.

"Scott, can I ask you something personal?"

"Sure, shoot, Bro."

"Have you ever played around with another woman since you've been married to Alicia?"

"Hell, no, man. I have no reason to. Sure, I look at big legs and pretty asses." He threw his palms up as a sign of innocence and shook his head at the same time. "But, that's as far as it goes. I'm not taking a chance on losing what I have for a pretty ass. Now, when are you going into practice with Neil?"

"In two months. Right now we're having the office expanded. It's a good location, on the corner of Wilshire and Fairfax."

Scott looked at their glasses and they were half-empty. "We'd better get back by the time Mom is finished cooking. You know how she hates waiting."

Early the next morning, Travis jogged on the pier and watched the silver dawn filter palely through a fine autumn mist that cloaked the streets.

After he finished jogging, he went back inside and phoned Tracey and asked her to meet him at the pier in Marina Del Rey. It was cool outside but the skies were clear and blue. It was a place that Travis often went when he needed to think clearly. He would walk up and down the pier and smell the fresh air and look out at the clear sea, the boats, people laughing and having a good time.

In the early mornings it was quiet until it got close to noon.

As he dusted the sand off his long, hard legs he could see Tracey walking toward him. She was wearing a pair of shorts and a jean jacket. She looked young, no more than twenty-five. Her hair hung past her shoulders, and the curls blew in her face. She wore sunglasses and her purse hung on her shoulder.

"I wasn't sure that you would come."

"I was rather surprised when you called," she answered. "Do you run out here often?"

"Yes. When I want to think and clear my head. It's peaceful and I love the water. I can walk here from my apartment. I don't know why you were surprised. I've told you more than once that I want you." He leaned on the rail looking out at sea and so did she.

She didn't say anything as she tapped her fingers up and down.

"I've been thinking of our situation. How we can solve the problem or if it can even be solved. I still haven't told my mother about Susan. I don't want to see her hurt. But, I don't want you uncomfortable either. By the way, have you told his mother about Susan?"

She jerked her head fast and looked at him. She seemed surprised that he asked her that question. He turned to face her, waiting for her answer. But he was sure that she hadn't.

She began to sputter. "You don't understand, Travis. You're not the one who was hurt by Donald and Susan." And now she felt as if she had been unfair, or insensitive. But it was different. Donald and Susan didn't hurt him. They hurt her.

"So, did you or didn't you tell Donald's mother?" Travis demanded.

"I didn't actually tell her. My sister didn't know that I hadn't and out of bitterness she brought the matter up."

He folded his arms in front of him. "Why didn't you tell her when you found out?"

Tracey cleared her throat. "Where are you going with this conversation?"

"I want you to tell me the truth, Tracey."

"Okay, I didn't tell her because it wasn't any of her business. I didn't want to hurt her. You see, she didn't think that Donald could do any wrong. She always thought he was perfect."

"The same way my mother thinks of Susan. Funny, how you don't mind hurting her," he said in an icy tone of voice.

Tracey seemed to be at a loss for words. "I don't want to see your mother hurt. But I was hurt more than anyone by your sister."

"And your husband. You seem to conveniently forget his part in it," he said, with an edge to his voice.

"I haven't forgotten." She turned her head looking over the water. "I know that it's hard for you to understand. It's hard for me, too. I think we need more time to think about it."

He grasped her shoulders. "I have done all the thinking that I'm going to do. I've told you how I feel about you, that I want to marry you. So maybe you should be the one to think about it.

"Let me get this right," he said, his mouth in a grim line. "You wanted to spare your mother-in-law's feeling, but you don't give a damn about my mother's. Maybe you're not the person that I thought you were. Or maybe being in love with you prevented me from seeing who you really are." He let her go and looked out at the sea again as if he couldn't look at her any longer.

Tracey was shaken by his hard words, his cold eyes. She'd never seen this side of Travis. If only he would look at her, if only he could understand how hurt she had been by her husband and his sister. But no, he only thought she was selfish, unfeeling toward his mother.

"Travis, I didn't mean it the way it sounds. You don't know how hurt I was the night I walked into that hospital. I keep trying to forget. The other night at your mother's house was just too much, too soon. Maybe in time we can work something out. I don't know what to say," she whispered and looked at him.

His expression remained impassive. His eyes looked like stone cold marbles. She wondered if she had said anything to make him understand how she felt. And as she looked at him she realized that he was a part of her recovering from all the hurt and pain she had gone through. He was always there for her. She didn't want to lose him, or stop seeing him, and he said that he loved her. *God, how could she make him understand?*

He turned to face her and stood close. "Tracey, I'm leaving it entirely up to you. You think about it and make the decision. I won't bother you anymore." He kissed her on the cheek and turned to walk away.

Suddenly Tracey's jaws seemed frozen shut. She wanted to call him, but something held her back. After he was down the beach and becoming smaller and smaller on the horizon, she was able to speak again.

"Travis, you're not bothering me. You've never been a bother. . . ." her voice trailed off in the wind like a sinking ship. He was gone.

She stood there watching him, wanting to call him back, wanting to run to him and fall into his arms. But, she just stood there, motionless and watched him walk away without looking back at her. Tracey went to her car and sat there for half an hour before she drove home. It was over. She had lost him.

Twenty-five

Tracey was standing on a kitchen chair, wrestling a dead lightbulb from a socket, when the doorbell rang, startling and sudden. It rang three times before she got to it. It was Robin, standing as if she was getting impatient.

"What took you so long? It's freezing out here today."

"I was changing a lightbulb in the kitchen. And I had just pulled my luggage out of the closet so I can start packing. Come on in the den with me," she said walking in front of Robin. Tracey looked over her shoulder. "Besides, you're always cold."

"Did you say luggage? Are you going somewhere?"

"Yes. Guess what? Wendy is getting married!"

Robin sat in the leather chair and crossed her leg. "Marrying who?"

"Don't you remember that I told you that she had met a man?" Tracey sat on the couch.

Robin shook her head in amazement. "Do you mean to tell me that she is marrying someone else so soon? Has she lost all her senses? Really, Tracey, I don't know what to say about her anymore."

"Then don't say anything. I really don't understand you, Robin. Wendy and I have been friends since we were in grammar school. And what is wrong with her marrying again?" Tracey snapped, tears forming in her eyes.

Robin looked at her strangely. "Hey, what is it, Tracey? I know you're not crying because of what I said about that nutcase. What is it, honey?" she asked, and looked genuinely concerned. She walked over to the couch and put her arm around Tracey's shoulders.

Tracey wiped her eyes. "Travis and I had a fight. No, it was not a fight. We're just not seeing each other anymore."

Robin pulled away so she could see Tracey's face. "Why, what happened? It seemed like everything was going so well."

"I thought so, too, until I went to his mother's house for dinner."

"What does she have to do with it?"

"Nothing really. She talked about her daughter like she was a saint or a queen or something. I was sick to my stomach every time she said Susan's name." Tracey mimicked Travis's mother. "'Susan this, and Susan that,' 'Susan was such a good person, a smart person.'

"Robin, I just couldn't take any more of it. Travis won't tell her the truth about his sister."

"Which is?"

"About her and Donald, of course."

Robin sat up straight. "Now wait a minute. You jumped all over me for telling Mildred about Donald and you want him to tell his mother? Mildred wouldn't know today if I hadn't opened my big mouth, and you had no intention of telling her. Now, what kind of fairness is that?"

"I just don't think that I can see him and go around his mother and listen to her talk about her wonderful daughter."

"If that's the way you feel, then you can't see Travis anymore." Tracey looked at her as if she had been expecting Robin to encourage her to see him again.

"That's right. Hate his sister more than you love him. Expect a mother to turn her back on her daughter because of one mistake and because of Donald. Remember, she didn't do this alone."

"You're supposed to be making me feel better, Robin, not worse." She started to cry again.

"Tracey, what can I say? You want everything perfect, everything black or white, no in-betweens. You loved Donald, so you kept the perfect house, the perfect office, clothes, everything had to be perfect. When Mom and Dad died you were afraid that Aunt Flora wouldn't keep us, so you had to be perfect. But now you are an adult. And guess what? Everything is not perfect," Robin said ruefully. "You loved Mildred so you didn't want to hurt her by telling her that her son wasn't perfect. Why would you want to hurt Travis's mother?"

"I don't want to hurt her, Robin. I just want him to understand."

"There's nothing for him to understand. This is just a hangup that you have to get over and understand. You always have been a fair and sensible person, Tracey."

Tracey got up and paced the floor. "I know, but I'm not sure that I can."

"I sure hope you do. I thought something like this would get in the way, but I was certain that you could handle it. Guess I was wrong. You'd better think about this before it's too late, girlfriend."

"It may already be too late. We talked two nights ago and he seemed so disgusted with me. I think he's losing interest," she said sadly.

"Like I said, don't take too long. There are plenty of other women out there looking for a good man. And a doctor, too. Girl, do you love him, Tracey?"

"Yes. Talking to him the other night, I realized how much I do love him. Now I'm not certain if I've been thinking right or wrong about him telling his mother. I just know that I can't stand hearing her talk about her daughter."

"Mothers think that way of their children, Tracey. If you have a child, you will understand. She lost her only daughter, and Travis lost his only sister. You'll have to try and understand how they feel, too. You're not the only one who has lost someone. Now, you keep that in mind. But if you can't tolerate hearing the woman's name in your presence, then you should let him go," Robin said with an air of finality.

"That's easier said than done."

"You know it's been better for John and I, but it's not perfect, honey. John is John, and he'll always have some faults. But I want to keep my family together and I love my husband." Robin looked down at her hands and spoke in an embarrassed tone. "I had a tough time coping with Paul's death. I can still see him running across the street, the gun in his hand, yelling at me. I feel so awful some times. It has affected my attitude a lot, I know. But, I'm trying to get better."

"I'm glad that it's getting easier for you."

"When is Wendy getting married?" Robin asked as she got up and put on her navy blazer that matched the skirt that she was wearing.

"I'm leaving next weekend. But, I'll be back Sunday evening. I have lots of work to do."

"I don't know what to say about her. That girl jumps in and out of more relationships than anyone I know."

"She says that this marriage is different from the other three."

"She said that about that little bastard William, too. Look where it got her."

"I think she's changed, Robin. She's getting older now and she wants to be happy. We all do," she said wondering if it was meant for her to be happy, too.

Robin frowned. "Yeah, that girl is almost forty years old." She was walking toward the door and Tracey got up and walked with her.

"Aunt Flo and Eric went to church together Sunday," Tracey said with a smile.

"I know. She told me. She seems happy, too. You think they may fall in love again?"

"I don't know, Robin. I haven't thought too much about it."

Robin kissed her on the cheek. "I would like to see you happy again, Tracey. I hate seeing you so miserable. John and I thought you two looked so good together. He likes Travis. I know that I didn't want you with him at first. But he's a nice guy."

"What can I say? I have good taste. I just make bad choices."

They were standing at the door. "He's a good choice. You've got to learn to get over his sister and Donald."

Tracey stood in the door until Robin drove off. She walked back inside and turned the heater on and went back to her packing. She was happy to get away, but she knew that she would think of Travis.

Travis was sitting in his living room reading the newspaper when the phone rang. It was his mother.

"She's feeling better, Mom. Just the flu, that's all." He was not ready to tell his mother that he and Tracey may not see each other again. "Sure, Mom, I'll bring her over again soon. I'll give you a call tomorrow."

He hung up and started to call Tracey, but changed his mind. It would have to be her choice. He had tried everything he could to get her. If she was going to let two dead people stand in their way, so be it. There was nothing left that he could say to reach her and make her understand. But he understood her. She had been hurt, disappointed, and cheated on. But he was sure that her husband had told his sister a few lies, too. Who knows if Donald was really going to leave Tracey.

Poor Susan, he thought, and laid the paper down. It was so hard to believe that she was gone. She had loved San Francisco. Maybe if she would have worked and lived here, she wouldn't have met Donald. At least he could have seen that Donald was not the right man for his sister. After all, that's what brothers do when their sisters get involved with a man. But Susan had a mind of her own. She wanted to live in San Francisco where she finished school and that's where she was happy. He picked up the paper again to read. But, as always, Tracey was there in front of him to break his concentration.

Tracey stood outside Delta Airlines in Mississippi, waving for a taxi to stop. It had been raining again in

Mississippi. She was so cold that she could feel it deep in her bones. Why did she tell Wendy that she would take a taxi anyway? A car drove by fast and the water splashed against her new four-hundred-dollar boots. "Fools," she hissed, as she jumped from the curb, too late. "Damn fools," she said out loud and looked around to see if anyone was watching her.

"Hey, girl, you need a ride?"

At the sound of Wendy's voice, Tracey turned around so fast that she almost slipped off the curb. "What are you doing here? I told you not to come and pick me up, Wendy, with all you have to do."

"I don't have that much to do. Besides, you know that you are glad to see me," she said, and opened her arms to Tracey.

"I sure am, girl."

"Come on, the car is parked right down the street." Wendy grabbed one of Tracey's bags off the ground and Tracey picked up the other one.

In the car she noticed that Wendy had lost more weight; her hair was back in braids, tied back with a blue scarf the color of her dress. She looked so good and so happy. Tracey looked out the window as they passed a tall, brick building with people lined up in front of it.

"You lost more weight. You look younger, too. James must be treating you good."

"Yes he is. And I'm down to a size ten. Donna says I don't look like myself anymore."

"No. You look better, and I know you must feel better, too."

"I do now. Girl, I've been so nervous." Wendy clenched the steering wheel. "I thought the man was supposed to be nervous. But he seems to be calm about it. Sometimes I wonder if I'm making a mistake. You know I've made a few in my life." She paused at a stop sign and drove off again.

"Okay, now that we've talked about me, tell me what's

bothering you." She looked at Tracey. "I could hear it in your voice when we talked on the phone and I can see it in your face, Tracey."

"That night you called me, Travis and I had an argument. We're not seeing each other anymore. I haven't gotten a call from him in over two weeks now," she said sadly. "I'm miserable, Wendy, and I don't know what to do about it anymore."

"Have you called him?"

"No. I wouldn't know what to say to him. I just don't know. Maybe I'm not supposed to be happy. It never lasts too long for me."

"Tracey, you've got to get over Donald's affair with Travis's sister. Girl, they are dead. Maybe she was a nice woman, smart and pretty. But she fell in love with Donald. You don't know what he was telling her."

Tracey didn't say anything, but she was certainly thinking about what Wendy had said to her.

"When are you leaving?"

"I'm taking the four o'clock flight Saturday. I was going to stay until Sunday but I have too much to do. Besides, I'm terrible company for anyone to be around."

"But so soon, Tracey?"

"Honey, I really have a lot of work to do. Three deals going on at the same time. I have to meet an appraiser at nine on Monday morning, another at two. Both are twenty units, too. One of my clients is middle aged, always tense, and calls me every hour of the day."

Wendy turned the corner and stopped at the light. After she took off again they were home in ten minutes.

They got the luggage out of the trunk of the car. When they walked inside the house, the smell of coffee greeted them. Donna walked in the living room wearing a long white apron and wiping her hands with a paper towel.

"So, you made it, huh, girl?"

"Yes, and it's freezing out there," Tracey answered and hugged her.

"You're just not used to our winters. I have some fresh Danishes and coffee in the kitchen."

"I could use a good, hot cup of coffee. The coffee on the plane was terrible," Tracey said, frowning. She still had the bitter coffee taste in her mouth.

"Let's take your luggage upstairs first," Wendy said.

"And I have to get out of these boots, too. They're new and killing my feet."

"I'll be in the kitchen. You two finish and come down," Donna said.

Wendy and Tracey took the luggage up. Ten minutes later they came down again. Donna was pouring coffee and the Danishes were arranged on a plate in the center of the table. Tracey picked a plain doughnut and sipped her coffee.

"Wendy, what living arrangements have you and James made?" Tracey asked.

"I'm moving in with him. He has a nice, spacious two-bedroom house that's not too far from here. All I have to do is move in."

Tracey looked at Donna who looked disappointed.

"You two relax. I have a few calls to make," Wendy said looking at her watch. It was already past one. "After I finish, we can go to the supermarket and pick up a few things that I need. Oh, Donna, the caterer will be here at nine in the morning."

"What are they going to serve?" Tracey asked.

"Baked chicken, not fried. I have to watch my diet. Potato salad, fruit salad and some other side dish. The wedding is at eleven-thirty. It's small, only my family, his mother, daughter, sister, and her husband. It's mostly my family."

Donna sighed. "I'm going to miss Wendy in this big old house. I got used to having her here."

"Gee, Donna. We'll see each other every day at the office. It's not like I'm going back to LA. We won't be going on a honeymoon until summer."

They shopped, had lunch and dinner out. When they came back, they were all exhausted. They talked for a while, drank wine, and were in bed by ten. Saturday morning, the caterers were there at nine, the flowers delivered, and they were dressed and ready for the wedding. James was dressed in a black suit and white shirt. Wendy was dressed in a mint green dress and pumps, Tracey was dressed in her mint green dress as planned, and Donna wore her dark green suit.

The wedding was short, less than thirty minutes, and Tracey was glad that it took place at their house. After the ceremony, everyone met in the living room and chatted. James and Wendy were so happy and could hardly keep their hands off each other.

Tracey went to the bathroom to freshen her makeup. She was so happy for her friend that she'd cried all through the ceremony, feeling for once that she didn't have to worry about Wendy any longer. James's mother and Donna cried for both of them. Tracey figured theirs were tears of happiness, just as hers had been.

Tracey talked with Wendy's niece and brother, who came in after the ceremony was over. She met James's daughter, who she wasn't sure liked Wendy. She said very little about the wedding and was very cool when Wendy spoke to her. But, Donald's daughter wasn't too friendly with Tracey in the beginning, Tracey remembered as she saw James's daughter stare at Wendy. *What's with the grown daughters?* Tracey wondered. *One would think that they would want their fathers to be happy*.

Wendy and James left with everyone else. It was strange to Tracey, as if everyone had come just to see if they were really getting married so soon after they had met. She'd thought there would have been more of a celebration.

Donna and Tracey were tired after a long day. They sat in the kitchen and talked about the life that Wendy had lived in LA.

"I don't like James's family at all. They're so cold and

snobbish. Was this wedding so different from any other? And my brother was late at his own sister's wedding. I just don't understand how some people think. I know it's just been a month since they met, but that's their business, although I would never marry anyone so soon."

"At least Jerry had an excuse. He had to work late and got off as soon as he could. He seemed happy enough for Wendy."

"I guess so. But Wendy can forget about being friends with his family. I know the type, Tracey. Laugh in your face and talk as soon as you turn your back."

"Don't you worry about Wendy. She can take care of herself. Besides, she's not marrying his family anyway."

"You're right. I'm tired. It's been a long day. Let's go to bed."

Tracey was tired but couldn't sleep. She kept thinking of how happy Wendy and James were together and wondering if she would ever be that happy again.

The next morning Donna, Wendy, James, and Tracey went out to breakfast. Once they arrived at the airport, Wendy asked James and Donna to wait in the car. She wanted to walk Tracey to the gate so they could have a few minutes alone.

"How did you sleep last night, Tracey? You look tired."

"I was too tired to sleep last night. How did you sleep?" she asked with a wicked smile.

Wendy laughed out loud. "I didn't get much either, but not for the same reason as you. You were too unhappy to sleep. Why don't you give him a call when you get home?" Wendy's voice became somber. "Weddings bring all the unhappiness out and make people take a look at their own lives. You can have a nice one if you just let go, forget."

They were standing at the large window. Tracey looked out at the men servicing the planes in the rain.

"Right now I have too much to do. Maybe after I close

the sales on the deals I'm working on, I can think more clearly about my life."

"That could be months, Tracey. Why wait that long?"

Tracey shook her head, confused, not knowing what to do about her life, or if she was following the right course. *But what was the right thing?* she wondered, more uncertain now than ever. Was she really as unfair as Travis accused her of being?

"Don't worry about me, Wendy. I'll do what's best."

"Yeah, sure. You'll work six days a week. Then what, Tracey?"

Tracey threw her hands up. "I don't know, Wendy. I can only take one day at a time. Sometimes life just gets to be too monumental. Right now, I don't know what I'm going to do, or where my life is going. Everything moved so fast this year, so much has happened." She heard the voice over the loudspeaker say it was time to board the plane to Los Angeles, and she welcomed the interruption.

"That's me, honey." She hugged Wendy and felt her eyes water. For some strange reason she felt sad to leave Wendy, as if they wouldn't see each other for a long time. They had always lived so close to each other.

"Take care of yourself, girl. Don't have me worrying about you," Tracey said.

"Like the way you got me worrying about you? Maybe James and I will be going to your wedding soon, I hope." Wendy kissed her on the cheek and Tracey pulled away in a hurry to board the plane. Wendy stood there until Tracey was gone.

Twenty-six

"When did you get back, Tracey?" Flora asked, surprised to see her niece. Tracey was standing in the doorway. "Come on in out of the rain."

"I don't believe this. When I left it was raining, and it rained the entire time I was in Mississippi. I get back home, and it's still raining," she said as she took off her coat.

"No, it just started back today, but the weatherman says it's going to clear up."

"At least it's not cold here. It was freezing in Mississippi, and I hated going out in that terrible weather."

"Tell me about Wendy's wedding." Flora said, motioning for Tracey to sit next to her.

"She's happy, Aunt Flo. The wedding was small. His family didn't seem too excited about it." She put her finger on her cheek and pondered the situation. "I guess you can say his mother was happy but the rest were very dry. Have you seen Robin since I was gone?"

"Yes. She and Lisa took me to lunch yesterday."

"And what about Eric?"

"He's in Dallas with his son. He'll be gone for a week," Flora said.

Tracey looked at her. Flora was dressed comfortably in a quilted dress and slippers. Her hair had grown back as if she had never gotten it cut.

"Do you miss him, Aunt Flo?"

Flora was quiet for a few seconds as though she had to

think about it before answering. "Yes I miss him. But, he has his life and I have mine," she said casually.

"Aunt Flo, do you think that one day you and Eric may become close again?"

Flora patted Tracey's hand. "Maybe. But we're older, and we think differently now. We may never be more than friends. We like and respect each other and that's enough for me."

"Have you forgiven him for leaving and not writing you?"

"Of course, Tracey. That's forgotten. Besides, if he would have kept writing, David and I would never have met and gotten married." She patted Tracey's hand. "You have to forgive and forget. There are reasons why you meet, and reasons why you part. Nothing ever goes as planned. Nothing's perfect. If you don't forget what's behind you, then how can you go forward? I met David and fell in love, again. Eric had made his choice, so I made mine." She looked at Tracey again, her head held high. She looked so much like Tracey's mother, Flora's late sister.

"Aunt Flo, you have no feelings for Eric at all?"

"Sure. He's still a very handsome man. But we're different now, older," Flora said in a bittersweet tone. "We're becoming very good friends, which is more than what we had when we were younger. If anything happens between us, it will be for different reasons than it was before. You have to like the person as much as you love them."

The wisdom of that simple statement resonated with Tracey. "I never thought of it that way, Aunt Flo. I'll keep that in mind."

"Eric and I represent companionship for each other, friendship and trust. Not being so much in love that we can't see the forest for the trees. That's for young lovers, like you, honey."

Tracey was stunned by Flora's words.

"You should be very much in love and enjoying every minute of it. When I was young and in love with Eric, I didn't think that I would ever love another." She shook her head remembering. "He was the first man that I ever loved."

"He and I were having lunch one day. It was before he had any idea that I was your niece, of course. He said that he was in love with you, too, and that he thought of you all through his marriage."

"I thought of him, too. But that's life. Are you sure that I can't get you anything, dear? I baked an apple pie with fresh apples that Robin gave me."

"No thanks, Aunt Flo. I ate too much in Mississippi. Donna still loves to cook."

Tracey picked her purse up off the coffee table. "It was nice visiting you, Aunt Flo. But, it's time I leave. I'm going to the office for a while."

Flora looked at her watch. "It's six o'clock, and it's the weekend, Tracey. You should be out on a date, not working."

Tracey almost laughed out loud at the thought of a date.

Tracey worked until nine-thirty that night. She was alone in the office and sipped on coffee to keep herself awake. She checked her answering machine again to make sure that she didn't miss any of her messages. There was no message from Travis, not that she really thought there would be.

Tracey sat behind her desk and stared out the window at the passing cars and the winds that was blowing the light rain against the window. As she returned the folders to the filing cabinet, the phone rang, and she grabbed it on the first ring. When she answered it, she heard a click. Wrong number, she supposed. At ten, she decided to go home and get an early start in the morning.

It was a warm, clear morning and Tracey was at the office at eight-thirty and Michelle at nine. At noon, Robin walked in.

"The rain stopped, and the weather is too beautiful to be

stuck inside. It's the end of April. I hope the rain is gone until winter," Robin said, and sat in the chair facing Tracey's desk.

They sat and talked for a while. Michelle finished her lunch and went to sign up for a real estate class. "I'll only take half an hour."

"Take your time. You deserve a break," Tracey answered as she cleared the table.

"What time did you come in here this morning?" Robin asked.

"I got in around eight or eight-thirty. Escrow has to close on Erin's loan by Thursday and I have another one closing next week. Dealing with the bank that he selected is a disaster. They're so picky," she said and looked at Robin's face. "Are you all right?"

Robin sighed and shook her head in disgust. "Yes. Well, no. I had the worst nightmare last night. Paul was chasing me down this long, dark alley with a gun in his hand."

"That's terrible. How awful."

"Looks like I'll never get him entirely out of my life. A dead man haunting me. I made one mistake, the one that men have made since the beginning of time, and I'm being punished for the rest of my life," she said sadly, and stood up to leave. "It's just not fair."

"No, you won't be punished for the rest of your life. It's only been months, you know. You're dealing with it better than you think. How is everything else going at home?" Tracey put one hand up. "Wait, let me answer the phone." She pulled out her pad and started to take notes. Robin leaned against her desk and waited.

"Okay, you were saying?"

"You asked how are things at home? Everything's going all right. We are married, you know? One week it's all good, the next week it's business as usual."

Tracey frowned. "What a way to describe a marriage."

"That's the story of my life, honey. That is my life." She looked at her watch. "I gotta get out of here."

"I'm glad you stopped by."

Robin was about to open the door and turned around again. "I called Aunt Flo today but she was talking long distance with Eric. Sounds like he's missing her if you ask me." She waved her hand and walked out the door.

Tracey watched Robin as she walked to her car. She thought of Flora and Eric. Who knows what could happen?

It was past one and Travis had finished his shift at the hospital. He took one last look in the mirror at his hair. He needed a haircut but it would have to wait until Thursday. All he really wanted today was to go home to peace and serenity.

On Travis's way home he decided to stop by Tracey's office to see that she was all right. What harm could it do; after all, he was still in love with her. He knew that she needed time, but he couldn't wait to see her any longer.

There was only one woman that he wanted, and it was Tracey. He didn't want to play the dating game, meet officious women that only wanted him for his money, or to play games. There was always one of the nurses at the hospital that tried to get him, but he wanted Tracey. Maybe since he missed her so much, she might miss him, too. He had made love to her twice, and both times she needed him as much as he needed her. She cared for him, that much he knew. But she just had to work this thing out about her husband and his sister. Soon or later she would accept that they are dead and she is still alive, he thought as he drove in the direction of her office.

"Hello, Tracey, it's Carl Johnson."

Tracey frowned with petulance when she heard his voice, but it was too late for her to hang up. *What does he want,* she wondered?

"Hello, Carl. Are you in town?"

"Yes. And today I'm in the branch and I've checked on your client's loan. Looks like the documents will be delivered today so he can sign."

"That's so nice of you, Carl. I was going to call for the status on the documents myself," she said. "How's the weather in San Diego?" Tracey picked up a magazine that was delivered in the mail. Tyra Banks was on the front cover.

"The weather is nice, about the same as here. Tell you what, Tracey . . ."

"What," Tracey asked and laid the magazine facedown in front of her.

"I'll be going your way in about twenty minutes. I can drop the documents off. That should give you an extra day for funding."

"That would be nice, Carl. Let me give you the address to my office."

After she hung up, Tracey opened her drawer and read the card that Travis had sent to her months ago. She still couldn't get him out of her mind and as the weeks passed, she thought of him constantly. She opened the envelope with trembling hands and tried to read between the lines. As she read it, she wondered what was he thinking as he signed his name. Did he love her once, had he forgotten her, and did he still have deep feelings for her? She just didn't know anymore. She placed the card back in the drawer and tried to get some work done.

The door opened and it was Carl. He was wearing a navy, tailored suit and white shirt. Tracey smiled as she looked at him and recognized the fact that he was undeniably very good-looking. His eyes sparkled as he looked at her.

Tracey got up from her desk and extend her hand to Carl, but instead of shaking her hand, Carl slowly placed the palm of her hand against his warm lips.

"Have a seat, Carl. Can I get you a cup of coffee, a Coke?"

"No thanks," he said and smiled. If he told her what she could give him, she would throw him out of her office. He placed the thick, white envelope on her desk.

"I owe you one, Carl. Saving me the trip of picking the documents up really helped."

"Yes, you do owe me. How about dinner and a little dancing one night while I'm here?"

Tracey nodded, but she had no interest of sharing one evening with this man. She pushed her hair from her face. "Sorry, but lunch is the best that I can do for the next two weeks."

Carl threw up both hands. "Lunch is better than nothing. And I better get going to my meeting. It's all the way downtown." He stood up and pushed both hands into his pockets.

"Wait! I'll walk you outside. I've been stuck inside since I got here today."

Tracey and Carl walked to his car. "Don't John and your sister have a teenage daughter?"

"Yes," Tracey answered.

"I have a couple of movie tickets in the car. Here, you can give them to her. Looks like I won't be needing them, unless, of course, I can get you to go to a movie with me," he teased.

Tracey laughed out loud. "Give me the tickets, man." She stepped off the curve as a speeding car was coming close. Carl grabbed her around her waist and pulled her near him.

"Lord, what fool was that?" Carl said. "That car could have hit us."

Tracey legs were so weak she was sure they would give in. She held on to Carl, her head lay against his shoulder and his arm was still around her waist.

Carl felt her body trembling against his. "Are you all right, sweetheart?" He led her back inside her office. Once they were inside Carl gave Tracey a glass of water.

No one noticed that a black Mercedes had stopped and then took off again. Travis was shocked that Tracey would show such affection in public, unless it was a man that she was in love with. Damn, he had been such a fool. And to think that he was about to make a bigger fool of himself. Well, he thought, he didn't have to wonder if they were going to get back together again. How had he misjudged her so?

Twenty-seven

June 2000

As the month of June wore on, things settled down somewhat, eventually. Tracey was beginning to wrap up her escrows. She was so tired that she lay across the bed still wearing her black suit and shoes. She lay on her back, and closed her eyes for twenty minutes before she got up and changed into a short blue bathrobe. She looked at her slippers beside her bed but walked right past them.

After she listened to her messages, she went into the kitchen and made herself a turkey sandwich and emptied the remaining potato chips onto her plate. She finished eating, then sat in the patio, looking at how beautifully her roses had bloomed, and how green the grass had become after such rainy winter. She hadn't realized until now that it was already June again.

The weather was sunny and beautiful. She loved the summer, the warmth and the lovely nights in Southern California. Only she had been spending them alone, working all day and all hours of the night. She didn't quite understand why she felt so lonely today, so blue.

She phoned Flora before she left the office, but Flora and Eric were going out to dinner and to a movie. Michelle and Larry Gross were dating and deeply in love. They had become so close that Tracey was sure that in less than a year they would be married. "You go, girl." She smiled, balled up her fist and pulled her elbow down in the "Yes" sign.

Robin was sleeping better at night without the miserable nightmares of Paul chasing her or trying to kill her.

It was summer again and everyone in her life was happy. She had worked herself into a frenzy trying to close all three escrows simultaneously. She would never drive herself that hard again.

She had made a lot of money, but she felt almost as if she had lost some of her sanity along the way. She went back inside and sat on the couch, feeling restless, trapped in a life with no place to turn, no one to go to.

Tracey decided to take a long shower, hoping it would help her relax and fight the anxiety that she was feeling; her emotions were clamoring for attention. She had been thinking more and more of Travis lately.

Was he dating? Had he forgotten about her? But she knew that she couldn't blame him if he had, and she knew that he would never tell his mother about his sister. That was all right, too. It just didn't seem to matter any longer. He loved his mother and why should he hurt her? Too bad she hadn't understood when he tried to explain it to her.

She couldn't stay inside any longer, she needed to get out for a while and get some air. Take a drive or go to the beach. Tracey grabbed her purse and keys and walked out of the house.

At the very moment that Tracey was thinking of him, Travis picked up the phone to dial her number but changed his mind and hung up. He couldn't seem to get the picture of Tracey and the man embracing in front of her office. *But, what if the man was a family member, or someone she hadn't seen in a long time?*

He had to know. Travis had to hear her say that she didn't want him. He wouldn't call her. It was time they looked each other in the eye once and for all. Or maybe it was time that he moved on to someone else. He learned a long time ago that you couldn't have everything you wanted, or everyone you wanted. Perhaps Tracey wasn't the girl for him but it was time he found out.

He wanted a wife to come home to at night, to travel with and spend the rest of his life with. Maybe Tracey had no intentions of ever getting married again. He sighed and looked at his watch. It was only seven, still early. Damn, he thought. Only one way to find out if she wants me. Why keep playing this waiting game when I can come right out and ask her? He combed his hair, put on a T-shirt and shorts. He was going to talk to her. Either way, he had to know.

Travis stopped and bought a dozen red roses. He parked his car in front of her house and walked right up to her door. He didn't know what to expect. She may have someone else there, but again, he had to find out once and for all.

He rang the doorbell but got no answer. He rang the bell four times, hearing her telephone ring at the same time. She wasn't home. Out of disappointment, he almost flung the roses down. But he didn't want her to come home and see them on the ground. Didn't want her to know that he had come to see her. Travis wasn't entirely certain if he would ever come back again.

Tracey inhaled the fresh, warm air as she walked along the pier with her shoes in her hand. She wore a pair of white shorts and white T-shirt, her hair tied back in a ponytail. She felt so young and relaxed. This was what she needed, the freedom to feel alive, as free as a child walking in the warm sand, feeling it fall between her toes and the sun warming her face.

Suddenly she saw Donald's face appear in front of her and wondered how many women he'd had while they were married. The trips to Fresno were as frequent as the ones to San Francisco. But they stopped once he had completed the project that was being built.

A thought hit her with shocking clarity. Maybe she had

known all along that there were other women, maybe she was just afraid that her perfect world and perfect life would crumble around her if she admitted it to herself. So she closed her eyes and went on like nothing or no one would come between them. Lately, she had learned that there's no perfect world.

She saw a man walking in her direction. He stopped and looked at her. She couldn't see his face because of the bright glare of the sun in her eyes.

He walked closer; she stopped and stared at him. Tracey froze, afraid to try and walk on her legs that had suddenly grown so weak. Her heart was racing. Was she dreaming, was it really him?

"You're walking in my domain, lady. But it's okay. I know you're here to apologize for making my life hell for the last few months, to tell me that you love me and will be my wife." He took another step closer to her.

"You've never come here before, so it must be to say those words to me," he said with so much confidence that it almost frightened her. But she sighed and relaxed. She trusted him. He loved her. She could see it in his eyes as he looked at her.

"I know. I'd never come here until we met here the last time we were together," she said, hearing her voice trembling. She wanted to look away but couldn't. He looked so tall, so muscular, his legs long and hard.

"I'm happy to see you, Tracey Woods."

He was so close she couldn't breath. "Do you really love me, Travis? Are you really happy to see me? Because I'm in love with you, too."

"Yes, baby, I do love you."

Tracey couldn't keep quiet any longer. "I've missed you, I've been so lonely without you, Travis. Why haven't you come to me before now?" Her words stumbled out in a rush.

He grabbed her and held her tight in his arms.

"I love you, woman. I want to spend the rest of my life with you." He held her face, his hand under her chin, and looked in her eyes. "Tell me that you love me again and again, Tracey."

"I love you, Travis. I want to be with you forever and ever." Tears streamed down her face.

Slowly, he kissed her wet face from her eyelashes, to her cheeks, to her lips.

He took her hand and led her to a bench that was only a few feet away. They sat there and faced each other.

"I still can't bring myself to tell my mother about Susan and Donald. I've thought about it . . ."

"No, Travis. Don't tell her. It's not something she needs to know. I've given it a lot of thought. And you know what, love?"

"What, baby?"

"It doesn't matter anymore. I've gotten over Donald. I have my life to live now. What they did doesn't matter anymore."

He took her hand. "Do you want to get married again?"

"I've thought of that, too. Only if I can marry you," she said, looking into his eyes. She saw so much love there, and she felt so safe.

"Will you marry me, Tracey Woods?"

"Yes, love. I will marry you."

He took her hand. "Come on. I have something for you. He led her to his car and gave her the dozen roses.

"I bought these for you. I had just left your house and decided to walk on the pier before going home."

They were walking in the direction of his apartment. She held her roses with one hand and Travis held her other hand. Tracey inhaled the scent of the roses, and the fragrant air that blew in from the pier. She turned her face up toward the streaming rays of sun.

It had been quite a year. She'd lost her husband and found a new love—Travis. A year ago, it had been a dreary, rainy June—when she didn't think that she would ever be warm again, and the real summer might never come. But now she was warm and life didn't feel cold at all anymore.

Grab These Other
Dafina Novels
(hardcover editions)

__**Some Sunday**   1-57566-916-1 $24.00US/$33.00CAN
   by Margaret Johnson-Hodge

__**Forever**   1-57566-757-6 $22.00US/$29.00CAN
   by Timmothy McCann

__**Soul Mates Dissipate**   1-57566-913-7 $24.00US/$33.00CAN
   by Mary Morrison

__**It's A Thin Line**   1-57566-629-4 $23.00US/$32.00CAN
   by Kimberla Lawson Roby

Call toll free **1-888-345-BOOK** to order by phone or use this coupon to order by mail.

Name _____

Address _____

City _____ State_____ Zip_____

Please send me the books that I checked above.

I am enclosing $_____

Plus postage and handling* $_____

Sales tax (in NY, TN, and DC) $_____

Total amount enclosed $_____

*Add $2.50 for the first book and $.50 for each additional book.

Send check or money order (no cash or CODs) to: **Arabesque Books, Dept. C.O., 850 Third Avenue 16th Floor, New York, NY 10022**

Prices and numbers subject to change without notice.

All orders subject to availability.

Visit our website at **www.kensingtonbooks.com.**

Grab These Other
Dafina Novels

(trade paperback editions)

More Women's Fiction
From Kensington